One Chance

Vee Taylor

Printed in the United States of America.
For more information, or to book an event, contact :
Vmtaylor04@gmail.com
http://www.veetaylorauthor.com
Cover design by Haya of Haya In Designs
Editing by Molly at Novel Mechanic

First Edition: July 2023

AUTHOR'S NOTE

While this book is strictly a work of fiction, it's not a horse-and-carriage romance. I do not condone these situations or actions between characters; it is simply a work of fiction. No characters in this book are based off of anyone as it is just part of my imagination.

This book contains heavy mentions of domestic violence, abuse, rape, CNC, dub con, drug/alcohol use, cursing, gun violence, gun use, kidnapping, masturbation, kink-play, drowning, anal-play, murder, and lots of morally gray activities. This book is not for those suffering from trauma and/or have triggers of abusive relationships or any of the above situations.

Some of the organizations in this book do not exist in today's world, so, since this is a work of fiction, we can also safely assume thatthese are stretched to fit our imagination.

To those who have been told they weren't good enough by others.
Let this be a reminder that you are.

And to those who have tried to tear you down. . .
fuck them.

PROLOGUE

TATUM

The world around me blurred as my mind disconnected from my body, leaving me a mere spectator of my own life. Every movement, every sound, every assault on my body was painfully vivid, yet I was powerless to intervene. It was as though I was watching a helpless ragdoll being tossed around, thrown into the depths of hell. It was a suffocating existence and an endless cycle of physical, emotional and sexual abuse. Color and light seemed to vanish from the world, leaving only a monotony in its wake. This was my reality, and I was entangled within its unforgiving grasp.

For years, I'd been trapped in a hellish existence with a man who gave no fucks, not even the ones that came from his pathetic excuse for a dick. Cameron didn't care about me as long as he got his daily dose of sex, leaving me to fend for myself in a world of pain and misery.

There was a time when we were happy. A time when I still had a spark in my eyes.

Rain began to pour outside, hitting the concrete walls of our dingy basement apartment like a mournful symphony. This place was a prison. Our "garden" apartment was a five-hundred-square-foot hole in the ground with bars on the windows and a musty stench that clung to everything. The windows were narrow slivers of glass that barely let in the morning light. As I lay on the bed, I tried to take stock of the few things that meant something to me. But nothing could make up for the fact that I was trapped in a dungeon with a man who cared only for himself.

This place has never felt like a home. Our small bed in the corner was adorned with what used to be a white sheet. It turned gray because, honestly, I didn't wash it much. We didn't have an in-unit washer or dryer. Don't get me wrong, there was space to put one in, but why would you need to have one when your prisoner could simply walk a few blocks to the closest laundromat to complete their weekly chore? The small couch looked like it was from your grandmother's old apartment. It had gray and white stripes, and you sank real deep into it. Finally, the kitchen had two plates, two chairs, two forks, two knives, two spoons, and two cups. For the last five years, I lived a life that made me want to crawl out of my body. Why was I still here?

I knew the only way to leave this relationship with Cam would be to leave the state. Still, the strength it took to fathom getting out of bed today left the thought of running away a far cry in the distance. It wasn't just Cam. It was the whole underworld he belonged to. There was always that lingering fear of someone coming for me.

Begrudgingly, I lifted myself out of bed and walked over to the tiny sink. I ran a callused hand over my face as I lifted my head to glance at the person in the mirror.

My light brown hair was matted in knots, and my eyes were sunken so deep that you could almost build moats inside the rings underneath my eyelids. I was malnourished to the point where I knew if I didn't get something inside my body in the next couple of days, it would go into shock from lack of nutrition. Between Cameron and any other threats coming for me, it was hard to concentrate enough to get any food down.

I ran my hands over my breasts. They were on the larger and perkier side of the average person and were littered with bruises. Some were still purple and throbbing as if they had their own heartbeat, and others were turning yellow as they recovered. Little did those pesky yellow bruises know that as soon as they turned flesh color, another throbbing purple bruise would take its place. I lifted my shirt gently to find an array of bruises similar to the ones on my chest, along with lash marks, teeth marks, and raw red skin in the shape of a handprint.

Then there were the scars. Scars permanently etched into my skin, signifying my place in Cam's world. They were trophies from the years of abuse. I pushed my shirt back down and moved my hands to trace my jawline.

A dry chuckle escaped my lips as I really looked at myself in the mirror again. I couldn't help but notice the cruel irony of a long, chiseled jawline and luscious lips that once complimented my porcelain skin. Strategically, my arms, legs, and face were absent from visible signs of physical pain, concealing my silent agony.

This was the very essence of my existence, wasn't it? Always suppressing my pain, keeping quiet, and putting on a façade of normalcy. A trip to the grocery store meant walking past people oblivious to the turmoil I faced behind closed doors. A life of striving for perfection while being broken inside.

As I snapped out of my reverie, I hastily brushed away tears trickling down my cheeks with the back of my hand. I refused to let myself break down and cry—not now, not ever. This was the path I had chosen. But the reflection staring back at me bore little resemblance to the person I was five years ago.

There was a time when I exuded vibrance. My long, wavy light brown hair cascaded down my back and billowed gently in the breeze, and my bright blue eyes were filled with adventure and mystery. That was the person Cameron had first encountered. He was a stunning, attractive mechanic who lent me a hand and escorted me to my car as I stumbled out of my overnight shift at a Chicago restaurant.

Cam was a hulking, burly man adorned head to toe in tattoos. So much so that even the one on the back of his neck extended down to his big toe. His jet-black hair was always slicked back, and his rough, calloused hands seemed capable of crushing anything in their path—a thought that sent a shiver down my spine. The attraction grew from a physical to an emotional one. When I first saw him, I was captivated by his rugged charm and undeniable allure. He was also incredibly kind, a trait that didn't go unnoticed. I'll never forget how he courted me with flowers, sweet compliments, and thoughtful gestures, waiting for me at the end of each shift and walking me to my car every time. It was a romantic haze that blinded me to the red flags. And as soon as he had me, his veneer of perfection quickly faded.

When I first met Cameron, I was a shattered, vulnerable girl craving the attention and affection that had been denied me for so long. I was miserable and alone, and my few friends could not alleviate the overwhelming sadness that consumed me. I was left to fend for myself, lost and alone in a world that seemed to have no place for me.

But something stirred in me with Cameron, making me crave the dangerous, thrilling sensations he offered. The life he promised was so vastly different from the one I knew, and I could not overlook the urge to break free from the cage I had been locked in for years. It was as though a bird that had been trapped for so long was finally given a chance to soar into the wide, open skies.

I can't pinpoint precisely what sparked this change in me, but I knew I had to seize this chance to escape the confines of my old life and discover what lay beyond. The need to fly, to break free from the cage that bound me, burned within me with a fierce intensity that I could no longer ignore.

1

TATUM

5 years ago

Meeting Cameron

As dawn began to break through the clouds, the jingling of the bell above the restaurant entrance caught my attention. I was stationed behind the counter, preparing coffee for the morning shift. The atmosphere was grimy, the fluorescent lighting casting a bright hue over the decor. The old-fashioned sixties theme was marred by the dilapidated condition of the seats, the grime that persistently clung to the bar area, and the coffee filter that desperately needed replacing. Despite my efforts to clean, the owner didn't seem to care much for updates. As long as the cash kept flowing, he once remarked.

With just five minutes left in my shift, I glanced at the clock and cursed my luck. Towering over six feet, he exuded an intimidating aura that permeated the entire space. Dark, slicked-back hair framed his face, concealing his thoughts as he slouched onto a worn stool at the counter.

My eyes were irresistibly drawn to him. Slowly, as if my steps were weighed down by concrete bricks, I carried a small mug of coffee toward him, feeling a strange mix of anticipation and apprehension.

As I neared him, he remained lost in his own world, yet a charged energy crackled in the air between us. It was puzzling that I felt so drawn to him, especially considering the lack of male attention I had received in years. Maybe it was the long shifts when strangers often approached me at the diner, but something distinct set him apart. The desire to introduce myself, to embrace him, tugged at my core, but the intensity of his presence held me back, intimidating and intriguing.

Finally, I arrived at his side around the counter with the pot of coffee in hand. Pouring a cup, I couldn't shake the unsettling feeling that something significant was on the verge of happening.

"Coffee's on the house," I said when I finally got to where he was. I brought him a cup with a little milk on the side. I felt bad for him. He looked tired and maybe part of me wanted to care for him in some way.

His gaze met mine. Without a word, he pulled out the stool beside him, a gesture demanding I join him.

"Sit," he commanded, his voice's deep, rough timbre sending a shiver down my spine.

"I can't. I'm working." I gestured around the deserted restaurant. It was sort of the story of my life, being constantly alone even though I was surrounded by the patrons at work.

I had been on my own since I was seventeen, abandoned by parents who believed I had disgraced our family. I was meant to follow the path of a perfect, respectable citizen, donning tulle dresses and revering men destined for success as if they were divine beings walking this earth.

But I rebelled against my parents' expectations and their high-society lifestyle. Growing up in the privileged confines of the upper class had its perks, yet being forced to conform to their ideals and shield the family name from humiliation was something I failed to achieve. I excelled at being the wayward girl.

In high school, I dared to love someone that didn't run in the same circle as my parents. It was just a fling, but it cost me the final string of trust and connection with my family. My mother's battle with mental illness and my father's inability to care provided them the perfect excuse to sever ties with me. From then on, our relationship was a facade, void of love and warmth.

My mother was diagnosed with obsessive-compulsive disorder when I was in elementary school. She was absent during my childhood, constantly in and out of hospitals and rehab centers while my dad tried to fix her and her illness. His life was consumed with getting her better, so I was raised by nannies.

She came home for good after she went to a facility in Malibu. She was very different, but unfortunately, the damage was done. She didn't need everything to come in eights or obsessively clean door handles, but she was broken.

My parents didn't raise me when I needed it the most, so the bond a child has with their parents never developed. Hindsight bias, I should have known it wasn't her fault for going through what she was, but as a kid, all I wanted was to have my family together. Thus, I think my parents saw me as this big cold inconvenience in their life after that moment.

My mom got better and began to insert herself in with the Chicago elite families. She was very good at sucking up and doing the most to move up the social ladder. This came at a sacrifice to me, who continued to be raised by nannies as they attended event after event. This was my life until I was able to get out of the house after high school. My parent's disowned me the moment I told them that I wanted to be a photographer. They told me that they wouldn't be able to tell their high society friends that their daughter was a 'lowly' photographer.

On the day of my eighteenth birthday, I decided to break free. I told my parents I needed to leave, and that was the end of it. I found solace in a diner that offered me a night shift, allowing me to attend school during the day. I secured a modest apartment on the third floor of a worn-out walk-up building, transforming the space into a burst of color. I had a little inheritance that I got on my birthday, which helped my day-to-day living.

I vividly recall thrifting a vibrant pink rug and a bed clearly meant for a child's room, but I fell in love with the orange headboard and painted the walls the brightest shade of yellow imaginable. My apartment became a sanctuary of happiness, curated with hues and cherished secondhand treasures. Day after day, the routine repeated. I attended art school to nurture my photography skills, headed straight to the diner, and returned home to repeat the cycle.

My thoughts snapped back to the stranger in front of me, gesturing to the vacant seat beside him. He appeared worn out and broken. It almost looked like I was staring into a mirror that reflected my own lost self. I sat on the pulled-out stool. "Only for a minute."

"What's your name?" There was an undeniable pull compelling me to reveal my actual name and not the one I made up to deter creeps.

"Tatum. What about you?" I replied, my curiosity piqued. Despite my usual inclination to fabricate a name when customers—mostly men—asked, he evoked a different response. His commanding presence and intense aura both intimidated and intrigued me.

"Cameron," he replied. Then, in an unexpected confession, he declared, "You are truly one of the most beautiful humans I've ever met."

His words caught me off guard, leaving me stunned by the raw transparency and bluntness. Despite the swiftness of his admission, I couldn't deny the tingling sensation that stirred within me.

My face scrunched in both question and curiosity. At the end of the day, this was just a creepy stranger, and I should leave. I desperately searched for a way to escape, but his hand gripped my arm with force before I could move. The slight tinge of pain that shot up my arm was uncomfortable yet strangely thrilling.

My father had always been meek, mild, and emotionally distant, and my past boyfriends provided physical satisfaction without any emotional connection. But this man was different, and I couldn't help but feel drawn to him. It was curiosity that drove me to want to learn more about him. Despite my doubts and fears, I knew this was a risk worth taking.

"No, sit back down," his voice had a commanding authority that brooked no resistance, compelling me to comply without question.

"Your eyes are a captivating shade of blue, deeper and more profound than any jewel. Yet, behind their beauty, I sense a profound sadness. Working late nights as a waitress in this rundown diner in the shittiest part of town.. I can only assume my guess is correct. " he uttered.

His grip on my wrist tightened, sending a shiver down my arms. It felt as if he peered into the depths of my soul, seeing through the facade I desperately tried to uphold. The happy-go-lucky image I tried to present in the diner and in my house was just a cloud for the deep pain I felt about practically being abandoned by my parents. In that moment, the weight of my monotonous routine seemed to momentarily lift, and I felt truly seen. At twenty, I was supposed to be living my best life, yet I was trapped in an endless cycle of work and school.

"Thank you, I suppose," I whispered in the charged atmosphere.

"I'm going to walk you to your car this morning. You shouldn't leave here alone. The after-hours bar crowd isn't safe," he declared with concern.

"Unless you have someone who walks with you," he smirked with amusement.

"If you're asking whether I have a boyfriend, the answer is no. I appreciated your directness earlier instead of dancing around the question," I retorted, a hint of a smile tugging at my lips.

He chuckled, a sound that resonated deep within me and filled the air with a tantalizing mix of mystery. A bell rang, and I looked at a customer who had just walked in. Thank goodness. Just the escape I needed.

"I'm going to wait for you. It's not safe for you to be walking alone to your car." He glanced at the guy who stumbled in, clearly from a night out at the nearby bars.

That shift, he actually waited and walked me to my car, just like he said he would. He didn't say a word, just watched me as I headed to my car and drove off. We didn't exchange any words, but it felt like he wrapped me in a warm blanket of protection by accompanying me out of the diner. When I got back to my apartment that morning, I closed my eyes, realizing it had been ages since someone genuinely cared about my safety. Little did I know, this was just the start of something unexpected.

2

TATUM

Present

The morning rain was the perfect catalyst for my long-awaited departure. With every drop that hit my window, I felt a surge of determination to finally make it happen. I had attempted this escape seven times before, but this eighth try would be different.

As a child, my mother's obsession with the number eight was suffocating, but now, it was my lucky number. I used to have to keep eight stuffed animals on my bed, and we practically had eight of everything else in the house, or else my mother would force me to get rid of something until the number was right.

Today, as I packed my bags for the eighth time, the irony of the situation was not lost on me. I was finally leaving, and it would be with my lucky number, the one that brought comfort and pain throughout my life.

I grabbed the few clothes I had and stuffed them into the backpack my friend Jackie gave me when I asked if she had a spare. She was always kind enough to me. She was sleeping with one of the other mechanics at the shop and was the only girlfriend I had been allowed to talk to besides Betty, who lived a floor above us with her grandchildren. Although I only ran into Betty at the laundromat down the block from us, our conversations were pleasant, and I know she heard the screams below her. She always gave me a reassuring look with a wrinkle of her nose, reminding me of my pain but never asking or making me talk about it.

Jackie was considered a safe person. She knew the shop's rules and probably suffered herself, so Cameron deemed her someone I could sit around and chat with. About a month ago, I told Jackie I wanted to surprise Cameron with a little trip but had nothing to put our clothes in. She didn't think twice because she had no idea what kind of person he was behind closed doors or at least never let on that she did. She fawned over me with an 'aww' and 'how cute' before handing me a ragged black backpack. It was large enough to hold my few outfits, some toiletries I would need, and other small personal items.

I ran around the apartment, trying to find a piece of paper and pen to write a note to Cameron. I don't know why I felt like I owed him this, but something inside me remembered our first year together and how good it was. How there was happiness and joy.

I will never forget Cameron making me smile when he walked me home from the diner every night. And I'll never forget how he rubbed my feet after long shifts. Honestly, a tiny part of me felt that writing him a note would mean this was final. I prayed he wouldn't come after me. It felt like the last bit of string tying me to him, and I wanted to make sure he understood the rope was cut after I left. I wanted no part of him...ever again.

As I started to write, I couldn't help but think about the other times I attempted to leave. The first three tries were a joke. I got a few blocks away with clothes in my hand and realized I had nowhere to go and no one to go to. I had maybe twenty dollars in my pocket, so quite frankly, it was laughable. One time, I walked into Betty's apartment and just started crying. She sat me down with a cup of tea by her fireplace and let me weep into my hands before I walked back downstairs to our apartment. The fourth time, I came up with a plan. I had a bus schedule, a hundred dollars I kept from the change of shopping trips over three months, and a destination. Montana. It went swimmingly until Cameron found my bus schedule tucked under my pillow and flipped out. The bruising from that beating lasted over a month, and I was banned from going to the shop.

Some of his shop buddies caught me the fifth and sixth times. They found me at the bus stop and forced me to the shop with them, exclaiming that his 'little lady' was trying to bolt. Because of the embarrassment of his buddies finding me and the fact that he couldn't keep his woman in check, I was punished tremendously. He never struck me in the face until those two times, and then he forced me to stay in the apartment until the bruises healed.

The last attempt was something different. I made sure everyone was eating lunch at the shop while the bus was scheduled to leave. Cameron was at a pickup from another club. I got on the bus and headed toward Indiana. My final destination was West Virginia, where a distant cousin offered to let me crash on her couch after telling her I was looking to relocate. I cried when the bus pulled out of the station. I figured this was it, my shot at freedom.

Until it all went wrong. . . with me. Sitting on the five-hour bus ride to Indiana, I realized I couldn't leave. Who would help him with dinners? Who would clean up for him? How was I going to hide and escape from him completely? My heart started to beat out of my chest, and my palms would not stop sweating from anxiety. What if the grass wasn't greener on the other side when I got to West Virginia? What if I ended up with a meek man like my father? Cameron hurt me, but he made up for it by giving me protection and love. After hitting me, he always showered me with love and affection. He gave me gifts and took me out of the house to different places, sometimes even on dates where he would hold my hand and kiss my body lovingly and gently. He would include me in the shop events and fawn over me, which I loved.

I loved when he obsessed over my clothes and stopped the creepy guys at the diner from following me out of my shifts. It felt like a form of protection and desire, which I missed in my childhood. Why wouldn't I look for it as an adult?

On this incredibly long bus ride, I thought about all our good and loving times. My brain couldn't focus on the trauma and pain I experienced and only let me remember the good. Happy memories flashed through my head, like meeting at the diner, our first dates, and when he disclosed his darkest and deepest secrets to me.

When I finally arrived in Indiana, I got off the bus and immediately walked to the ticket counter. My body panicked at the idea that it would be separated from the only thing it longed for and desired. I immediately requested a ticket on the next bus back to Chicago.

I knew Cameron would come home the next day around lunchtime, so I got on the overnight bus back. I used the last of the money I saved to grab food and hopped back on the bus. When I got home, Cameron was fortunately still not there. I quickly grabbed my stuff from the garbage bag I was carrying it in and took the trash out so he wouldn't see any of the receipts. That night, he punched me so hard on the hip that I couldn't walk straight for a month because I wasn't home in time to make dinner. That was six months ago.

I blinked a few times and returned to the reality of my shitty apartment, where I sat with my stuff strewn all over the bed. I don't know what snapped in me or when it did, I just knew I needed to get very far away from this place. Only going a few hours away by bus wouldn't get me far enough. I knew I needed enough money to last a couple of months while I got on my feet.

I was allowed to work at the laundromat during the day for a few hours, helping people with the machines and earning a few dollars an hour. I also kept the change from any errand I was told to go on. It was dangerous, but I knew I needed a couple thousand dollars to get far away from here and on my feet. I also knew I would turn around again if I left on a bus. I needed a mode of transportation that I couldn't control, so I booked a plane ticket. I couldn't get them to turn the plane around because I needed to return to my abusive boyfriend.

It was riskier because it left more of a paper trail. If Cameron didn't leave when he said he was going to, the plane would still take off with or without me, and I would be screwed. But everything was falling into place.

He was leaving on an overnight trip for the shop to grab supplies, my plane was on time, and I was ready to go. I had flown a few times to see my mom in her rehab facilities as a kid, so the thought of flying didn't give me anxiety. What made me nervous was myself. I didn't want to disappoint myself. I wanted to get out of here and not look back.

Looking at places I could go to on the map, I immediately thought of California. My mom had gone to a facility in Malibu, so I considered going to LA, but the prices to get settled were too much for me. I scrolled down the map until I saw San Diego. There were neighborhoods by the border where I knew I could afford a little apartment, and the restaurant industry was booming. I could work at a diner or restaurant there and explore my photography more. San Diego was full of cliffs and had beaches for miles, hiking, and lots of people using it as a destination spot to get married. It was the perfect location for me.

My flight was leaving in a few hours, so I needed to hurry before catching the bus to the airport. I sighed and looked at the paper, not knowing how to say what I wanted to. Part of me just wanted to say, "Fuck you," which is how I truly felt. But I couldn't write that. I needed him to know how much I hurt. My hand shook as I started to write from my heart.

Cameron,

You used to have this incredible hold on me, drawing me in with your presence. We had this connection that made me believe we'd be together forever. When I was with you, I thought I felt alive and free, but I've come to realize how much you wore me down over the years.

Something changed, and you started draining the color out of my life, replacing it with terrifying darkness. You broke me down mentally and physically until I was nothing but an empty shell. Your protectiveness turned suffocating and overwhelming. And you put me in dangerous situations that could've gotten me killed. You left me marked by your shady lifestyle.

Now, I need to leave—for both our sakes. If you truly love me, please let me go. I'm not coming back, and I don't want you to try to find me or bring me back home.

I am done.

-Tatum

Tears streamed down my face as I scribbled my name at the end. This was it. The end. I finally reached my breaking point, and it was time to move on. I knew the road ahead would be a challenging climb with only a few thousand dollars to my name, but I was ready.

The taste of freedom was tantalizingly close, and the ember of my inner glow pulsated with newfound strength. For the first time in a long time, I was excited to uncover who I was meant to be. I grabbed my backpack and looked at the clock.

Shit. I would be late if I didn't catch the next bus. I picked up my stuff, left my phone, and looked around the apartment once more. I gently wiped my tears away and realized I wasn't crying because I was sad about leaving this place. I cried because my future seemed so bright and vibrant for the first time in a long time. I cried because today was the day I began the journey of healing and independence.

I looked up to where Betty lived and saw her in the window, making food for her grandchildren. She couldn't see me from where I was on the street, even though her apartment was street-level. I smiled, knowing she would enjoy the quiet of the apartment. The screaming would stop, and the girl below her would finally get to fly. It was time to go.

I quickened my pace as I made my way to the bus stop, ducking behind a tree to hide from prying eyes. As I gazed up at the branches, I noticed buds forming, signaling summer's start. A car raced by, followed closely by a mother and child, oblivious to the journey I was about to undertake. The challenges ahead seemed insignificant compared to the endless years of pain that came before. Clutching my ticket tightly, I let out a deep sigh and felt the weight on my chest lift. For far too long, I held in the pain, but now, finally, I was free.

I saw the gray bus approach and stay hidden until it stopped and the doors swung open. I looked around to confirm it was clear and immediately walked on and into a seat. I sat close to the window to watch the city slowly disappear as we made our way to the airport.

I checked into my flight an hour later and sat at the gate. I splurged and got a sandwich before takeoff. As I watched everyone walk by, I clutched my long sleeve shirt and pulled it past my wrist. I winced as I pressed a spot where a bruise was. Never again. I would never allow a man to hold that much power over me.

I was now living life for me.

"Now boarding for flight five-fifty-three to San Diego, California."

Determined, I rose from my seat and headed toward the line, each step feeling like a deliberate move in the new chapter in my life. As they scanned my ticket and I made my way onto the plane, I knew there was no turning back. This was it, the moment I had been waiting for. Taking my seat at the back of the plane, I peered out the window and listened to the flight attendants as the boarding process ended. After a brief delay, the plane began to back away from the terminal, guided by the soft glow of the airport lights. I couldn't help but wonder about the other passengers on the flight, imagining them off to see family, conduct business, or simply return to loved ones.

But me?

I'm going to find a home.

3

Tatum

6 Months Later

I jolted awake as the blinding rays of morning sunlight filled my room.
Panic set in as I realized I had overslept and would be late for work.
In a frenzy, I dashed to my cramped closet, which was barely big enough
to fit my meager wardrobe. My studio apartment was sparsely furnished,
with only a thrifted couch and a makeshift kitchen table that doubled
as a desk. I couldn't afford much, but I made do with what I had. My
camera gear sat on a shelf, a constant reminder of my passion, and a small
bookshelf housed my guilty pleasure—a collection of smutty romance
novels perfect for days spent lounging at the beach.

I lived in an up-and-coming area outside the city, in a casita at the back
of someone's property. I saw an ad on Craigslist after a month of living

in Airbnbs and initially thought living on someone else's property was weird, but beggars can't be choosers.

Tony and Samuel lived in the main house and never bothered me. Tony often reminded me of Betty. She sometimes left pastries she cooked at my door for breakfast, and her husband always kept the yard clean.

The casita was small but had a little kitchen, bathroom, and everything I could need.

Fumbling through my closet, I grabbed a denim skirt and work shirt. I splashed water on my face and threw my hair up in a large bun. My first few months out here were for healing myself. I spent days at the beach just soaking up the sun. I went to the drugstore and bought a brush and some makeup to feel feminine again. I was determined to bring the glow back into my life.

I knew my money would run out quickly, so I looked for a job. I saw a lady doing a photography session on the beach one evening when I was watching the sunset. I don't know what possessed me to approach her, but I asked if she needed an assistant for her shoots. She introduced herself as Lacey and, after asking a little about my experience, offered to let me assist her with a few weddings she had coming up. She was willing to pay me twenty-five dollars an hour, and I had to control my reaction because I didn't think I had ever been paid that much.

I helped with a few weddings that month and learned that she was intense, to say the least. She was harsh and blunt. I couldn't spend much time with her outside of work, even though she invited me to coffee or showed me around the city, because something about her reminded me of Cameron. I was making every effort not to be reminded of him.

I constantly checked over my shoulder and even installed deadbolts on my door in case he found me. I got a new phone with a California number as soon as I arrived. And I'd never had a bank account or anything, so I wasn't super traceable. The money I made on the weekends working for Lacey was fine but not enough to let me stay here full-time, so I got a job at a bougie brunch spot during the day. The manager said he liked my vibe and style, and I was hired on sight. Between working brunch shifts during the day and weddings on the weekend, I could pay rent and my few bills.

I even had enough to buy a little beater car to get to and from work. For once in my life, it felt like everything was fitting into the little puzzle that I called my life. Maybe my mom was onto something, and the magic number was eight.

I dabbed a little makeup on my eyes and really looked at the person in the mirror. She was still broken and small, but she was finding herself. From the small brightly colored bath towel to the bedspread, she was slowly getting her color back.

I grabbed a somewhat over-ripe banana off the kitchen counter, the keys from the hook on the wall, and a jacket. Even with the sun, the fall mornings in California could be chilly. I looked around my small, one-room apartment and took a deep breath. There were days that this life felt like it was becoming something mundane and hard again, but glancing around, I saw everything I had worked so hard on these last few months. This was my independence, and a beam of pride lit my core. This was me now. No one would hurt me or tell me what I could or couldn't do. I survived.

I hurriedly slammed the door, locking the many sets of locks on the top and bottom. I always shook the handle again to confirm everything was locked before walking to my car in the carport.

"Agh," I yelped. I looked down and noticed that I had stepped on one of the succulents that lined the carport area.

"I don't have time for this, damn it," I said out loud. I pulled out the bristle that went into my sandal, jumped into the car so I didn't step on anything else, and started the engine. I pulled out of the driveway and drove to work.

When I finally got to work and found a parking spot, I was greeted by my new favorite people in San Diego, who also worked at the restaurant—Daphne, Maeve, and Chelsea, aka Chels. They were the three people who made me feel like this place could become a home when I moved here and found this job working the brunch shift. They were a devilish bunch and always encouraged me to find the best version of myself.

I met Maeve first and quickly became close to her. She was very motherly to me and had kids. The relationship with her children's father didn't work out because he fell in love with another person. She worked the brunch shift while her kids were in school, so she was always a bit late because of school drop-off. Her long blonde hair and fair skin complimented her bright blue eyes. She smelled of spring flowers blooming. We called her Mother often because of her nurturing soul.

"Look who slept in," Maeve called from the break room as she got her apron on.

"Ugh, don't get me started. My alarm clock didn't go off, and I stepped on one of those damn cactus things." I looked down at my toe and prayed it wouldn't start bleeding.

"Those suckers can be gnarly," Daphne chimed in from the bathroom area.

Daphne was the free spirit of the group. She loved all things historical and old. When I met her, she was the first person to show me around the city and tell me all about the history of San Diego. She also loved to garden and sometimes made bouquets and wedding arrangements for Lacey's clients. Her shorter black hair was cut into a fashionable bob.

"I forget you're from the city of cold where they don't have cacti." Daphne joked.

"Hey, hey, I've been here for nearly six months. I'm practically a resident now," I retorted as I heard her snort.

"Hey, bitches!" Chels greeted as the breakroom door swung open.

"Ahh, you're late again. This time even later than Maeve, the Queen of Late." Daphne replied.

"Get outta here." Maeve punched Daphne playfully on the arm, and I immediately winced. Even if the interaction was fun and playful, something in me would always flinch at even the slightest physical contact. Thankfully, this group never attempted to hug or get physical with me. I had such an aversion to hugs, and they quickly learned that I was uncomfortable and never considered approaching me.

I looked back at the door as the last of our little group came in. Chelsea was the party girl. She was also permanently banned from working the weekend shift because she would either show up puking from her hangover or wouldn't come. I also thought she was the most beautiful of the group. Her long, bleach-blonde hair hung low down her back. She had piercing blue eyes and was the only one of us born and raised in San Diego. She echoed the stereotype of a "Cali girl" and wore it well. It fit her.

"Let's get out there and open the doors," I told the group.

"Are you working with the heartless b—" Chels was cut off when Maeve interrupted her.

"Chels was about to say we were going out later, but we wanted to know if you were working with Lacey." She accentuated Lacey because I knew Chels was about to call her a bitch. She deserved to be called one, too. If I didn't want to get involved in the photography community out here so badly, I would not be spending my time with her.

"Oh yeah, I have a wedding at one that I have to be at, so I gotta run outta here a little early."

"Boo." Chels chuckled from around the corner.

With nothing more to say, we opened the doors and started our shift. The time passed quickly, and soon I was packing up to head to my second job. I changed into all-black attire at the restaurant for the wedding I was photographing and slicked my hair back into a bun for a more formal look. I had already stored my cameras in my work locker, so I was ready to go. I hoped Lacey would let me take on more of a leadership role today instead of my usual quietness. But a girl can dream, right?

"Kill 'em, babe!" Maeve ran over and gave me a small pat on the shoulder. I appreciated the quick physical gesture.

"Don't let her push you around. I know she's your boss, but you have a voice, too. Remember that." She winked and walked off to her last table.

It was about a twenty-minute drive up the Five freeway to the little seaside town of Encinitas. Driving up felt like a decade. To say that my mouth was on the floor was possibly an understatement. I had been working weddings with Lacey for a few months, and the venues were always lux, but this was beyond.

I was greeted by a vast mansion with large white pillars. It was on top of a hill that overlooked the ocean, where you could hear the roar of the waves collapsing against the shoreline. The house was adorned with white flowers and eucalyptus spiraling down the pillars, and the large centerpieces at the front door gave off a modern and expensive boho wedding style. Since the ceremony wasn't for a couple hours, none of the guests had arrived yet, but the valet still greeted me and offered to park my car, which was rare since we were vendors, not guests.

"Wow," I spoke out loud to no one in general.

"I know. I am so excited whenever I get this assignment." I spun around to see one of the valets talking to me.

"I assume you're working with Lacey? The name is Jacob. If you need anything, just lemme know." He smiled and grabbed my keys before jumping into the car and driving away. They definitely didn't need my piece of trash clogging up the view of this mega-mansion.

I grabbed my gear and walked through the massive, wrought-iron double doors. The moment I stepped inside, my eyes went to a wall of windows. The backyard was set up for about one hundred and fifty guests, and florists worked on an arch made of the same white and green florals. The ballroom area was imposing, with gold and white accents in a modern but not gaudy way.

I heard some girls murmuring and walked upstairs toward them, assuming that was where Lacey and the bride would be. The bride was finishing her makeup, and I could see Lacey in the corner. She was an older lady who loved to dress boho and always had elaborate hairstyles on wedding days. She was setting up her cameras and wearing a burgundy maxi skirt and a flowy black top. Today, her hair was in two braids that tied in the back.

"Hey, Lacey," I said, and she looked up at me and scowled.

"Give me your camera. I need to put my SD card in it."

Oh, straight to the point. Today is going to be lovely.

"You got it." I smiled sweetly, hoping my positivity might shine into her soul.

"You'll be helping me set up the flatlay, and then I'll photograph it."

That is how it always was for us. I would set up the shot for her, and she would come in, take the photo and claim all the credit. It was okay, though. There was something about having to interact with the bride that made me anxious. I felt as though people could automatically read deep down inside of me, so sitting back and watching was where I felt comfortable.

"Okay, sounds good," I murmured as I gathered the flatlay items.

"Remember, Tatum, do not talk unless specifically spoken to by the bride, groom, or myself. Do you understand?" She looked sternly at me. Her voice was quiet so as not to let the other girls in the room hear her discipline me.

"Mm-hmm." I walked away, not giving her anything more.

I often shivered at the similarities between Lacey and Cameron. Part of me wondered why I allowed people like this to have such control over me and my actions. I knew moving here would physically put distance between me and my other life, but I wanted to heal the inner me so badly. I wanted to become someone I could tell my future kids I was proud of. By aligning myself with people like Lacey and depending on her, I knew I was only forcing myself to keep the pain and the rot inside. I needed to break free of any and all relationships that kept me thinking I was nobody.

I shook my head to restart my brain and return to reality. I began laying out the bridal details so I could go into creating the flatlay for Lacey, or where the invitation was photographed with the garter, earrings, jewelry, and rings. It was mindless work.

"Okay, girls, let's get into our matching pajamas and jump onto the bed with Macey in the front." I glanced at where Lacey was gathering the bridesmaids and the bride, Macey, to do cute photos on the bed.

I grabbed everything to work on and staged for the shot. I enjoyed watching Lacey work because, while I didn't love her personally, she was a boss professionally. She always had a smile on her face and was efficient and personable. My people-pleasing past prevented me from having the confidence to do this full-time.

Secretly, I was scared that if I started to build my social media more, then Cameron could find me. I barely had any socials. On Insta, I used an avatar of a girl resembling me and a different name. I wanted to keep him from accessing me or discovering where I was. Thus, working behind the scenes for Lacey was my perfect role.

After laying everything out, I walked over and tapped her on the shoulder. She glared at me and spoke when I gave her a small nod.

"Take over the girls, and I'll grab the flat lay." Before walking off, she whispered, "Don't fuck up."

I had never been allowed to take control of the bride, so this was a pleasant surprise.

"All right, girls, let's jump onto the bed. And go ahead and face the window."

A gaggle of excited giggles rang out as I tried to wrangle eight bridesmaids and the bride, who were busy chatting on the bed already.

"Let's get four girls behind the bride on your knees with arms around each other. The other four can be in front, sitting mermaid style on your hips." I motioned to everyone, my voice becoming more confident as I spoke.

"Make sure the hair ties are off your wrists, and let's do no shoes for this one." I glanced over at Lacey, who was busy photographing the details I laid out for her, and she looked over with a silent nod of approval. I didn't *need* her support, but knowing I was doing something right felt good.

"So, I know you just went on a bachelorette trip. Look at the girl who got the drunkest on the trip." A bunch of eyes looked to the bride. They laughed as they recounted different memories of their bachelorette trip as I snapped away, surprising myself at my confidence.

The rest of the afternoon flew by in a breeze. Every so often, instead of barking orders at me, Lacey would occasionally ask me to step in and photograph something while she was busy elsewhere. I had no idea what prompted this change, but I wouldn't complain about it.

When it was time for the ceremony, Lacey and I met beforehand to talk over the game plan since this was one of the critical parts of being a wedding photographer.

"You can stay at the back of the aisle, a little to the left, while the wedding party, the bride, and her dad walk toward me."

"All right, I'll grab a shot of them walking down the aisle."

"Do not step in front of me, whatever you do."

I nodded. Here I was, thinking a new Lacey was coming, but I was almost pleased when her old self reared its ugly head.

It was a warm day, with a slight breeze from the ocean wafting up the hill to the back garden where the ceremony space was set up.

The ceremony would start in about fifteen minutes, so I told Lacey I was running to the restroom.

After touching up the sweat dripping down my forehead and pulling my hair back into a sleek low ponytail, I returned to the ceremony space. After walking back to the space, I looked at Lacey, who was already in position and glaring at me disapprovingly.

Almost all the guests had piled in, and I went where I was instructed to stand right behind three large men in suits.

Just as the music began, my hands began to sweat. Being surrounded by this many people felt...unsafe. It felt like Cameron or one of his buddies could easily access me. It created uncertainty and tainted the professional identity I was supposed to uphold. Logically, I knew Cam wouldn't be here because this type of crowd screamed bougie. His friends were definitely not like this, but at the same time, I knew that the more eyes I had on me, the more likely he could gain access to me. Typically I stuck with more intimate weddings when working with Lacey, so this was my biggest one yet.

My breath became ragged, and my camera felt slick in my hands. The procession began, so I took long, slow breaths to power through my impending panic attack.

"You can break down at home," I told myself under my breath.

As I focused on what was happening before me, I snapped a few photos of the bridesmaids and groomsmen coming down the aisle. The music changed, and I knew this signaled the bride and her father to get in place.

My camera was attached to a strap that went across my body. It was bulky and leather but could support the camera if it fell to my side. But if the camera slipped from my hands and fell to my hip, I would be off balance.

Pulling my camera up to photograph the bride, I took a small step forward. Unbeknownst to me, a small rock was in my path. As soon as I stepped forward, the 'oh shit' moment I couldn't control flashed in my head.

My foot twisted slightly, and I let my camera drop toward my hip. The strap held onto the camera but knocked me more off balance than usual. I felt myself pitch forward into the middle of the aisle.

"Fuck," I gasped as I lurched forward, knowing damn well nothing would stop me. Lacey was going to fire me, and I'd probably end up on some YouTube video in those embarrassing wedding moments reels. Cam was most certainly going to find me.

I was totally and utterly fucked.

In a whirlwind of events, a beefy arm swiftly extended from one of the chairs in the last row as I was about to take a tumble. I felt a combination of fear and amusement as I shifted my focus from the bride to the person behind this unexpected move. He prevented me from an embarrassing fall, guiding me instead into the back of his chair, causing my camera to collide with his hip.

"Umph" was all I could say, and then I gave a huge sigh of relief when I realized no guest saw the potential kerfuffle. The bride walked down the aisle with her dad without a hitch.

I glanced at my savior and was frozen in shock. He was the epitome of male beauty, with piercing emerald eyes. His broad shoulders and strong arms were perfectly showcased in a designer suit that fit him like a glove. Every muscle in his body seemed to ripple under the fabric, and my eyes couldn't help but linger on the way it hugged his taut thighs. His tousled black curls had fallen across his face, drawing my attention to his sharp jawline and full lips.

He wasn't like any other man I'd ever seen—rugged, primal, and absolutely breathtaking.

"I am so incredibly sorry. Thank you so much. I don't know what happened. I must have tripped, or my ankle went out. . ." I rambled to the stranger.

"Hey, it's all good." His voice was smooth as silk, and a slow, seductive smile played on his lips. A breeze carried the scent of smoke and leather to my nostrils, and my heart started racing.

He winked at me, his gaze lingering on mine. My cheeks felt hot.

"Sorry again." I pulled away from his grasp, still holding onto my hips, preventing me from falling forward. I walked away to regain my composure, where the guests and Lacey couldn't see me.

My body was betraying me. Despite my best efforts to remain composed, his hand on my hip sent an electric shock through me that I couldn't ignore. It was a feeling I had never experienced with another man, especially never with Cameron.

Since moving out here, I was so focused on healing myself that I didn't put much thought into dating. Despite my friends' attempts to push me to socialize and date, I resisted. I knew I wasn't ready to open up to anyone else yet.

But that didn't mean I didn't have needs. I had my vibrator, Dominic. Though it had been years since I associated sex with anything other than lust and pain. My body responded in a way I wasn't ready for, leaving me vulnerable and exposed. I had to stop thinking.

I knew I needed to get back out there and continue photographing the ceremony; otherwise, Lacey would have my head for breakfast tomorrow. I grabbed my phone from my fanny pack and quickly texted Maeve.

Tatum: *Shit. Shit. Shit. I have so much to tell you. No, not about Lacey. I almost ruined a wedding. Meet for coffee tomorrow?*

I knew we both had off the next day, so I quickly shoved my phone into my pocket without waiting for a response and ran back to the ceremony. Lacey was too busy photographing the ceremony to notice I'd left and returned. I grabbed my camera and began walking around the aisles, snapping photos of guests and tearful bridesmaids blotting the tears from their cheeks. I was lost in the grandiosity of the event that it wasn't until the very end that my eyes looked to the last row.

When I saw him there, all I could see were bright eyes staring at me as if they had been fixated there the entire time. A slight smirk crept on his face, and my cheeks warmed immediately. I looked down and walked toward the back of the aisle as Lacey captured the new husband and wife's first kiss.

As the man clapped for the new couple, I couldn't help but really look at him. His carnal energy was still there. He was primal yet fit into this world so well.

His square jawline was stubbled, and it cracked from side to side as if he was thinking about something. I lowered my eyes to his hands and saw that they were the most enormous hands I had ever seen. They could probably grab my waist and hoist me up.

I blinked, erasing whatever fantasy was about to cloud my vision. No. I was not going to do this. This is my job. I will behave and act professionally. Plus, this man is so far out of my league. He is at a fancy wedding and just helped me not make an ass of myself. There is absolutely nothing more happening here.

"Get a grip," I whispered to myself.

Finally, the bride and groom headed back down the aisle together. When everyone leaped from their chairs excitedly and clapped, I noticed how tall the stranger was. He must have been solidly over six-foot-six. My eyes moved down to his taut ass, and I sucked in what might have been a bit of drool from my mouth.

I haven't been this sexually attracted to someone in so long. A memory of Cam at the diner flashed in my mind. The way he looked at me, cherished me and held me. . . But this wasn't Cam. This was something so much. . . more.

4

TATUM

Five and a half years ago

After our initial encounter, Cameron became a regular at the diner. As time passed, I grew more comfortable with him walking me to my car each night. It was a small gesture but made me feel safe and protected. The feeling was addictive, something I craved. It was a stand-in for the support I never received from my family. Even on my days off, I drove to the diner, waiting for him to arrive like clockwork an hour before my shift would have ended. I would sneak off to the bathroom to freshen up, knowing he would be there waiting for me. As ridiculous as it sounded to go in before four a.m., even on my days off, I was obsessed with him. On the days I worked, we had a routine. He would order a hot cup of coffee and occasionally some food. His order was always the same—scrambled eggs with a side of bacon. Simple and no-frills.

I could sense his arrival before he even stepped inside the diner. The pungent scent of car grease would precede him, and his piercing gaze would fixate on me, even if I was at a different table. It was as if his presence demanded my attention, his eyes silently begging mine to meet his. Despite the danger he exuded, I couldn't help but feel a strange comfort in his arrival that I had longed for.

When the clock struck four, he would wait for me to pack up and walk me to my car, only exchanging a few words. It didn't take that long to get to my car, but we asked each other simple questions. Despite the brevity of our conversations, I found myself longing for them, eager to be in his company.

"What's your favorite color?" After learning the basics about where he lived, what he did, it felt like another typical question to ask.

All I had gathered during previous conversations was that he was twenty-seven, lived in the area, and worked as a mechanic.

"Why?"

"I dunno. I suppose your favorite color tells a lot about you."

He chuckled. "Black then, if I had to have a favorite."

Of course, it was black. He was a walking billboard for the color black.

"I figured." I shrugged.

When we finally reached my car, he opened his palm and gestured toward my keys.

"What? You want my keys?" I asked inquisitively.

"Tatum, I just want to open the door for you." I schooled my facial expression and gave him my keys. He opened the door and jumped in, starting the engine. Just as fast as he jumped in, he came right back out.

"Why did you do that?"

"Just wanted to make sure everything was ok with your car when it started up."

I looked down at my piece of shit Mustang and was instantly embarrassed. He was a mechanic and probably judged me for not taking care of my car. It was never a priority for me between going to work and school.

"Maybe I can check it out at the shop one day."

As he saw me get anxious, he quickly interjected. "You know, just for some maintenance."

As soon as he said it, he slipped away to his car. I stood in the parking lot as the sky turned from blue to purple to pink. These exchanges with him were strange. Quick and often, if he said too much, he would just run away as he did today.

I went home that morning, showered, and lay in bed before my first class started. Everything inside me said this was weird. It was fast, illogical, and I'm not even sure what else. I didn't know what the outcome would be. Was this someone I would date? I laughed because Cameron didn't seem like the kind of person you dated. Fucked, maybe, in a quiet, brooding sense, but imagining us in public holding hands and going to a fine dining restaurant made me laugh out loud.

Honestly, it was times like this I wished I had a girlfriend or parents I could vent to. Sure, I had friends from school, but I never got to go out with them and was never super close. I know to them it seems like I work all the time, but I had to if I wanted to do what I loved, which was being a photographer.

Day turned into night, and I was back at the diner.

When he walked in that morning, he was different. Angry. His brooding sense was more domineering, and when the clock turned four, he looked over at me with eyes filled with rage and frustration.

"Get your shit. I don't have time to fuck around today." He looked directly at me when I dropped his coffee on the counter, spilling it a little.

"I never said you had to wait or walk me to the car. I'm perfectly capable of doing it myself."

"At this point, you've made it MY responsibility to care for your safety."

I was pissed.

"What the f—"

He grabbed my chin, bringing it so close to his lips.

"Do not finish that sentence. Come with me. It's for your safety, Tatum."

"My safety?" I could barely speak. He gripped my cheeks hard as he pulled me close to his lips. I could smell the perspiration as he slowly moved his face down to meet mine.

"I am doing this for you. I do this only for you," he whispered.

I didn't argue with him again. I conceded because his grip tightened on my face, and I needed to get out of there. To process later, I told myself. I grabbed my purse from the back and folded up my apron. When I returned to the front, he was pacing by the door.

We left the restaurant, and he looked obsessively from left to right and back again.

"What's your problem?" I muttered.

"You. You are my fucking problem right now because I have to make sure you're always safe."

ONE CHANCE

"You literally do not have to do this." I was so anxious about this exchange. I cursed under my breath that this would be the last of whatever the fuck this was.

I always asked him, "How are you a mechanic and work during the nights? I've never met a mechanic that works at night." He told me whenever I was working that he had just gotten off of work at 4am. He would laugh and shake his head, always saying something about cars needing to be worked on at all hours of the day in his line of work, even at night.

That's the thing about abusers. Everyone always asks, "But didn't you see the red flags?" I want to be like, of course I did. But I never really did. I was literally clouded by love.

This day was no different from any other shift. Until it was. As we headed to the car, a man dressed in all black and a leather jacket stopped Cameron. The words exchanged imprinted in my head as a core memory. A memory that would later predict the future.

5

TATUM

Present

I followed Lacey to where she gathered the bridal party and family for the formal photos following the ceremony.

"I don't need you here."

I had no idea what to do at this point, still flustered by that strange man at the ceremony.

"Don't just stand there. Go to cocktail hour and get candids. It's becoming quite annoying having to constantly baby you. You should know what you're doing by now." She quickly shooed me away and turned her attention to the family.

I shook my head as I understood her words and tucked them deep into my head. Walking over to the cocktail hour, I took the candids of people and details of the reception. I looked up from my camera and spotted the strange man chatting with other men in similar suits.

The guys sitting next to him at the ceremony were standing beside him, but it didn't seem like they were engaging in his conversations. You could see his strong jawline, and as he spoke and held his glass of wine, he had this aura of ease, and yet his stance said of an assertive man. My eyes moved up and down his body. I must have been staring for an uncomfortable amount of time because suddenly, I realized he was staring right back and walking in my direction.

He approached me with a sly grin that sent anticipation coursing through me. His seductive smile, mischievous eyes, and graceful movements had a captivating effect. I remembered his breath on my skin, his scent enveloping me, and desire grew within. With confident allure, he walked, his hips swaying in a rhythm that stirred longing. His magnetic smile drew me closer, intoxicating me with sensuality. As he neared, his gaze softened, yet the underlying passion remained. Weak-kneed and eager, I was desperate for more.

The two men trailed behind him like bodyguards. One was tall and imposing, with broad shoulders, a muscular build, and a five-o'clock shadow accentuating his chiseled jawline. His dark blonde hair was short and neatly trimmed, and his piercing brown eyes darted around, watching everything. He wore a fitted black suit that hugged his toned physique, and his shoes were polished to a high shine.

The second man was shorter but no less intimidating. He had a thick neck and a powerful build that suggested he could easily take down anyone. His shaved head gleamed under the harsh sunlight, and his eyes surveyed the room with a cold detachment. Together, the two men made for an intimidating sight, and it was clear that they were not to be trifled with.

I knew I had to do something other than gawk, so I pretended to be fascinated by the flowers in front of me.

"Are they ready for their close-up?" a low, raspy voice asked, causing a shiver to run down my spine.

I turned to see him standing dangerously close, his body radiating an intense energy that made my heart race. I stuttered, struggling to form coherent words.

"The flowers, I mean. Are they camera-ready?" he clarified with a smirk, his hand rubbing his stubbled jawline.

I blushed, feeling exposed under his intense gaze. I nodded because the words weren't coming out. I stood there for an embarrassing amount of time, just fucking smiling.

"How long have you been a wedding photographer?" he asked, his voice smooth and seductive.

I knew I should back away and escape, but I was trapped in his gravitational pull.

"Not a photographer, actually. I just work with one," I managed to reply, trying to inch away. He stepped forward, and my heart skipped a beat, but he didn't touch me. Instead, he stood his ground, his eyes holding me captive.

"Are you okay from earlier?" He leaned down before whispering, "I did, after all, save you from falling."

Nope. This was not going to happen. I had to get out of here. I felt something awakened in my core. My hands were sweaty, and if I walked closer to him, I would be engulfed by his beautifully handsome and large arms.

"What is going on here?" a very familiar voice asked over my shoulder. It was stern but still professional, as this man was still a guest; I assumed Lacey didn't want to discipline me in front of him.

"I was just photographing cocktail hour like you requested," I said quietly, hoping this would appease her and not earn me a lecture.

"The cocktail hour is over there." She gestured a few feet away where the mingling guests were.

"Yes, I was just over there. But I came over to do some detail shots and—" I was abruptly cut off before finishing my sentence.

"She was showing me something. I am a guest at this wedding, but I'm not acquainted with you...?"

"Oh, I'm sorry, sir. My name is Lacey, and I am a part of Lacey Ann Photography. I was hired to shoot the wedding. Tatum is my assistant." She gestured to me, standing off to the side.

"Mm-hmm," I muttered under my breath, rolling my eyes in a break in professionalism. The stranger's lips curled in a smile. Shit, he heard me. My mind raced with thoughts of what he must think of me, cursing my slip-up. I felt a rush of embarrassment wash over me.

"Tatum," he repeated just low enough for me to hear it. His baritone voice reverberated inside my brain, and I could feel myself dripping underneath my clothes.

He spoke again. "Well, Lacey. Tatum was just showing me some of the best spots to photograph. Since I'm an old friend of the groom, I think it best that you allow her to continue as she was."

The two men I had forgotten until this moment were just behind him and stepped closer to Lacey. Their presence was staggeringly assertive.

"Yes. Yes, of course. Please, Tatum, continue. And go ahead and finish photographing the rest of the guests." She spoke with a slight annoyance.

The stranger's tone dominated the conversation.

"I think it would be best if *you* continue photographing the guests. Since you are the wedding photographer today, as you previously stated." His smirk could probably be seen across the ocean.

"Oh. Okay, sir."

She looked in my direction before saying, "See you when you're ready."

She walked toward the crowd, eventually disappearing into the sea of people. The two men took a few steps back to their original position. Watching Lacey be put in her place like a sad little puppy made me too happy.

"You shouldn't let her speak to you like that," he growled.

"I'm just her assistant. I really don't want to get in trouble." I started to gather my stuff before I looked over my shoulder to get one last look.

"Thank you, though. This was probably the first time in my life that anyone stood up for me."

With that, I left to find Lacey and didn't look back. When I got to her, she barely acknowledged me.

I was silent the rest of the evening as Lacey quietly instructed me on what to do, and I listened. Never once did I set eyes in the direction of the strange man in fear of being sucked into his captivating aura.

When the night ended, Lacey and I parted ways with no more than a short goodbye. I went to the valet station, where my car was parked.

"Here to get your car?" Jacob, the valet who parked my car at the start of the day, asked.

"Yes, please." I smiled politely at him.

"You know, some guy was asking what car you drove. A little strange if you ask me, but I didn't say anything and made sure he left, so there won't be anyone stalking you or anything if you're worried," he rambled.

"Oh. How scary. Did you, by any chance, get his name?"

My voice hitched. Please, God, don't let it be Cam. Please let me be safe. Please let me be free of him and the shop.

"Naw, but he was one of the guests. Big guy with a navy blue suit."

I breathed a sigh of relief. It wasn't Cam.

I grabbed my car and thanked Jacob before heading home. I couldn't stop thinking about the scent of the strange man.

When I got home, no one from the main house was up, so I quietly slipped into my little casita. I took a warm shower and lay in bed, hoping sleep would wash over me. But that didn't happen. I stirred in my bed, full of anxious excitement. I stared at the ceiling, letting the evening play out in my mind. The handsome man, the way he stood up to Lacey, and fearing that Cam would find me at any turn that I took.

I needed a release from the anxiety bubbling up in my chest. I turned over and opened the top drawer of my nightstand.

"Well, Dominic, today is your lucky day," I whispered as I grabbed my vibrator.

I shifted under the covers and placed the vibrator over my throbbing core. I shut my eyes and thought of the handsome stranger. I let my mind wander over his thick muscled body and the size of his hands as I stroked myself, touching my clit as I pressed the vibrator closer to my opening. A shiver fell through my body as my mind quieted and lust filled in.

I thought of how the strange man walked over to me with a confidence I hadn't seen in a long time. I circled my opening using my fingers and let the vibrator plunge inside me. The smaller vibrating area helped my fingers as I circled slowly and flicked my clit. The other part of this particular vibrator had a thrusting feature that slowly slid into my wet core. I gasped and pumped it in and out. I shifted on the bed so I could press the vibrator deeper into my and used my free hand to explore.

I moaned as my thoughts shifted from what was to what could be. Thinking of his fingers trailing down my stomach and circling the same spot my hands were.

"Open up for me," he would whisper as his mouth moved lower. I felt my release build as I pictured his mouth sucking on my clit and gently pressing his tongue against me. I became wetter as I imagined his mouth ravishing me.

The thought of him touching me in ways no one had before made me sweat and pick the pace of my fingers. I wanted his mouth to trail up toward my breasts and touch them tenderly yet possessively.

His mouth would trail up my neck, placing delicate kisses as he moved to my jawline and across my face, finally stopping over my mouth. My hands were busy, letting the vibrator sink deeper into me.

As he whispered one final word against my lips, I felt the power of his voice travel through my body and reverberate in my core.

"*Tatum.*"

His voice was solid and steady. His touch was gentle and not overwhelming.

That was it. I exploded in overwhelming lust.

After a few ragged breaths, I pulled the vibrator out and threw it to the floor. I felt my wetness leak onto the bed. In all my twenty-five years, I don't think I've ever masturbated to a man whose name I didn't know.

I allowed myself to fully relax, and my eyelids grew heavy. My body begged for rest, and I could have slept for years. It was the perfect ending to a day of unexpected excitement.

But as much as I wanted more, I knew that the handsome stranger would need to remain just that—a stranger. It was a bittersweet feeling. I was grateful for the experience but mourned what could have been.

6

TATUM

Present

The next morning, I woke up and stretched as I remembered my night. The situation yesterday was bittersweet. I would probably never see that man again. A part of me wondered what he could have wanted with my car. I was still nervous that he was associated with Cam somehow. Maybe even hired to take me back to Chicago.

I shook my head and reached for my phone on the nightstand. I had a text from Maeve.

Maeve: *You never texted me back last night. I am DYING to know what happened. Wanna grab a coffee at Superblooms and walk around the bay?*

I had so much to share with her, and some fresh air was absolutely needed.

Tatum: *For sure. Meet at ten?*

I slipped into a buttery yellow sundress, the soft fabric hugging my curves and falling to a mid-calf length. The dress made me feel feminine and carefree. I slid on a pair of comfy white Vans to match my casual look, anticipating how much walking we'd be doing. After grabbing my keys and my favorite sunglasses, I noticed Tony working in the backyard.

"Hi, Tony!" I was so excited to see my neighbor. She was one of the first friends I had made here, and it brought me such joy to sit on her porch or help her around the yard.

"Hey, sweet girl. We didn't see you much yesterday. Busy day at work?" Tony was an older lady who was stout in stature. She worked during the week nannying for a family down the road. On the weekends, she tended to her garden or spent the day reading in the sun on her small porch with her husband, Samuel.

My exhaustion was evident to Tony in my voice as I responded.

"Ugh, yes. I worked a shift at the restaurant in the morning and then had a wedding to shoot in the evening."

Tony clicked her tongue in disapproval. "Geez, girl! You need to take a break. Unless, of course, you're trying to catch a man. In that case, keep up the grind to make time to meet someone and date.." She gave me a sly wink, not knowing about my encounter with a strange man the day before.

I shook my head. "No, no, nothing like that. Do you need any help today? I was going to grab a coffee with a friend, but I can always come and help later."

Tony smiled warmly. "You're always so willing to lend a hand. But no, go enjoy your day. I plan on making some blueberry muffins after I finish these bushes, so I'll drop some off at your doorstep when you get home."

I was so grateful for her kindness. "You're too kind to me. What did I do to deserve you guys?"

Tony patted my shoulder. "You're the blessing, dear girl." I returned her smile and waved as I made my way back to my car, avoiding the cactus that had given me grief the day before.

As I pulled into the coffee shop, I caught sight of Maeve waiting in line. Her gorgeous hair was pulled back in a high ponytail, with a burnt orange headband. Oversized boyfriend shorts and a large cream button-up completed her outfit, but her two little girls in the stroller stole the show. Kelsie was the oldest at five, and her sister Kinsley was four. They both had the curliest blonde hair; seeing them made me wonder what it would be like to have kids. It was such a foreign concept, but Maeve made it seem effortless. Her ex-husband left her for his partner, Stephen but the four of them all remained cordial and parented the girls together. Maeve's parents took her in after the divorce and they had been living together while she worked at the restaurant.

"Hi, girls," I said, patting the two little ones on the head.

"I know you have good chisme." Maeve clicked her tongue, referring to my ominous text from yesterday.

Maeve smiled as she got to the front of the line and gave the cashier our coffee order.

"I'll have one medium iced americano, and my friend will have a large, iced vanilla latte, please. Oh, could I also get two small orange juices? If you have kid's sizes, that would be awesome."

Working in the breakfast restaurant world, it wasn't difficult for Maeve to remember my coffee order. We paid the bill and waited for our drinks, and I watched the little ones. Once we had our beverages, I found a cozy spot to sit.

"Okay, I'll spill, but I'm not ready to tell the other girls yet." Meaning Daphne and Chels.

"I promise I won't say anything until you're ready. Oh my god. Is this a 'you met someone and boinked them at the wedding' sort of conversation?" she exclaimed, emphasizing the boink.

"Auntie T, what is boink?" Kelsie asked.

Maeve and I looked at each other and laughed. Whenever we were around the girls, we had to use code words for things we didn't want little ears to hear. But really, it left us explaining things we still couldn't explain.

"Kels, do you like lollipops?"

Kelsie nodded.

"What's your favorite flavor?"

Maeve's face scrunched up with confusion as she stared at me, clearly lost about the conversation.

"I like strawberry lollipops," she shared enthusiastically.

"That's a good flavor." The little girls ran down to the beach that was connected to the coffee shop, and while they played on the shore and we watched then I turned to Maeve.

"Yesterday, Auntie T found a lollipop she wanted to lick until it was gone. Unfortunately, the lollipop disappeared before she got off work. She couldn't find it anymore." I continued the lollipop analogy.

Maeve's mouth dropped.

"You see, I found this very handsomely tasty lollipop that even told mean girl Lacey to be quiet while the lollipop continued to get as close as the lollipop could to my lips. Right when I was going to give it a little taste, though, silly Auntie T pulled away quickly and blamed work. Even worse, Auntie T didn't get this lucky lollipop's name or number."

"SHUT. UP," Maeve exclaimed loudly. A few customers sitting next to us turned their heads. "T, you better spill right now," Maeve said.

So, I told her about my interaction with the stranger and what happened with Lacey. I left out details about what happened that night with my vibrator, but I mentioned that I couldn't stop thinking about him.

I shifted in my seat, trying to ignore the heat building in my cheeks as I talked about him. Maeve's eyes widened as I gave her more details, and I could tell she was intrigued.

"You need to go find the bride on Instagram or some other socials and message her for the guy's name."

"Absolutely not! Not only would that directly violate my contract with Lacey, but she would slit my throat. She's also the type of person to ruin my reputation in the wedding industry."

"What contract?" Maeve eyed me.

"When I started working with her, Lacey made me sign something like an NDA. It essentially says that I wouldn't contact her clients or share on social media."

"Shit." We sat back in our seats as we thought about me never seeing that guy again.

"Trust me, I have tried to think of every way to contact him. I guess I thought it was just a sign for me or something?"

"What do you mean?"

"When I first arrived here, the feeling of loneliness overwhelmed me. I had just left a relationship that tore me apart, leaving me with scars. The last six months had been an uphill battle to regain the trust and confidence in myself. To believe that I was worthy of love again." I took a long pull of my coffee while staring out at the bay ahead of me

"It's like every time I start to feel like I'm getting back on my feet, life throws another curveball at me. And it's not just the fact that I don't have this guy's name or number. It's the fear that I'll never find someone who will love me the way I deserve. That I'll never be able to fully trust someone again after what happened with my ex. It's a constant battle with my mind, and I don't know if I'm strong enough to win it," I continued, my voice trembling with the weight of my emotions.

I never told my friends the full story of what happened with Cam in Chicago, but they knew I was in a toxic relationship with someone who mistreated me.

"Hey, you know you don't have to go on this journey alone. It's okay to let someone in and see where it takes you. Don't be afraid to let your guard down and give someone a chance." Maeve grasped my hand with hers.

I mustered a weak smile. "I know, but it's not that simple." Maeve didn't seem to hear me and just continued.

"I don't need to know what happened in Chicago, but I want you to fully embrace this fresh start. Only then can you open yourself up to the possibility of moving on. Grab onto the opportunity when it presents itself instead of turning away from it."

She was right. The realization that it wouldn't be with my mystery man didn't mean there wouldn't be another chance for me. I needed to keep my heart open to the possibility of love.

"Yeah, you're right," I said softly, a flicker of resolve in my voice.

We walked around the bay, discussing work and planning the next girls' night get-together. When Kelsie and Kinsley got fussy, we knew our visit was over. I waved goodbye and went home.

I insisted on helping Tony with the rest of the gardening. We got knee-deep in mud, planting different varieties of blueberry bushes. The late summer heat created a mess with the harvest, so I helped the best I could with the little knowledge I had. As the sun dipped past the horizon, Samuel brought us red wine, and we sat outside to drink it, watching the neighborhood kids playing in the cul-de-sac.

7

TATUM

Present

On Sunday, I could sleep in because I didn't have to be at the restaurant until eleven for the second shift. My next wedding with Lacey wasn't for a while, so it was a nice reprieve from working early mornings. Letting myself drink a little too much was my treat last night, knowing I didn't have to be in until later.

I was still in the lazy haze of the morning when I wasn't exactly awake but wasn't in a deep sleep either. I kept hearing a buzzing sound in my ear. It was almost as if a hive of bees were in my bedroom. Did Tony decide to take up beekeeping? If so, why was she doing it so early in the freaking morning? The buzzing was unending.

"Okay, okay," I shouted in my empty bedroom.

I opened my eyes and realized I was being bombarded with text messages in the work group chat.

Daphne: *I AM SO MAD AT YOU TATUM.*

Chels: *Why the heck is there a very hot man in a freaking suit asking for you, Tatum?!*

Daphne: *WAKE UP!!!!!!*

Daphne: *I will continue to blow your phone up until you answer us. He isn't leaving until you come in, he says.*

Chels: *He's sitting in Maeve's section and she seems to know who this mystery man is. If you've been hiding this delicious piece of ass from us, your ass is dead.*

Chels: *HE EVEN SMELLS LIKE MANLY HEAVEN.*

Oh no. No. Absolutely-freaking-not. What the heck is happening right now? My barely awake brain could hardly process the flurry of text messages that kept coming through. I quickly swiped away from the group chat to realize that Maeve had texted me separately.

Maeve: *Get down here now! A man in a tight suit is looking for you, and he's not leaving until he sees you.*

My mind raced with questions. Is it the man from the wedding? How on earth did he find me at work? What did he want? Was it Cam? Panic began to set in, and I felt my hands shake.

Maeve: *Hurry up, girl! He's not going anywhere and asking for you by name.*

I took a deep breath, trying to calm my racing heart. I needed to hurry, but I also wanted to look good. I rushed to the bathroom, frantically grabbing my curling iron and makeup bag. As I curled my hair and applied my makeup, my mind raced with a million different scenarios.

It couldn't be Cam if the guy was in a suit. Cam didn't even own a suit, leaving me with one option.

I finally threw on my uniform, grabbed my keys and sunglasses, and rushed out the door with my heart pounding. Samuel wished me a good day at work, but I couldn't even respond. In less than twenty minutes, I would be face to face with the man from the wedding. My palms were sweaty, and my stomach was in knots. I didn't know what to expect, but I knew I had to be prepared for anything.

In less than twenty minutes, I knew I would be face to face with my mystery man from the wedding. I didn't know what I would say or do. Was there a protocol for this sort of thing?

"Oh hey, I masturbated to you the other night and didn't even know your name."

That would be ridiculous. This whole thing is freaking absurd. Why was I so nervous?

"Deep breaths. In and out," I spoke out loud.

When I finally pulled into work, my legs felt so heavy that I wondered if I could walk.

Tatum: *I'm here*

I walked in through the staff door to the break room. Within seconds of opening the door, my three friends materialized.

"Why didn't you tell us you met some hot man?" Daphne practically screamed the moment she walked into the room.

"Shh." I looked behind them to see if anyone from the front saw.

"Where is he?" I asked.

"He is in my section. He's been sitting there since eight this morning and refuses to leave," Maeve responded.

"Also, two tall, chiseled, and intimidating looking men are in my section. They haven't moved either," Chels said.

Those guys had to be the two bodyguard figures trailing him around the wedding. Who the heck was this guy that he required bodyguards?

I don't know what came over me, but I urgently asked Maeve, "What did he order?"

"*That's* what you're curious about?" Daphne protested in disbelief.

This time both Chels and Maeve hushed her sternly, realizing the gravity of the situation.

"He ordered a coffee that I've been refilling for the last three hours and one of the house omelet specials."

"The two burly guys got the same but double omelet orders. They eat like freaking horses," Chels added.

"You gotta go out there, T," Maeve said quietly.

I knew she was referring to our conversation yesterday about opening myself up to love; this could be my chance. I knew taking this opportunity could be what I was waiting for, but I felt hesitant and unsure if I was truly ready for it. The scars of my last relationship still lingered, and the fear of getting hurt again loomed over me like a dark cloud.

Yet, there was something about this moment that felt different. Maybe it was how he stood up for me with Lacey or how my heart skipped when our eyes met. Was the universe telling me to take this chance and finally let go of the past? To embrace a new beginning? But could I really do it? Could I put myself out there again and risk getting hurt?

"Okay," I whispered after coming to a decision.

My friends all looked at me sympathetically. My lips turned up in a slight smile.

"I really love you guys." Tears threatened to fall, and I quickly wiped my eyes. I had never had a group of friends who cared about me or rooted for me.

"If anything, just think of this as practice flirting with a hottie." Daphne winked and went out to her tables.

"She's right. This is nothing but a little flirtation," Chels said and followed. Finally, it was just Maeve and me in the small, cramped break room.

"This might be it."

"Get outta here. He's clearly too rich and who knows what sorta stuff he's into with his bodyguard men trailing him," I said jokingly.

I gathered my courage and grabbed my notepad from my locker. It really was now or never. Straightening my apron, I walked out into the restaurant.

8

Tatum

Five and a half years ago

The day was no different from any other shift—until it was. As we headed toward the car, a man dressed in all black and a leather jacket stopped Cameron. The words exchanged were imprinted in my head like a core memory.

"You never finished the exhaust rebuild on the car, Cam," hissed the shadow man.

"Not here." Cameron suddenly pushed me behind him.

"It's gotta be done, Cam. The Knights are pissing on me to get this shit done yesterday." The guy looked around Cameron and walked to where I was hiding.

He asked, "This your lady?"

Cameron hesitated. You could hear the hitch in his voice, and then he mumbled something I couldn't make out.

Finally, Cameron pronounced, "It'll get done, Donny. By this afternoon. I'll get it done."

"You always do, Cammy Boy." As quickly as he came, the man huffed and slipped into a black Camero and sped out of the parking lot with the tires screeching.

The memory of that exchange was seared into my mind. I couldn't hide the shock and terror that must have been written all over my face. But then, something unexpected happened. Cameron hugged me. Without a word, he gestured toward his car, holding the door open for me like a gentleman. I didn't hesitate to follow him, still trembling with fear as I gathered my bag.

He told me he wanted to show me around the city and explain what that man wanted with him.

"Was it an angry customer of yours?" I asked inquisitively.

"Something like that," he said in a low growl.

Once he sped off, it was completely silent in the car until we got to where he was taking me, stopping for some breakfast burritos.

As we drove around an area outside the city I couldn't help but notice the cheap, dingy buildings that lined the streets. We were in the deep part of town. The air was thick with the scent of gasoline and exhaust fumes, and the few people we saw on the streets gave off a dangerous vibe. The silence was palpable, and even the hum of the engine couldn't break it.

Finally, he pulled into the driveway of a gray concrete building with big red letters spelling out "Cam's Shop." I could see the wear and tear on the place. The garage bay doors were open, and a few men dressed in black worked on motorcycles, scattered beer cans crunching underfoot.

Without a word, he got out and walked around to my door, seething as the men in the garage turned their attention to us. I stepped out, closed the door, and followed him towards the open doors, 90s rock blasting from inside. I remember that the guys worked all night here since it was a twenty-four seven shop.

As we got closer, I could see that most of the men were covered in dark gray and black tattoos, their sleeves rolled up, and their arms stained with grease. Some of the older men had gray hair and long beards, and the younger ones, probably in their mid-twenties to thirties, had the same vibe as Cameron.

In the back, I noticed a few young women on some of the guys' laps. They had on skin-tight tops and high-waisted shorts that maybe covered their bits, but if they moved too much, I wouldn't be surprised if I didn't see any underwear.

We approached the entrance with Cam leading the way. I asked innocently, "Is this where you work, Cam?"

"Be quiet. Don't speak unless I specifically tell you to." His voice was low and gruff, resonating with a dangerous masculinity that made my heart race.

As we walked deeper into the garage, one of the younger guys shouted, "Cammy Boy! Gracing us with your presence today?" The girl on his lap was tossed aside, but she didn't seem to mind, quickly settling in with another guy.

Cam's face turned dark with anger, and I could feel the tension as he replied, "I just have to check up on the bike for Donny. He stopped me in the parking lot of my lady's work. Some shit about The Knights getting pissed."

I followed Cam, keeping my head down and trying not to draw attention to myself and stopped when he spoke to the guy.

Cam's voice was low and harsh, like the growl of a ferocious beast. His tone was unnerving and left a chill down my spine. Honestly, the word "frightening" couldn't even describe how terrifying he was. He pulled me closer to his side, and I could feel his muscles tense beneath his leather jacket as he spoke to the man.

"Let's go to the back and finish this conversation."

"No." Cameron's voice was even more feral and possessive than before.

"We don't talk business in front of our ladies." The man motioned to me.

I was frozen, unsure how to react in this situation. I didn't know what was happening or what sort of business they were talking about. I looked at Cameron for clues on how to react, but he was like a statue, with no fear showing on his face.

"Doesn't matter. She's with me." He glanced at me, and I saw nothing but ice in his eyes.

The man gestured to us, and we followed him down the hallway to a very small office in the back. Upon initial inspection of the room, it was nothing unusual. There were boxes of paper stacked in the corner and a small wooden desk with a few computers and a leather chair. But something about this particular office felt ominous and foreboding.

I half-expected Cameron to sit opposite the large chair that signified it was for the boss. But he walked past the man to the leather chair. This completely shocked me. I didn't know to stand, so I froze at the door. The other man took the chair in front of Cameron. That's when Cameron gestured for me to come to him.

"Sit," he commanded.

I looked around, trying to figure out where, and finally noticed the piercing look on his face. He looked down at his lap and slowly back at me. It suddenly clicked that while he was talking business, he wanted me to sit. . . on his freaking lap.

I slowly started to shake my head no, but his voice echoed again. "I said sit."

I glanced over at his associate, who just stared at this exchange. It dawned on me that this might be a power play between them. If Cameron couldn't control who everyone assumed was his woman, then who could he control? To please him, I would have to do what he asked. It went against any feminist ideas. I had to sit on a man's lap while he conducted a business meeting. Still, I felt like I had no choice in this scenario.

I walked over to Cameron and did exactly what he said. I slowly let myself rest on one of his muscular thighs, and he wrapped his arm around me to pull me tighter against him until my ass was literally in his lap. He kept that arm around my waist while he grabbed a pen and what I assumed was the anticipation of what would be said during this so-called business meeting.

Cam finally exhaled and spoke. "All right, tell me why the fucking bike hasn't been done and whose ass I need to kick."

"Listen, we put Tiny on the mod for the new bike, but because he's just a new initiate, it's been taking him a minute to figure out how to mod it so that the crew can put max amount of. . ."

He trailed off as if he didn't wanna say anything else. His eyes looked back and forth between Cam to me.

"Spit it out, Tommy," Cam barked at him.

"All right, don't get your fucking panties in a twist. The amount of. . . product. . . that Orlando wants us to mod for isn't going to be possible. He's going to hand us our asses."

Cameron's free hand slams onto the desk, making me jump and yelp in fear. His hand wrapped around my waist and squeezed even tighter. A moan of pain replaced my scream of surprise.

"It needs to be possible. This is non-negotiable. Get the new kid off the project and put yourself on it. I will not let the fucking other chapter head asshole bark orders at us."

"Man, I was working on the 1969 Shelby and almost finished the engine rebuild."

Cam glared at him.

"The Mustang is a project for a legit client. Right now, getting that bike mod done is the only thing keeping The Knights from burning this place down and burning your fucking face off after I personally put a bullet through it and leave you here for them to find."

I was so uncomfortable during this conversation that I didn't know what to do or where to look. I kept my eyes down and fidgeted with my nails, picking off the paint from my manicure. I counted how many hangnails I took off to keep from saying anything. Tears threatened to fall because the air in the room was heavy and warm and Cam's hand was getting painful.

"You got it, boss." Tommy stood up and walked out of the office. The moment he left, I tried taking a breath in but was hyper-aware of the large arm squeezing me against a large chest.

"Don't say anything in here."

He heaved me off his lap and set me on my feet. The gesture felt so foreign and the opposite of what had happened in the last few minutes. I just nodded my head and continued to look at the floor.

He grabbed a few papers and signed his name at the bottom before grabbing my hand and leading me out of the office. Walking back through the shop, I noticed Tommy was standing next to whom I presumed was Tiny.

It was clear that Tommy was disciplining Tiny for something as they looked over a small, completely broken-down motorcycle, the parts on the floor.

Before leaving the large open doors, Cam turned to Tommy.

"I signed the papers to finish off the Honda and the other Mustang." Tommy looked up and nodded before Cameron gave him a pat on the back and walked out, still hand-in-hand with me.

He went over to his car and opened the door for me. As he walked around to the driver's side, I noticed the harsh look still on his face. When he entered the car and closed the door, he looked at me, and his cold business face fell and immediately warmth flooded the car as he pulled away.

"Let's go talk, honey," he said, taking my hand and pressing his lips to the back of it. I was speechless at the sudden shift in energy between us. One moment he was a boss, probably involved in some illicit business, and the next, he was opening car doors for me and treating me with tenderness.

That whole thing had me hooked. I was so intrigued and wanted to dig deep and unravel what made him tick. But at the same time, I couldn't help but feel for the guy. It must've been tough to always wear a mask and live a life that only showed a fraction of his true self.

"Precious," he drawled and pulled my arm toward his while driving, leaving a trail of kisses up my arm while still looking at the road.

"You were so good. I knew you were going to be the one."

I just blinked and let him continue kissing my arm. Looking out the window, I was startled because I recognized the neighborhood and saw him heading toward my house. If I didn't have enough questions swirling through my mind, I would have added how and why he knew where I lived. Instead, I just let him take me home. I was utterly exhausted, and whatever game we played tired me.

I should have been scared when he pulled into my parking spot at my apartment. I shouldn't have let him open my door and walk me up or kept the door open a little longer, allowing him to come inside. A part of me knew that by leaving the door open, I was allowing him inside my world. Or rather, allowing his world to take over mine.

9

TATUM

Present

As I approached the man, his large frame made the chair seem small. He sat there, with his dark hair, tapping furiously on his phone. His features were distinct, and his demeanor seemed anxious. Despite the strange circumstances, I couldn't help but feel drawn to him.

Glancing at the table behind him, I recognized the other men from the wedding. They looked like the guys Cam used to keep around—dangerous. Yet, this felt different, and I could sense that the man didn't have a weapon on him. The molded suit left little room for hidden weapons. The bodyguards didn't appear as terrifying as the men I was used to being around.

I looked at the stranger before taking my final steps toward him. My feet moved forward, but my mind was stuck in a whirlwind of questions. When I finally met his gaze, we locked eyes.

"Hi."

My voice was quiet. On the drive to work, I practiced a whole speech about why it was weird to stalk someone and seek them out, but the moment I came face to face with him, it was like the words had disappeared, and it didn't matter anymore.

His usual intimidating demeanor melted away, replaced with an unexpected tenderness that left the atmosphere safe and comfortable. In a moment, I saw a different side of him than what he presented to the world and couldn't help but feel a dark desire ignite.

"Hey," he whispered back, matching my tone. He followed it quickly with, "Do you have a minute to sit?"

I was taken aback, half expecting him to bark orders at me. While I looked around the restaurant, it was pretty slow for a Sunday. My friends were busy waiting at their tables, but they were looking at us. Maeve simply nodded her head, an understanding between the two of us that she'd take over my tables.

"Sure." I shrugged and began pulling out the chair next to him.

"No, please, let me." He stood up quickly, grabbed the chair the rest of the way, and waited for me to sit. When I did, he tucked it back into the table. Once he sat down, our knees barely grazed, sending a jolt of electricity through my heart to my core.

"How did you find me?"

He chuckled and said, "I had a feeling that would be your first question." His smile warmed my heart even more, enveloping me like a cozy blanket on a chilly day. Despite his devilish good looks, he exuded a sense of calm. It sounded silly, considering I barely knew the guy, but I felt a completely different vibe from him than when I first met Cam. The stranger exuded warmth and sensuality, drawing me in.

"I know it probably seems strange that I'm here, but I promise it isn't as bad as it sounds." His smile was so warm it felt like I had stepped off the plane into the California sun for the first time.

"It seems a little stalker-y." I remained stoic yet I could feel a tug of need pulling at me in the back of my mind.

"It does, doesn't it? When I was leaving the wedding, I couldn't find you, so I asked the valet about your car. I wanted to leave a note with my number on the windshield. Except the valet refused to show me where your car was." His hand looked a little unsteady as it ran through his stubble.

He seemed frustrated that his plan went awry, his jaw ticking. I felt myself tense and flinch because the gesture was familiar and not in a good way. But I kept listening to his story.

"Let's just say I'm not used to not getting my way and needed to see you again. I wanted to talk to you and look at you again. I wanted to see if those flowers looked good in those photos." I laughed remembering what he said when he approached me.

My hands lurched toward my face to cover my heated cheeks. I knew I was blushing and couldn't do anything to stop it.

It was as if he noticed I was uncomfortable and quickly shifted the conversation. "I looked up your employer after she told me her business name and contacted her. She also wouldn't give me your personal phone number but mentioned where you worked on your days off from her."

Oh—

"So, you decided just to come here?" I asked.

"Yes," he replied matter-of-factly.

"And you planned to wait all day?" I questioned yet again.

"Yeah. If you weren't here today then I would have come back tomorrow and the next day."

Oh, I was right.

"I needed to see you, Tatum."

A warm flush spread across my cheeks as I felt a surge of heat between my thighs. "Can I at least know your name?"

"Julian." His voice was low, and his chin tilted as he said his name, looking me right in the eyes. Almost like he wanted to reach out and cup my jaw, but I could see his hands gripped tightly together like he was forcing them by his side.

Julian. His name was Julian, and now I knew exactly what name to cry out next time I needed a release.

"Are you satisfied?" I don't know why that question slipped out of my mouth, but it did.

"Am I happy with what's in front of me? You have been the object of my obsession over the last few days. I was desperate for a taste of you, even a little smell of the sweet lavender, to melt into your blue eyes. I haven't been able to focus on anything BUT you the last few days, little bear."

"Little bear?"

"Don't worry about it. You remind me of something or rather someone."

As he spoke, I couldn't help but notice how his eyes sparkled, and his curly black hair lay atop like a crown on his head. He smiled like he knew something I didn't, and the little smirk on his face only added to the mysterious and sensual aura surrounding him, heightening the chemistry between us.

"Let me take you out? As much as I would love to sit here all day and watch you work, I know your time is limited."

He gestured to the restaurant, already filling up with the brunch crowd.

My heart raced as memories flooded back of another man who had approached me the same way. I yearned for a proper date that didn't involve a bedroom or someone trying to control me. Still, I hesitated.

"I'm not sure that's a good idea."

With a sly grin, Julian leaned in closer. "You see, little bear, I wasn't really asking."

His voice dripped with command but not the possessiveness I had experienced before. I tensed as he leaned in, wondering if he could sense my fear of physical touch. He never laid a finger on me, and I found myself drawn in by his respect of my boundaries unlike Cam.

"I don't like being told what to do," I quipped back.

Julian chuckled. "I love a good challenge. Give me your number, and we'll take it from there. No pressure, just whenever you're ready."

As he spoke, I felt myself melting under his gaze. He was demanding and possessive in all the right ways, yet still, he showed me respect and care. With excitement in my stomach, I knew this man was different from anyone I had ever known.

"What will it be, Tatum?" I loved the way he said my name in two distinct syllables.

This could just be a little trist. A fun exchange between two people in very different tax brackets. I didn't live in a fairytale where a man wealthy enough for bodyguards would ever be interested in a romantic relationship with a waitress and photography assistant. I needed a little romp and deserved it after what happened in Chicago. Something serious was the last thing on my mind.

"Fine. Just one date."

He started to speak up, but I quickly interrupted him. "With one rule. Tell me who the men are that always follow you."

He showed no expression at first, then pulled his mouth into a half grin that I couldn't quite interpret.

"Deal."

I grabbed a napkin, pulled a pen from my work apron, and quickly jotted my number on the napkin. "So you don't have to accost me at work again. Just let me know when and where."

He smiled, and I felt myself get wet almost instantly. Shit, I was going to have to freaking change my underwear all the time if he kept this up.

I got up from my chair, and he immediately did the same. "It was a pleasure to see you again, little bear."

With that, he walked out the door with his two bodyguards. I shook my head, unable to process our conversation and decided it was best if I just got right to work.

I started my shift, running food and shooing away my friends who tried to get me to talk about what had happened. The next few hours passed quickly, and our shift was finally over.

My friends pulled me over to one of the empty tables. "I'm grabbing us some coffee and asking the chef to bring us a plate of pancakes to figure out what the heck just happened." Maeve gestured to a little booth in the corner, where we slid in together. When she finally came back with the coffee and pancakes, we dug in.

Chels was the first to break the silence. "Do not make us sit here all day, T."

"Okay, okay. It's wild, and I don't even know where to begin. His name is Julian. . ."

"Now that is a hot name. Can you imagine it rolling off your tongue when you're doing the—"

Maeve punched Daphne in the arm before she finished her sentence.

"What? I am just saying it's a good sex name." Daphne shrugged and shoved a forkful of pancakes in her mouth.

I laughed at her confession and replied, "It would be a good sex name."

"He told me that Lacey wouldn't give him my number but mentioned I worked here."

"That might be the first smart thing Lacey has done in a while," Chels grumbled.

"I know. I was grateful she didn't just go around sharing my number. Then told me he wanted to take me out, like on a real date."

"What!?" the three girls exclaimed at the same time.

"We need to get you ready," Chels mentioned too enthusiastically.

"What are you going to wear?"

But Maeve asked quietly, "How do you feel about it?"

I took a second before answering any of their questions. How did I feel about it? Good, I think. I knew that I was excited, but I was anxious about how or why I felt this way.

"I am a little nervous. Excited though, and I did agree to it."

I added, "He also called me something different. He called me little bear."

"Little bear?" Maeve questioned.

"Yeah, but don't ask me why because he said he would tell me later."

76

"I don't get it." Chels looked puzzled.

"I agree. I don't get it either, but I guess if that's the weirdest thing this guy does—"

"Other than demanding to see you at your place of work? Sure," Maeve said, interrupting.

I knew she was looking out for me, but she had a point. My thoughts were interrupted when Daphne chimed in.

"Is it weird? Sure. I'm the first person to side with Maeve as someone who is incredibly cynical of love, but I can also see that this has potential for you, T. This could be the gateway to opening up and getting your glow back like you always talk about."

"I agree with Daphne. This is your new chapter, and if the strangest thing is that he calls you little bear, I don't think it's all that weird. Plus, it's nice that he wasn't aggressive or weird with any of us. He just wanted to see you and ask you out."

All this encouragement made me feel like a different person. I felt like a fire was lit under my ass and said, "Let's fucking do it."

That afternoon, I went with Chels to get my nails done. Afterward, Maeve and Daphne met us at a small boutique in La Jolla. The clothes were far too expensive for us, but it was a treat yourself kind of moment. After browsing the racks, I headed to the dressing room with an outfit selected by each of them. I also picked out something that felt the most like me. The girls gave me feedback after I tried on their picks. It was either too much, too little, or nothing super special.

Finally, I put on the outfit I selected. It was a low-cut, pale pink bodysuit with see-through sleeves and delicate bows at each shoulder. It made me feel feminine and delicate, and the color wasn't too bold or in your face. I paired it with high-waisted, light wash jeans. When I finally felt ready, I walked out to the girls.

"That is it!" they squealed with joy.

"What if he doesn't text, though?" I asked hesitantly.

"Then you still have a kickass outfit to wear to a club that we'll take you to." Maeve winked at me, and the other girls nodded in agreement.

"Okay, I'll take it." I grabbed the outfit, went back into the dressing room, and changed back into the clothes I came in.

I almost put everything away when the cashier told me the price. Never in my life had I considered buying an outfit of this price. It was a hundred for the whole set, which, while not outrageous, was more than I'd ever spent on something new for myself.

"Get your glow back," I quietly whispered after handing the cashier my money. I grabbed the bags, and we walked outside.

Chels insisted that I needed a wax. She said it was "just in case."

10

TATUM

Present

A long afternoon of prepping for a date that wasn't happening that day turned into evening. I told my friends I wasn't even sure when it would happen. They insisted he would text me soon and it would happen. I kept checking my phone, but nothing came through.

I finally got home at dusk and threw myself on my bed, exhausted from today's whirlwind. The last few days felt like I was living in a movie. Like I had a life that wasn't mine but imagined I could have. My eyes felt heavy, and even though I still had my clothes on, I immediately succumbed to the darkness and drifted into a peaceful sleep.

Suddenly, my phone buzzed, jolting me awake. I missed a call from an unknown number, and I never to answered calls from people I didn't know. But what if it was Julian? I couldn't let this opportunity slip through my fingers. The thought made my heart race with anticipation.

I sat for a minute, but soon, my phone signaled a new text coming through.

Unknown: *I tried calling. It's Julian. Save this number as mine. I want to see you as soon as possible. I'll have a car pick you up tonight at 7:30.*

I texted him the address of the main house for safety reasons then glanced over at the clock—six-thirty. Shit! I only had an hour and no time to prepare mentally or physically for this. I jumped out of bed and turned on my curling iron. I had curled my hair this morning, so it only needed a touch-up. Then I redid my makeup, opting for a natural look to represent my most authentic self. I slipped into my new outfit, silently thanking my friends for convincing me to get it.

I grabbed my nude heels and some dainty gold earrings. After spraying on my favorite perfume, I glanced in the mirror.

The person was both recognizable and not in the same breath. I saw my long brown hair and blue eyes. My breasts were perky as always, and I had gotten curves since moving to San Diego. I ran a hand slowly down my arms, shivering as I realized I could wear outfits with sheer sleeves. There was nothing to hide anymore. Nothing to fear. A tear threatened to fall.

"It's okay. You're safe," I spoke in the mirror. After glancing at the clock, I realized it was seven-thirty.

I heard a small knock on the door of the casita.

"Sweetie, there's a man out front who says he's here to pick you up." Tony's voice echoed from outside the door.

"Coming!" I grabbed my purse and quickly went out the door.

"Now, look at you. You look absolutely ravishing. Between this and the black car sitting out front, I think you are in for an amazing night, my darling."

"Ugh. It's a first date, so who knows." I shrugged and left the gate leading to the house's front.

"Hi. I'm Tatum."

"Hello. My name is Christian." The man reached out to shake my hand. I recognized him immediately. He had blond hair and bright blue eyes. He towered over me, his build similar to Julian's but bigger. Everything about him was intimidating.

"Hey, you're one of the guys from the wedding and the restaurant."

"I am," he said curtly and opened the door for me.

Before I got in, I said, "Who is he? Why does he need security?"

The man only nodded.

"That's not my place to say, but I've worked for the boss for ten years now, and if you ask again, he will tell you." With that, Christian shut the door.

It took about thirty minutes to get where we were going, and while I didn't completely recognize the area, I knew it was up the coast and by the water. When we finally arrived, I looked outside in awe. The restaurant had a small pathway leading to it, and looking at it from the parking lot, you could see it was on stilts over the ocean. The roar of the ocean was just beyond, and suddenly I wished I had worn something fancier than these jeans.

I felt my hands start to sweat and wished I had driven my car. I shook my head and mustered my courage to open the door.

Just as my hand was on the handle, it opened, causing me to stumble out slightly.

"Are you okay?" Christian held my hand, steadying and surveying me with concern.

"I'm okay. Sorry, I was going to open it."

"No need. I've got it. Let me help you. Julian is waiting."

"Thank you, you don't have to."

I sensed him as I straightened. I turned and caught a whiff of his scent—leather and the smoky aroma of an old-fashioned. It was intoxicating and familiar, sending a shiver down my spine. Standing tall and confident and more commanding than I remembered, he was there. He looked delicious, and I couldn't help but be drawn to him.

He had ditched the suit for a more casual look of khaki pants and a white button-up shirt that hugged his chest muscles in all the right ways. Time seemed to slow down as he approached me, and I couldn't take my eyes off him. When he finally reached me, he leaned in to kiss my cheek. His lips felt soft and warm, and I felt a surge of electricity run through my body.

"Tatum," he finally said as he pulled away.

"Hi," I responded shakily. I struggled to get the words out of my throat. Everything about this felt different. But it felt. . . right.

"Come." Almost as if his hands weren't touching the small of my back, he gestured for me to walk inside. The touch felt intimate and inviting. I didn't realize men could be so gentle yet so powerful.

"Please?" He looked at me when I hesitated momentarily. This was the second time he had asked me politely for something. "I'm sorry I got caught up with something at work and couldn't get you in time." I grabbed his hand, appreciating his excuse and followed him in. I realized we were the only two people there.

"Is it too late for dinner?" I asked out loud.

Julian only chuckled. "Oh, little bear, I reserved the restaurant for us."

My eyes widened.

"No worries. I work with the guy who owns this place, and he owes me a favor, so I just called it in tonight. This way."

He nodded at a table for two right at the very edge of the restaurant. We were inside, but the vast windows made it feel like we were outside. It was a beautiful modern restaurant with plush cream chairs and gold accents.

"Gosh, this is beautiful," I said as I sat in the chair he pulled out for me.

"Have you ever been up here to Del Mar?"

"I think I was here for a wedding once but I don't come up north that often." I added, "I don't actually do much outside of work and, well, more work,"

"Have you worked as a photographer very long?" he asked, genuinely curious as he leaned closer.

"Oh, no. I'm not an actual photographer." I laughed softly before saying, "I'm just an assistant."

"You said that before, but it seems like you could have your own company. You had great control over the wedding party, and I noticed..."

"You noticed that I was about to fall on my ass into the middle of the aisle. I was seconds away from being a YouTube star but not for the right reasons." I sighed.

He looked at me, and after a bit, his lips turned up into the smile that made me melt inside. The one it seemed that he only reserved when we were together—the one that was so different from the exterior he held around Lacey. "Hey, a star is a star, is it not?"

I rolled my eyes. "Who wants to be known as the girl who ruined a wedding?" I grabbed the napkin off the table and fumbled to place it on my lap.

"Why don't you start your own business?" he asked.

"I just moved here a few months ago, so I'm not ready yet."

Thankfully, the waiter came over for our drink order.

"Would you like something to drink?" Julian asked me first.

I was being given an option. It was the first time anyone had taken me out on a date and given me a choice. I shivered and felt almost. . . empowered? It was a ridiculous reaction to a glass of wine, but it was the first time I had been asked what I wanted and was not told.

"I'll have whatever you're having. I'm not picky."

He turned toward the waiter and instructed, "Get us a bottle of the 2016 Baldacci Cabernet Stags Leap."

"That sounds so fancy," I giggled. It was so obnoxious that even I rolled my eyes at it.

"I like my wine fine and my company finer." My laughter echoed in the empty restaurant at the ridiculous line.

"Do you use that line on all your women?" I quickly retorted.

"Not all women. Just you." He winked.

I needed to change where this conversation was going because it was flirting I wasn't ready for.

"So, will you keep your promise and tell me why you have two men following you? Well, and why one of them picked me up today. It was

84

kind of impersonal if I'm being honest. I kind of expected you to be there."

God, this bold new person was really coming out, and I couldn't rein her in. How embarrassing.

His face flushed red, and I wanted to bury myself in the ground. He dragged his hand through his hair and looked down at the table.

"I am so sorry. I had a meeting to finish up. Please know if I could have, I would. I promise to tell you about the bodyguards, but I'd really like to get to know you first."

I pouted, sticking my lower lip out a little.

"Do you know your nose crinkles a little when you get frustrated? It's fucking adorable."

"If we're getting to know each other, why don't you tell me what you do for work? You're fancy enough to attend bougie weddings and wear very. . . tailored suits."

He almost spat out his water. His eyes turned into the widest grin and it was hard to ignore the tight jawline and beautiful plush lips. I couldn't help but think how incredibly handsome he looked in this moment.

"Tailored suits, eh? You've been looking, then?" he teased.

"No. I just know that the better the suit fits, the more expensive it is." I was playing coy. I didn't even care that he knew I was too. The banter between us was perfect, like a sweet symphony.

"Ah." His lip tilted up on one side.

"So, tell me. What do you do for work?"

"Such a curious little bear." He smiled tightly and ran a hand through his hair, letting it fall slightly to the side.

I looked at him tight-lipped. There was no way he was getting out of this. Between the flashy cars, fancy suits, and protection, I needed to know what he did.

"I work with money—wealth management. I'm a middleman who helps companies work with each other."

"Obviously, it's been successful?" I ask inquisitively.

"It was something I fell into, a family business. But to answer your question, yes, it's been quite successful since I took over."

"Cocky, aren't we?" I mused.

"There is no such thing. I like to think of myself as confident."

The waiter came with the wine, and I realized I hadn't even looked at the menu. I was so engrossed in the conversation and trying to understand him better.

Julian thanked him as he poured the wine. The waiter nodded and left as quickly as he came. I took a sip and almost moaned in ecstasy.

"It's good?" Julian mused.

"Good? It's absolutely amazing. You have amazing taste, thank you." I batted my eyelashes and looked up in his direction. "Do you always treat your dates this well?"

He didn't speak for a moment. Instead, he looked into my eyes. In an incredibly slow and sensual move. His eyes locked into mine and then slid down my body. This movement forced my cheeks to blush. A hiss of air escaped my mouth before he looked back up.

"Only ones I am trying to impress." He spoke each word deliberately and asked, "So, where did you move from?"

I wasn't expecting this question. It was such an innocent question to ask someone, but the story behind the move—running away from my dangerous ex-boyfriend, who may or may not be trying to find me—was so much more complex.

"I moved here from the Midwest," I said blankly and matter-of-factly. He studied me.

"It's a story you'll tell me later."

He didn't press me for anything else, but responded with a hint of empathy. Immediately, I let out a small breath I didn't realize I was holding out.

"Thank you," I said quietly.

"May I?" he asked, reaching out his hand and gesturing for mine. Cam's touch still haunted me, and unwanted physical contact caused me tangible anxiety. Julian asking permission was different and felt safe.

His large hand reached toward my fingers on the table. He slowly circled the top of my hand with a finger, almost as if asking for it to open for him. When I finally consented, he took my whole hand into his. I felt myself melt at such a tender yet caring gesture and was grateful for the small act of kindness.

Any self-doubt eased then, and the constant drone of hesitation in my brain quieted. I leaned toward him, desperate to taste him. He brought my hand to his lips and slowly pressed a kiss to the back of my hand. He released it and quietly moaned.

Fuck. I needed to get laid.

"You smell like lavender."

I tore my eyes away from his hands and glanced at his face. His eyes, dark with lust and desire, stared back at me.

"Thanks," I said. "I have Tony to thank for that."

When I said the name, he let go of my hand and sat back. It was so sudden it took me a second to process why he let go. My first instinct was that he was rejecting me. He didn't like what I said, or I spoke out of turn. After a few seconds, the reason clicked in my head.

"Wait, no! I live in a casita on her and Samuel's property." I emphasized the *she* when I described my landlady.

"Ah. I misunderstood. I thought I had misjudged."

"No." I laughed. "I didn't come out here with much, and they gave me a killer deal on the house at the back of their property. I help in their garden when I can, hence the lavender smell."

"You need to tend to it more if this is how you smell after." He lifted my hand back up and inhaled.

The waiter came over and set two plates of the most beautiful grilled salmon, Wagyu steak cooked to perfection, and the fluffiest-looking risotto in front of us.

"I had them make my favorite meal here. It's the best thing on the menu." He looked at me and noticed my hesitation.

"Unless you're a vegetarian or vegan. They can cook anything you'd want—"

I interrupted him. "No, no. This is perfect. I've just never had anyone put much thought into a meal like this." I smiled.

"You deserve to be put first. I told you before, and I'll say it again. It's not often I'm told no, but that doesn't mean your opinion doesn't matter. Your voice matters here, which includes not wanting this. I'll have them make something else for you."

"No, I appreciate it. Seriously. This looks delicious." To convince him, I take a bite.

"Mmm," I moaned.

He laughed and looked at his food.

"I think it's time you tell me what the deal is with the bodyguards," I finally said after a few moments of eating in comfortable silence.

"You are so curious, little bear."

"While you are at it, I'd also like the little bear's explanation," I asked.

"Okay, okay." He set his fork down, and I followed suit.

"In my line of business, I manage companies that may not always like how I work with their money. Or they want me to make a quick withdrawal that I cannot. I have to be certain that there are no threats against me. Hence, Christian and James." He looked behind him, and I realized the two men from before, including the one who drove me, were in the back of the restaurant. He waved at them, and they nodded back.

I'm not an idiot. I've been around enough crime to know what this meant. The whole gross underworld is what Cam got me wrapped into. It's a scenario where once you're in, there's no way out besides a bullet to the head. You're broken down into a shell of a human by drugs or, in my situation, being trapped as the very person I hope I never have to see again.

I shifted in my seat, feeling uncomfortable. This wasn't the kind of conversation I expected on a first date. I sipped my drink and looked around the restaurant, trying to figure out the quickest exit strategy. But something about the way he spoke made me want to stay and listen. Maybe it was the vulnerability in his voice or the way he looked at me with his intense eyes.

"I'm sorry if this is too much for a first date," he said, noticing my unease. "I just wanted to be honest with you. I understand if you want to leave now."

I shook my head. "No, it's okay. I appreciate your honesty. It's just...a lot to take in." How involved was he really? Were my suspicions on the right track or just ramblings of fears of my past?

"Is this all legal?" My voice was barely above a whisper.

He hesitated for a moment, his gaze searching mine. "No," he finally admitted, his voice low. "It's not."

My heart sank, and I could feel the color drain from my face. The underworld again? A life of crime and dangerous dealings was exactly what I ran away from. The thought was terrifying, and I couldn't help but wonder what I had gotten myself into.

"Again, I understand if you want to leave," he said, his voice gentle. "But please know that I would never put you in danger." I looked at him and considered his words.

"But by admitting this to me, you're placing me in some danger if I know the truth right off the bat?" I didn't expect him to agree, but he nodded slowly.

My breath quickened before I said, "Where's your gun?"

Julian's lips turned up slightly, and he cocked his head to the side, pondering my question.

"Do you really want to know the answer to that question?" He looked me dead in the eyes. This was exciting him in some twisted way.

"Who are you, little bear?" he asked again when I didn't answer his first question. His once relaxed posture was replaced by that of an icy-cold businessman. But that didn't scare me.

"Show me. Where is it?" I didn't falter and gathered my courage. I'd been here before, and I wanted to know if he was also in the same world I had just escaped from.

Without breaking eye contact, he pushed his chair back and lifted his right foot onto his left knee so I could see what he was doing.

"I will always tell you the truth, little bear, even if it means you may be in danger of knowing what that is. I never lie." His raised pant leg showed a black Smith & Wesson strapped to his ankle.

"I fucking knew it. You are part of a dangerous world," my voice coming out barely above a whisper yet laced with an undying determination.

I'm done. I couldn't get involved in this world again. Been there, done that, and it practically killed me. No, it was worse because it beat me down until I couldn't recognize the person in the mirror.

"It was nice to meet you, Julian. Unfortunately, I don't mess around with people like you." I stood up and pushed my chair back. Simultaneously, Julian stood and followed me as I walked toward the door.

I could feel the presence of Christian and James and was infuriated. I knew this whole situation was too good to be true. A pain inside my chest pulsed, and an overwhelming feeling of pressure shot threw me.

The girl who was nervous and scared to come on this date flew out of the window the moment I felt myself sinking back into a world I knew well and had no desire to be a part of ever again.

I looked back at Julian and spoke firmly, "I'll call an Uber. Thank you for dinner, but I have to cut this short."

Before I could push the front door open, a large hand reached around me, holding the door shut. I whipped around. He hadn't touched me, but his body was inches from mine. His breath was ragged, but he only showed an unnerving calm.

"Who. Are. You?" he demanded. This time I knew he was not Julian, my date for tonight, but Julian, the nefarious businessman. He was on edge, and his tone was laced with steel. No more cute nicknames or bad pickup lines. Instead, I faced a terrifying man who dominated any room he was in.

"I'm nobody. I just—"

I gasped as he leaned down, and his nose traced from my ear to my neck. It was a mindfuck, to say the least. He was cold and demanding, yet his touch was soft and inviting. It sparked something deep inside me, and my body reacted to him. Instinctually, I tilted my head more to allow him more space to continue trending downward, feeling myself physically submit to him while my brain told me to run.

"You are. . ." His voice trailed off.

"I used to be a part of this world," I whispered, "and I don't want to do it again." Tears formed, and I squeezed my eyes shut so I couldn't see his face.

Instead of continuing down my neck, he pulled away. His cupped hand hovered next to my face where my tears threatened to fall if I didn't stop thinking. It was too much. All of this felt like a recipe for disaster.

His thumbs gently brushed under my, waiting to wipe away my tears. I looked at him through wet eyelashes and pleaded, "Please, don't bring me back into that world."

"Little bear," he murmured, wiping away a few rogue tears. "Who hurt you?"

Instead of saying anything, I just shook my head.

Julian's eyes searched mine, trying to understand. After a few moments of silence, he let out a deep sigh. I could see his internal struggle as if he debated with himself about what to say next.

"You're right," he finally said. "I shouldn't have brought you into this without warning you."

He leaned closer. "But I need you to understand that I'm not like them. I may be in the same world, but I operate differently. I have my own code, and my own morals. Most of all, I would never let anyone in on the secret without protecting them." I looked at him skeptically.

He searched my eyes for whatever answer he was looking for, and his eyes softened into something gentler. I still couldn't bring myself to do this with him. This world was too much for me, however he said he existed in it. It was too painful, and I had no power. I was a meek, lost female.

"I can't," I said softly.

He nodded and, without further question, moved his hand away from the door to let me walk out. I began to turn around when he cleared his throat.

His voice cracked when he said, "Please. Let Christian drive you home. No strings, just so you don't have to worry about getting there safely."

Then, soft enough that I had to strain to hear, he whispered, "So I know you're safe."

I couldn't look him in the eyes but nodded in agreement. Christian materialized from behind Julian and walked ahead to open the door. The wind whipped around as I stepped outside and got into the car.

It was as if he was frozen in time, and the world around him was moving, but he was not. As I got into the car, I looked out once more. He looked so defeated, like he had lost something important to him. I wondered what he was thinking, what was going through his mind. Did he regret telling me about his work? Did he regret meeting me?

As Christian drove me home, I couldn't shake the sadness and confusion inside me. My past and present had collided, but I didn't know how to move forward.

In that moment, pity consumed me. My mind was a tangled mess, struggling to unravel what I wanted from what I needed. I longed for a mind that wasn't haunted by the trauma of my relationship with Cam. It was as if his dark energy still lingered around me, constantly reminding me of the pain and fear I had endured. I could only hope that one day, the scars of that chapter in my life would heal and I could find peace.

We drove the rest of the way in silence. Christian opened the door for me when we arrived, and I stepped out.

"I may be stepping out of line, but the boss is a good man."

I smiled sadly at Christian.

"I'm sure he is, but I cannot be around this world. I barely survived it before," I said cryptically.

I walked along the path to the backyard and opened my door, turning on the light to the quiet place I called home. I locked and relocked the three locks, ensuring each one was turned tightly. I laughed cynically, realizing that my subconscious was obsessing over knowing everything was secure.

"This is why I cannot deal with that world. I have no space for more locks."

11

TATUM

Five and a half years ago

When Cameron and I entered my apartment, he looked around curiously.

"This is a lot of. . . color," he said surprisedly.

"I grew up in a very cold house, so I wanted to make sure where I lived felt alive," I admitted while gesturing to the bright pink couch. He looked around the apartment, his mouth turned down in disgust.

"I know you have a lot of questions," he said when we were both seated.

"I do."

He grabbed my hand and held it tightly in his. It was a gesture that felt sweet and possessive as if he didn't want to let me go and held on in desperation.

"I own a mechanic shop; that part is true. But I'm also the president of a motorcycle club."

I wasn't surprised, but hearing those words from him felt different than seeing him in action.

"What exactly is a motorcycle club?" I asked hesitantly, not sure if I wanted that answer.

"We do import and export. And I'm in charge of modifying bikes and cars to fit the product we export." He looked at me intensely, his gaze and hands not leaving my own.

"How did you get into it?" I asked meekly.

"I sorta fell into it. I was using drugs when I was younger and owed the club a bunch of money. I asked to work off my debt because I was training in mechanics. Years passed, and next thing I knew, I was head honcho."

How did I process something like this? It felt so intense and so fast. I was half expecting to have to drag the answers out of him, but he offered them up so easily. Something I had grown to like about him was the bluntness I hadn't ever experienced before.

Growing up, my mother's OCD ruled our lives. My father didn't escape that authority. He adjusted his job, work hours, where we lived, and how he acted toward me based on her wants and needs. Nobody considered what I needed as a child because I was quickly dismissed. My thoughts and actions told me I was stupid and unworthy of having a voice in the family.

"Why did I have to sit on your lap earlier?"

"Oh baby, that's just where it's getting good." He licked his lips as he spoke.

"I realized earlier that you're the missing link to my life. When I saw you working in the diner last month, I knew you'd be a perfect match. You're beautiful and so willing. . ." he trailed off, not finishing his sentence.

"Willing?" I questioned.

"You and I will be the fucking king and queen, baby. How does that sound? You wanna wear a crown and be my queen?"

It all felt so sudden, like a rollercoaster I couldn't get off. I knew I should be cautious, but my heart yearned for this man and the chance at a real connection. At the same time, my brain screamed warnings about the dangers of getting involved with a motorcycle club leader. I had never been exposed to this lifestyle before, with the drugs and illegal activities. It was all so foreign to me.

But despite my fears, I couldn't deny the magnetic pull I felt towards him. I wanted him with a hunger that consumed me every time I thought about him. And now he was laying it all on the line for me. How could I say no to that? The thought of walking away made me with longing and fear all at once.

My heart screamed so loud I could feel it outside of my body. This man was baring his entire career, life, and soul to me. How could I say no to him? I craved him when I went to work and waited for him until he showed up.

"What am I going to do about work?"

"Oh my queen, you're gonna quit. There's no need to work." He tugged my arm and pulled me so I was on his lap. I could feel his erection growing the longer I sat and looked at him.

It was euphoric to feel desired. At this moment, feeling his hard body pressed and growing tighter against mine, I knew saying no wasn't an option.

I leaned in and whispered, "If I do this, I want to keep my apartment. It means so much to me and my story that I keep it."

I looked around my beautifully furnished home. It was bright and joyous like I was. While others may view it as juvenile, it was the first place I called home. I spent hours carefully curating the things that felt uniquely me.

"Of course, baby," he said smugly.

"Okay. I'll be your queen, and you'll be my king." I pulled away so he could see my face when I uttered those words.

His lips, demanding and painful, crashed over mine like a predator finally catching his prey. As I gave into the pleasure and pain, I couldn't help but wonder if being queen was worth giving up my apartment, my job, and possibly my freedom.

12

TATUM

Present

The next morning I woke to my alarm going off. I kicked off the covers and groaned loudly. It was officially November, and the colder winter weather had started seeping through windows. Although cold to a San Diego native was summer for someone who grew up in Chicago, I told myself my body was still acclimating.

I was dreading seeing my friends at work. I loved them, but explaining what happened on the date made me anxious. I started my morning routine and tried to pretend yesterday didn't happen when I heard a slight knock at the door. It was so quiet that I thought it was the wind at first.

"Tatum, are you in here?" I heard Samuel on the other side of the door.

After a sigh of relief, I threw my robe over my pajamas and ran to the door.

"Sorry, dear. Someone dropped something off for you, and I thought you'd enjoy it now."

"I'm so sorry that people keep dropping off my things at your door. I swear, I indicated that my house was the one through the alley on all delivery instructions."

"It's really okay, dear. Anyway, I figure you may want to see this sooner rather than later. It looks like it's from someone pretty special."

"Oh?" I questioned.

"Will you help me grab it?" Samuel had a small smirk on his lips like he knew a secret I didn't.

"Of course." I smiled and followed him to the garden where Tony was unloading lavender bushes.

"What is this?!" I exclaimed.

"I don't know where we'll put all this lavender." Tony smiled, her cheeks bright with joy.

"Where did this come from?" I asked.

"A truck dropped it off a little bit ago. They kept unloading bushels of this beautiful lavender plant. Oh! There was a note. Samuel, give it to her."

He handed me a handwritten letter. I didn't need to open it to know who it was from. I already had a suspicion after seeing the lavender. Still, I grabbed the note, wanting to open it when I got in my house.

"I would help you plant these, but I have to get to work."

"Honey, you have to read the note." Tony nodded toward the backdoor, where a few people were coming out.

"They're here to plant it around your casita and make sure it has the right soil. But whoever did this thought of everything."

She winked at me and excitedly put on her gardening gloves. I thanked them and then walked into the house.

With shaky hands, I pulled the note out of my pocket and opened it.

Tatum,

I'm sorry for how our dinner ended last night. I cannot seem to get my mind off of you and wanted to make sure the next time I saw you, you were drenched in the smell of lavender.

-J

I dropped my head back and threw my hands up in frustration.

"Why do you have to be so suave?" I blurted out in the emptiness of my car.

How could he be so charming and why did it make me feel so vulnerable? He gave me a beautiful present that I loved, but it also made me uneasy. I remember how quickly that world seemed attractive initially. Love bombing was something I could not do again.

I felt conflicted. On the one hand, I wanted to give in to the temptation and see if this could lead anywhere. But on the other, I knew the risks and consequences. The memory of how quickly I was drawn into that world the last time haunted me. I quickly ran into the house to get dressed and then to work. As much as I wanted to indulge in this forbidden fantasy, I couldn't afford to lose myself again. I needed to stay focused on my job and my safety.

When I got to work, Maeve was the only one on shift with me, but she was late so I didn't have to dodge any questions, although I was sure they were coming.

I held my head high and spent the next few hours focusing on my tables. Even when Maeve arrived, I only nodded curtly before going about my job. Work was easy. I was used to the routine and predictability of it. The restaurant industry was fast-paced and didn't always leave room to dwell on your thoughts before the next task needed to be done.

My shift flew by and then was over. I was in the break room, avoiding confrontation and trying to get my things before Maeve came in.

"Nope. Not today, sister. I can read your face." She looked at me with an apologetic smile.

"Yeah, nope, to you too. Go pick up your kids at school or something," I barked at her and winced internally. It came out much meaner than I expected.

"Okay, rookie. Watch it. You sound like Kelsie when she doesn't get her treat after dinner." Maeve turned away and opened her small locker to grab her purse.

"I'm sorry. I didn't mean for it to come out like that. I just had such a night."

"I assume he didn't call?" she questioned.

I realized I hadn't told them I was going out with him. And everything happened so quickly afterward that I wasn't in the mood to send an update when I got home.

"Worse." It was all I could get out.

"Coffee?" she asked, her face filled with concern.

"I think we'll need more than coffee for this one."

"Drinks then! Let's go, T."

We walked to a little hole-in-the-wall bar a couple of blocks away. It was only two in the afternoon, but the bar was open and packed.

It reeked of old beer and piss from the wood paneling and musty interior. Entering a bar before the sunset was a new low for me, especially since I wasn't a big drinker.

We sat on bar stools with fabric pilling on them.

"What happened?" Maeve asked after ordering us two whiskey sours.

I recounted last night's events, even sharing about the gun and the bodyguards. I was tired of hiding the truth from those who cared about me. The need to spill everything consumed me. I shared the intense sadness I felt walking away from him and the gravitational pull sitting across from him. I explained how much I wanted to explore this but couldn't. Throughout my venting, Maeve held my hand, nodded in agreement, and wiped my tears when I couldn't hold them anymore.

"It's just a world I was involved in already and cannot go back there. It's what I'm running away from. I cannot get involved in that again," I concluded through sobs.

After a few beats, Maeve spoke gently. "While I don't fully understand, I just think if there's something about him that calls to you, you need to trust your gut."

"My gut is broken. It didn't tell me that my ex would be the devil reincarnate. He hurt me, Maeve. And I'm not talking about the cheating kind of pain, either. He used to. . . hurt me."

I attempted to run my fingers through my hair, but they were getting stuck in knots because I didn't have time to brush it this morning. Of course, the mats in my hair were just another reminder of the person I was before.

"Turn to the side." Maeve swiveled me on the stool so my back was facing her.

She gently ran her fingers through my hair, working out the knots one by one, then slowly started braiding my hair. The gesture was so maternal, making the ache inside hurt more.

I felt so vulnerable that I shared everything I had experienced with Cam in Chicago. I was forced into a club, and the abuse quickly followed and came under the guise that everything I did was for the greater good of the club and our relationship. He took me with his strength and power, making me feel little and useless. He broke me down and used me to get further into the club's pockets.

When I finally finished sharing, I realized that Maeve was finished with my hair. I slowly turned around on the stool and saw her face wet with tears like mine.

"We must look like fools to anyone else in this bar." I laughed through the pain.

"I love you," she spoke softly.

"Thank you." I reached my arms out, an invitation to embrace her.

She held me, and I realized our friendship was stronger and more intimate than any other relationship I had. Sometimes friendships were as rich as romantic relationships.

We wiped our faces and took long sips from our drinks.

"What're we gonna do about this Julian guy? And before you say anything, we're in this together."

My shoulders slumped because I was emotionally exhausted after sharing my story. "I have no idea."

"You said your ex was involved with a motorcycle club? They dealt with drugs, from what I know on TV shows and stuff, right?" she asked quietly so no one could hear us.

"Yeah. It's all like that in real life—maybe worse."

"Well, this new guy is wealthy, which is the opposite of your ex. He also was kind and never forced you to be involved in part of his life. He asked if you were sure you wanted to know, and you encouraged him to share."

"You're right." I looked up, digesting her words.

"Plus, the way you described it, he does something like managing money between different companies, right?"

"Also correct."

"So, these seem like different worlds. Even though apparently, neither of them plays within the legal system." She emphasized the last world as if everything she was saying seemed utterly ridiculous. It was.

"If we set all that aside and look at him as a person, he didn't force you into anything. And you didn't go to his place of work for your first date, right? No, you went to a nice restaurant like a normal person. While he might operate somewhere outside the legal realm professionally, he seemed like he wanted to get to know you."

"This sounds like terrible advice." I laughed for a moment, and Maeve smiled at me.

"Ugh, I know. I just replayed that back in my head, but it's true. What I'm trying to say is that you deserve a chance. We don't know anything about this guy. Maybe give it a bit to settle in before making any rash decisions? Decisions should be like wine; the longer you mull on them, the sweeter they taste."

I took her words and let them sink into my brain. I often felt whiny and meek because I was molded into that for most of my young adulthood. It's hard for me to step outside that mold and look at the bigger picture. I should have known to glance at the whole thing versus focusing on one thing.

"I see what you're saying. While they might operate in the same realm, the worlds are different in what my involvement would be."

"Exactly!" She was so excited she chugged the rest of her drink and slammed it on the bar counter.

"I'm not saying you have to go out with him again, but if the attraction was there and it was so profound for you, then I think you should. Just think about it." She looked up as her voice lowered an octave as she finished the sentence.

"I can't promise anything, but I'll think about it."

She nodded and said, "I gotta get the girls from school. Will you be okay? You can come with me if you want."

"No, no. I'll be okay. I gotta go see the lavender mess at my house." I laughed.

"Thank you again," I reiterated.

We paid the tab and hopped off the bar stools. After walking to our car silently for the first time, Maeve hugged me. Instead of cowering in anxiety or fear, I embraced the hug. I walked into the car and drove home.

I parked in my spot and walked to my casita, half expecting a mess, but what I stumbled on left me breathless. Lavender was planted around all the edges of my casita, and beautiful string lights hung from my house to the main house, creating a little fairytale land over the patio. The smell of the lavender was so strong it smelled like a whole farm was packed into this little yard.

Tony and Samuel sat on crafted, wooden Adirondack chairs that seemed so luxurious you could sink into them.

"Wow. New chairs?" I asked as I approached them. They had two glasses of wine over the fire.

"Yes." Tony smiled and continued, "From the lavender man." She winked at me.

"You must have some lucky charm," Samuel echoed his wife.

"I must." I smiled hesitantly and then waved goodnight. It was early evening, but I was exhausted. After a warm shower, I texted my friends the story I told Maeve. I left out the stuff that happened in my past and focused on what happened with Julian. Chels was screaming at me, telling me to call him immediately, while Daphne was more hesitant. She assured me my feelings were valid and trusted I knew where to go.

I lay in bed and scrolled through the wedding pictures I took in my editing software. It was then that I noticed Julian. The picture was taken during cocktail hour, and while I was focused on someone in front of him, I could see him clearly in the background. He was with people I remember him talking to, but his eyes weren't on the group. No, his bright emerald eyes were focused on my camera. On me. They were laced with lust and a fevered appetite. I quickly shut my laptop and groaned. Why were the easiest decisions the hardest to make?

The next morning, my phone chimed to wake me up.

Unknown Number: *I introduced you to my favorite dinner, so I hope you enjoy my ideal breakfast. XO*

I wasn't scared that it was Cam because I knew whose number it was. It was Julian's; apparently, I never saved it the other night. I had no idea what he was talking about, but I went to the window to see if he was in the courtyard.

A small package was at my doorstep, so after unlocking the many locks on my door, I grabbed it and walked back inside.

The smell immediately hit me, and I was transported to a bakery. It smelled delectable, and I quickly opened the package. Inside were three of the most golden, flaky croissants I had ever seen. One was clearly chocolate, and the other had a lavender smell. I pulled the mystery one out, broke it open, and realized it was filled with raspberry curd. I took a bite and melted into food heaven. It was moist and so good. While I was slightly weirded out that he had been at my doorstep at dawn, this package made up for it.

I didn't respond to his text but indulged in the treat. The day continued as normal, with no additional conversations or messages from him. After work, I half-expected to come home to another surprise and was silently disappointed when I walked into a house that remained untouched.

The next few weeks passed, and we got further into the month and the chilly weather. Each day was started with a new surprise, either a handwritten note or a text from Julian. While I saved his number, I never responded. He gave me a variety of his favorites: coffee from Blackrock, Reese's, fruit (he bought an orange tree for us), and more.

It wasn't until today that I saw a familiar black car waiting out back when I got off work. I had to Uber because my car didn't start that morning, and I was worried about being late. I didn't bother calling a mechanic; if it was something with the engine, which I suspected, it would cost me far more than I could afford right now. The one positive thing I gained from Cam was knowledge of how to tinker with cars. I told myself I would figure out what was wrong with the car later.

A friendly face appeared from the driver's side door, and I immediately recognized Christian.

"Nice to see you, Miss Tatum." He spoke in a low voice but smiled when he finished.

"What are you doing here?" I questioned.

"Mr. Marchetti told me to drive you home."

I knew this was Julian's way of getting close to me. I also realized that he somehow knew I didn't drive to work. Somehow he knew enough to pick today of all days to send Christian.

"How did he know I didn't have a car here?" I asked.

He looked around the lot for effect and back at me before saying, "I don't see it."

Motherfucker.

"I am not getting in that car if he's in it."

"Mr. Marchetti isn't in the car."

Marchetti was quite a powerful last name, and I finally had a full name, so maybe Chels could do some social media stalking for me. I shot over a text to her.

Tatum:*Hey, do me a huge favor? Look up Julian Marchetti on socials and see what you find?*

Chels:*Already on it! We got a full name now? After all these weeks of wooing, I'm surprised it took this long.*

Tatum:*He sent a freaking car with one of his bodyguards to pick me up from work.*

Chels: *I would usually be freaking out, but it's about damn time.*

I stuffed my phone back into my purse and looked up at Christian.

"Are you ready now, Miss Tatum?"

"You have to swear to me he's not in there." I crossed my arms to prove I wasn't going anywhere yet.

"As I said before," Christian said, his tone laced with a hint of amusement. "Mr. Marchetti is not in the vehicle."

I reluctantly got in the back when Christian held the door open for me. It smelled like him. The combination of an old-fashioned and a hint of leather was even better than lavender, but I would never admit that out loud.

I rested my head against the seat back, my eyes drifting shut from exhaustion.

13

TATUM

Four and a half years ago

"Get your fucking ass over here," Cam growled when he got home from the shop.

We had just moved into our new apartment after Cam told me it would be better if we moved in together. He made me sell my couch because he said it was too girly for a shared apartment. I nodded in agreement, not wanting to upset him. Last year we spent every single day together. He wanted me to help him with meetings, so I would come to the shop and wait until he called me. Somehow he considered me his good luck charm.

I spent my days indulging in books I picked from the library until he beckoned me. After a hard day, his mood could get intense. He would come home, and the only way to satiate him was with sex. He would fuck me until he came and then pass out next to me, reeking of gasoline and sex.

"Yes?" I asked him when I appeared in the kitchen. I gave him a small smile, hoping that would help his mood.

"I need you, baby." He smugly mused while sliding over to where I was standing. It was very different from his earlier barks at me, but that is how Cam was. He was always hot and cold.

"What do you need, lovey?" I asked gently.

"I have a favor to ask you. It's huge, but you know how much of a queen you are to me. This is your time to shine, baby. This is your time." He smelled of cigarettes the closer he got to me. He pulled me tight against his body, crushing me to his chest.

I knew what these favors meant. He didn't even have to say what he wanted because I knew it would be illegal. A project they needed a Jane Doe to do. Sometimes the club got a shipment that was too risky to pick up or drop off, and they would send me. I was more inconspicuous than any of the guys because who expected an innocent female to pick up kilos of cocaine?

I'm not sure when it started, either. Over the last year, our relationship turned into something completely unexpected. I had been coerced to have sex, quit work, move out, and was controlled by the man I loved. It was a mind game because some days, he showered me with compliments and gifts, while on others, he would be degrading and cause pain.

My logical self and what I read in my books told me I trauma bonded to him, but most of the time, I believed he was different. I knew he loved me and was the same guy who was infatuated with me. Everything he did was to protect and care for me. At least that's what I told myself to sleep at night.

"What do you guys need?" I asked hesitantly.

"Baby, we got the news that this huge shipment was coming in, but the feds were gonna shut it down, so it got moved to our crew in Indianapolis. It's being brought in by the Devil's Den, another club on the East Coast. The problem is that if other feds are lurking, they already got most of our info out there."

"So, you need me to drive to Indy and get your drugs?" I asked in a monotone voice.

He pulled me tighter against his chest, and I let out a small gasp.

"You're the best, baby. I'm gonna make you my wife one day." He put his yellow-stained teeth against mine, pushing into me.

"When do you need me to go?" I mumbled between hurried kisses.

"Tomorrow."

"Okay." I was defeated.

"You are my queen. Stay quiet, do the job, and get the fuck outta there."

"Now, come over here." He threw me on the bed, and I stared at the ceiling while he ripped my clothes off.

How had I gone from working at a rundown diner to living a life of freaking crime? Sometimes, I wondered what would happen if I told him no and stuck with it. No, I don't want to sell your drugs. No, I don't want to pick up your drugs. I don't want to live a life of pain with you anymore.

Those were thoughts that lived permanently in my head. The reality was that life was so much more complicated than just saying 'no thank you.'

14

TATUM

Present

When the car slowed, I was startled to see that I was most definitely not back at home. I stared at a house that stood on top of a massive cliff. It was dark green with black accents.

I didn't recognize the area but, looking around at the other houses, deduced we were up north where the mansions were. At this point, I knew we were very far from home and clicking my heels would not get me there. The car pulled into the driveway, where Christian announced we had arrived.

Hell no. Just my freaking luck.

"Absolutely not, Christian. No disrespect, but you can tell your boss that I am not fucking getting out of this car."

Christian looked at me in the rearview mirror, then looked back and pulled into the garage opening for us. Which is when I saw a glint of silver.

"Is that my car?!" I screeched, shaking the seat in front of me in anger.

"Mr. Marchetti wanted to ensure it was fixed before you got off work. There was a small snag in our plans, and it wasn't ready until now, so I brought you to it."

Oh. If I was going to live an independent life, I didn't need a man swooping in to fix my problems.

"So, I can just grab the keys from you and be off on my merry way?" I asked inquisitively, knowing this was absolutely too good to be true.

"Yup." He smirked at me in the mirror. Something told me it wasn't going to be this easy.

"Okay. . . so, can I get my keys then?"

"Absolutely. They're being kept safe inside the house. Didn't want anyone coming to steal it or anything." You could tell Christian was seconds away from busting out laughing.

"What you're saying is that you were concerned that someone in *this* neighborhood wanted to steal my piece of junk car?"

"Thieves are thieves."

"Go get me the keys." I stared at him.

"No can do, Miss Tatum. You'll need to go grab them. Safety reasons, of course."

"This is fucking bullshit." I grabbed my purse, fuming.

Any sort of meek and mild mannerisms I had flew out the window as I angrily threw open the car door. The gifts he had been sending throughout the week were fine. In fact, I enjoyed them and could admit that. This, though. This was illegal. I didn't ask him to help with my car.

Just when I thought this man had a decent bone in his body, he freaking kidnapped me and stole my car!

As I stormed out of the car, the words echoed in my head, "I am not used to being told no." This will be a first for him, then. I was about to walk into this godforsaken mansion and say, nope, give me my keys. Then I'll turn around and walk out of here. I am done with these games.

I finally reached the door and went to knock when the door opened. An older lady in slacks and a sharply ironed button-up greeted me.

"Hello, Miss Tatum. Mr. Marchetti is waiting for you in the back."

How did this lady know my name? Of course. "The Boss" told her. I went on one date with this creep that ended early, and now he's all over me. I don't get why he won't let me go. They are all the freaking same. Anyone who works outside the law isn't used to being told no. They always get what they want, and I will not be a pawn in anyone's game.

I followed the lady, stomping my Doc Martins aggressively against the marble floor. I walked to the back of the house, and the breath inside my chest left. It was the coziest and most beautiful home I had ever seen. I was expecting a cold, minimalist home but was greeted by warm various greens and blacks. It was moody with European accents. A giant glass chandelier hung over the middle of the room, and an open fireplace in the center. Inside the fireplace were candles of different sizes, lighting the room warmly.

Big leather couches flanked the fireplace, and the paintings made the room look like a famous art gallery. In fact, it felt like I had walked into an old countryside cottage in the hills of Ireland instead of the California coast. It was absolutely breathtaking.

My eyes were fixed on the artwork when I felt Julian's presence enter the room. I slowly turned on my heel to see where he was.

He entranced me. I had forgotten how handsome he was. My eyes traced down the gray joggers and plain black T-shirt he wore. I hadn't seen him dress so casually before, and I wish I could have taken a photo.

Right before he got to the last step, my eyes dipped to the outline of his cock inside his pants. I gasped and threw my hands up to cover the surprise on my face. With each step toward me I could see every outline and bulge. My brain didn't stay loyal to my body when it started to imagine how his arousal would feel inside me.

As Julian walked towards me, his face betrayed a different emotion than his confident stature. He looked cautious, like he feared I would run away from him. I also couldn't help but notice the gun tucked in the waistband of his pants, no longer hidden as it was in the restaurant. Despite the fear that gripped me, Maeve's words resonated in my mind.

There was a certain lawlessness about Julian, different from Cam. He carried a pistol but was the kind of person who would fix my car just because he noticed something was wrong. He was a man of contradictions who dealt with thugs but secretly loved eating Reese's candy. The thought made me smile, and my cheeks grew warm.

I knew I couldn't be pulled back into a life I had no control over, but being around Julian made me feel alive in a way I couldn't explain. He watched me, a small smile turning up his lips. He removed his gun and set it on the kitchen counter before stepping in front of me.

"Tatum." He spoke each letter deliberately.

"I'm here—" I didn't finish because he got so close that I could smell the alcohol on his breath.

"I know, little bear."

As the words left his lips, his hand gently cradled my chin, tilting my head to him. My breath hitched as his lips trailed a feather-light kisses along my cheek, leaving goosebumps in their wake. My body was ablaze with desire, yearning for his soft lips to explore every inch of me.

I was initially hesitant about his touch but was quickly craving it. He had a gentle reverence, and his eyes silently asked for permission before his hands made contact. The way he handled me was intoxicating, and I couldn't help but feel weak in the knees. His fingers traced along my jawline, the roughness of his hands only adding to the intensity of the sensation.

"I just need my keys," I said breathily when I found the words.

He pulled away, looking at me with fierce intensity in his eyes.

"I haven't stopped thinking about you," he whispered in my ear.

"I have," I quipped, but the words rang flat.

"You have?" he said, tucking a few strands of hair behind my ear. Could he tell I was lying?

"Why did you take my car?" As if I snapped back into reality as his hands brushed my hair back, I pulled away from him and moved to the other side of the room.

He didn't falter and instead stalked to where I was.

"I've spent the last few weeks sending you pieces of who I am, Tatum." I leaned back and braced my hands against the kitchen counter.

"I've tried showing you that I'm just another human. My job is separate from my personal life. I just need a little extra security."

He drifted closer.

"You are an enigma, my little bear. A gorgeous package that I ache to unwrap." He was close enough that I could smell the leather scent I associated with him.

"I scoured the internet for information about you, but all traces vanished five years ago. Then you reappeared out of thin air. Where were you all this time?" His eyes glint with curiosity.

"When I found out you're scared of my world, yet you know so much about it, I needed to know. Before I stake my claim on you, am I getting in bed with the enemy?"

"You're not getting into any bed with me," I gritted.

His towering figure loomed over me as we walked the length of the room, and I found myself backed tightly against the counter with no escape. His chest was heaving with each breath, and the heat emanating from his body made my skin tingle with anticipation. The hard planes of his chest were just inches away from me; his sheer size was intimidating and exhilarating.

"I can do anything I want with you without a bed," he said, a playful glint in his eye. His face lit up with mischief, his lips curving into a suggestive smile that sent a shiver down my spine.

"I'll ask you again, sweetheart. Who are you, and why are you so damn irresistible?" He played with the ends of my hair, his eyes moving up from my chest to meet mine. They were filled with passion, and I couldn't help but feel a tingle spread through my body.

"You're stunning. What I wouldn't give for just a taste," he whispered, not letting me answer. A seductive smile curled his lips.

"Aren't you afraid I know who you are? Worried I might turn you over to the authorities?" I asked, my voice quivering slightly as his fingers twirled my hair.

"No," he said simply. "Ask me anything. I told you before I will always tell you the truth."

"Is your job dangerous?" I blurted out.

His fingers grazed the side of my breasts, and a rush of heat flooded me, igniting a desire I couldn't resist. My work shirt hugged my ample chest, and I felt my nipples harden in response to his touch. He leaned in closer, my body craving him and yearning for his skilled hands to explore every inch of me.

"It can be. It depends on how angry others are at me." He laughed gruffly, and his eyes locked onto mine.

"Have you ever had a girlfriend?"

I have no idea why I asked that. My heart was beating fast in anticipation, but I needed to know before considering giving him a piece of me.

"I don't have girlfriends, little bear. I love fucking women too much to commit to just one." The answer didn't shock me.

"But you told me about your world." I puffed my lips out and ran my tongue along the lower one. "Whether you wanted to or not, you brought me in unlike the other girls." His eyes dipped to my breasts before looking up into mine again, silently answering my statement. It was clear that I was different.

"Do you have blood on your hands?"

He pressed his chest against mine, and I couldn't help but feel a surge of consuming need course through me. Every time I exhaled, my nipples grazed against his shirt, and I felt my panties grow wetter with each passing moment.

A hot wave of pleasure washed over me as he leaned in, causing me to shiver with anticipation. Sensing my eagerness, he grabbed under my thighs and lifted me, and I wrapped my legs tightly around his waist. He gripped my waist and pulled me in. His hands found their way to my ass, and he squeezed, tilting his head to the side and breathing deeply into the shell of my ear.

"Yes." He dug his fingers into my skin, forcing me tighter against his chest. I was in a perfect position to feel him warm against me. "I would ask the same, but a little bear like you would never do something that dangerous."

Something deep inside of me surged at the thrill of this. The confident girl was back, and she wanted control. This wasn't her past. It was her present and future.

My hands grazed along his stubbled chin. I looked at his lips which were swollen and hungry for just a taste.

"Ask. Me." I emphasized each word when I spoke, speaking against his lips so we shared air.

He laughed and yanked away from me to leverage his hands onto the countertop. I was wrapped around him sitting on the oversized island, and he grabbed my jaw with one hand, his thumb tracing my mouth before pulling back completely.

"Have you?"

"Have I, what?" I barked back at him. My legs tightened against his waist, knowing he could feel the wetness through my jeans. The secrets I buried deep inside of me would surface.

He looked at me through hooded eyes while lust practically dripped from his lips. The electricity in the room was palpable.

"Have you killed anyone, little bear?" His fingers wrapped around my jawline, tightening slightly and bringing me closer to him. His thumb traced slow, sensual circles along my chin, sending a shiver down my spine. It was a subtle gesture that made me feel safe. I could feel his breath on my face, and his intense gaze made it clear that he was completely focused on me.

I dragged my tongue across my mouth and heard his deep moan. I threw my hands behind me, arching my back, and thrusting my hips against his erection again, letting him caress the curves of my body.

I pulled my head back up and licked along my lips before I held his gaze. I watched the desire ooze from him, knowing I had him where I wanted.

I gasped out in a soft whisper, "Yes."

15

TATUM

Four and a half years ago

It was raining, and we were holed up in a shitty motel outside the city limits. The rules for today were simple. I would get dropped off at the meeting spot, grab the bike pre-fitted with the drugs inside, and drive it back to the hotel. One of the guys would load it on their truck and head back to Chicago and Cam's shop.

While Cam slept like a log, I couldn't close my eyes. I stared at the popcorn ceiling peeling off in the corners and felt nothing. I tried to will myself to be mad or angry, but nothing came. It was as if I was just the carcass of a human—empty.

Cam shifted next to me, and I knew that he would be awake soon. He was in one of his good moods this week, whining and dining me and spoiling me with gifts. I knew this was his way of showing how much he loved and appreciated everything I did for him.

I should be scared. I should be worried about getting arrested or meeting somebody that isn't supposed to be there. The end of a barrel very well could be the last thing I see. Somehow, I trusted that Cam was doing this to protect us.

"Morning, my queen," he murmured and rolled toward me. His erection shoved against my ass.

"Not today. I have to focus, honey." I smiled warily at him, hoping he wouldn't be mad at my rejection.

"Yeah, I understand. Let's get dressed and rendezvous with the other guys to make sure the plan is all set."

After we grabbed our things and I threw on a pair of black jeans and a black T-shirt, we walked to the lobby where the guys had pretty much cleared out any lingering guests.

"Cam, we gonna let her pack some heat?" Tommy asked while I sat silently between them.

"She doesn't know how to fucking use this thing, but we can give her a quick lesson."

Cam pulled out his revolver and rested it on the table. I looked around and saw a hotel worker scurry out of the room when they realized who they were in the presence of. The club was pretty well known in the area. The men wore black leather vests with the club's initials on the back.

When I was forced to go into the shop with Cam, I noticed that some of the ol' ladies had the same tattoo. The ol' ladies were the guy's girlfriends/wives. They were vastly different from the mistresses that most members had and rarely came around except for official events. I was the only exception. Cam never had a mistress and always brought me to unofficial and official events.

"Naw, give her a lady gun or something." Cam smiled at me, but I only shook my head.

"I've never shot one," I whispered meekly, not wanting to speak out of turn.

"Don't worry, baby. We'll load it up for you. You just gotta point and shoot."

"But I won't need it, right?" I was nervous and asked Cam and Tommy.

"Naw," Cam said matter-of-factly.

At the same time, Tommy said, "Maybe."

"Shut up. She's all good. Nothing is gonna happen." Cam poked the barrel of the gun jokingly into Tommy's chest. It seemed like fun and games, but we knew if Tommy continued disagreeing with Cam, shit wouldn't be pretty.

"It'll go well, and I'll get the shipment to you." I was confident enough to ride a motorcycle since Cam had spent the last year teaching me. I even felt confident about getting this shipment and not getting caught.

"Let's fuckin' go," Cam bellowed, and with one swooping hand into the air, the rest of the crew stood up and walked outside.

The plan was for me to get dropped off at the spot, a small rest stop on the side of the highway. We went during the highway patrol's shift change, so it would happen around five p.m. I was meeting a new guy from the East Coast club.

Cam and Tommy would be a few stops down the highway, and I would have a tail in case something went wrong. The tail would be hidden in the woods behind the rest stop. I was supposed to text Cam when I was on the way back to the hotel so they could follow.

When we got to the stop, the boys dropped me off at precisely four fifty-five. These things happened fast, so I was excited to finish in the next ten minutes.

I got off the bike I rode with Cam and removed my helmet. He looked at me with pride shining brightly in his hooded eyes. I felt proud of myself for doing this for him and helping the club. I felt like I had been letting Cam down, so this moment was significant.

He slapped a long, rough kiss on my lips and beamed at me.

"I'll make you so proud, baby." I kissed him gently on the cheek.

He started pulling out the gun from the hotel.

"It's loaded with six bullets. You just gotta squeeze the trigger. Don't be getting all trigger-happy, though. Only do it if he compromises the load."

"Don't pull out the gun," I repeated.

"Exactly. If he shows up with anything other than the chopper, it's a bad run. Pull the trigger then, too." He seemed nervous as the time got closer to five.

"Listen, baby, this guy isn't gonna be expecting a woman. He's gonna try to talk some shit, so you need to put on your big girl panties and show up for me. You are the mother fucking queen of The Club," he said and kissed me again.

He signaled to my tail to hide. The rest of the crew revved their bikes and started to pile away. I grabbed my helmet and shoved the revolver inside my jeans, pulling my shirt out to cover it.

As the crew left, Cam took a last look at me and gave a quick wave. I grabbed my stuff, and a cold breeze blew through the trees. I couldn't tell if it was a figment of my anxiety or if it was actually getting cold out here. The unnerving calm before the storm was approaching. I stood by the run-down bathrooms with my helmet on the ground at my feet and felt the revolver's weight at my back.

The idea that I was holding something that could end a life turned me on in some twisted sense. I had so much power with one squeeze of my finger.

I thought briefly about using it on Cam's in his sleep.

Living a life where someone else controlled every aspect made me long for a taste of freedom. I knew I loved Cam, but at the same time, I felt so trapped.

I quickly shook my head and laughed to myself. I was being absolutely insane. The last year of my life had changed so dramatically between leaving my job, moving in with Cam, and our relationship. Cam loved me. He wanted me to be part of the club because I was his queen. He was my king and would do anything for me. Why wouldn't I do anything for him, including risking my own life?

The thoughts rambled in my head until I heard the deep reverberations of a chopper coming down the highway. It was go time. I looked over where I knew the tail was and gave a curt nod. I straightened my back and convinced myself I was a total badass. This was going to go smoothly. I just knew it.

I saw a man on the exact type of bike I was expecting pull into the run-down and mostly hidden rest stop. I needed to make it through the next couple of minutes for the hand-off, and then I would be on my way back into the safe and loving arms of my boyfriend.

The bike stopped slowly in front of where I stood. The person slowly dismounted, giving it two taps on the side so I could hear the fender was not hollow, meaning something was inside. The product. Thank god this was going how it was supposed to.

The man in the dark black helmet had an insignia on his leather vest of an American flag and a pin-up-looking woman next to it. He was wearing black jeans with visible stains on them, and I saw his hands stained with black dirt and grease as he approached. I stood up straight.

"You with The Club?" he asked skeptically.

He pulled off his helmet. He smiled when he looked at me and showed his several missing teeth, sending shivers down my arms. He was a tall guy but definitely not as meaty as Cam. He looked like he could hold his own in a fight, though. His hair was matted against his head and sweaty from the helmet. But his eyes were the scariest part of him. They were void of any life, and I instinctually moved my hand to the gun on my hip.

"I am safe," I whispered to convince myself.

"Are you deaf? Who do you belong to, lady?"

I coughed, blinked a few times, and redirected my eyes to the ground. "Yes, I'm with The Club." I didn't know what else to say.

"I'm just here to grab the bike from you." I reached my hand out for the keys he dangled from his fingers.

"They sent a pretty young thing like you out here to meet me? Those fuckers scared of a little fed finding them?" He threw his head back and laughed maniacally.

He stalked closer, the stomping of his boots echoing in the empty lot as he moved.

"Lemme get a closer look at you 'fore I hand off these keys. Haven't seen a woman in a while."

Once he got within arm's distance, his greasy hand grabbed my chin, pulling it toward him. My body lurched forward until I was practically chest-to-chest with the man. I focused on the collar of his shirt. So much inside of me was screaming to keep my cool and not look to where the tail was. I didn't want to give away that I had someone watching me unless I was desperate.

"I just need the keys, and you can go. I bet there's a bar nearby with some ladies," I said, fumbling with my words and hoping I didn't say something that got me deeper in trouble.

"Maybe. But why go to a bar when I have something right here to play with."

His hand held my chin as he pushed my body against the brick wall of the bathroom behind me. My legs were so weak from fear that I almost tripped over them, and by the time I had felt the cold wall, my breath was unsteady, and I was trying to find my balance.

"You want me, baby? I hear it in your voice," the man said, dragging his tongue across my cheek. It felt like sandpaper against my skin. At this moment, I knew I was totally fucked.

With a shaky voice, I said, "Please. Cameron will be so pissed if you touch me."

His maniacal laugh started again. "Oh, this is perfect. You're the boss's ol' lady? You taste like a sweet little ransom."

Ransom? Kidnapping? The thoughts raced through my head quickly.

"I'm gonna make you my little sex toy while your boyfriend freaks out looking for you." The way he emphasized boyfriend was horrific. His voice filled with a wave of maniacal anger.

This was the end. I looked around to see if anyone had come to the rest stop. Maybe if I was lucky and the shift change was quick, a highway patrol would swing by right about now. Who cares if I had a motorcycle full of drugs? I just needed to be saved from *this*.

"In fact," the man growled, "I think I'm gonna take a little taste right now."

He let go of my chin and wedged his thigh between my legs. I tried to twist out of the hold to escape him, but his grip was too tight. I willed my brain to focus and figure out how to get out of this.

As he pressed me into the wall, it clicked. The heavy weight of the gun dug into my back as he used his grimy fingers to undo the button of my pants. Two different scenarios played out in my head. I was either going to be raped and kidnapped, or I could use the opportunity to take matters into my own hands.

The man brushed against the top of my underwear, growling with pleasure. The closer he got to pulling my pants down, the clearer my plan became.

"You are gonna be so much fun to break." His breath blew over my face as he crashed his lips into mine. The taste of cigarettes and beer invaded my mouth. The more he breathed on me and assaulted me with his mouth and tongue, the more I knew what I had to do before I became his prisoner.

One thought tugged at my mind. Cam said not to use the gun unless the product was in trouble. I shouldn't threaten or harm him unless he compromised the load. But if the guy stole me, the load would be alone in a parking lot. Wouldn't that be a threat to the product? It would be. Not only would I not be here, but a very illegal amount of a very illegal product would be sitting in a rest stop off the highway where a patrol car could come by at any second. This was all I needed to convince myself to go ahead with my plan. I knew exactly what I needed to do to save myself.

"Anyone could drive by," I gritted in between smelly breaths and kisses he tried to force on my lips.

"You're right. Let's get going." He motioned to the extra bike in the lot on the far corner.

When he tugged my arms, I practically screamed, "Wait!"

He stopped but never took his greasy hands off me, looking like he was seconds away from killing me.

"Lower your voice, girl," he threatened.

"You can have me right now. Let's just go to the back of the building where no one from the parking lot can see." I pointed to the grassy area behind the building.

It was my last-ditch attempt to show the tail in the forest that something was wrong. At that exact moment, I felt my phone vibrate in my pocket. I knew it was Cam. It had been way too long since I texted. This drop was only supposed to be a few minutes, and it's already gone way over that.

He pulled me behind him, and I stumbled over my feet again. I kept looking into the wooded area where the tail was, but there wasn't any movement. He was there, right?

"Motherfucker," I muttered.

"Okay now, take off your clothes."

He pawed at my shirt with his vile hands. *It's go time, Tatum.* Clearly, no one else was coming to save me, so I had to save myself.

"Let me strip for you," I murmured, trying to make my voice sultry.

I might be twisted, but the thought of pointing the gun at this slime ball made me wet. The power I had in my hands... He had no idea I was packing because most clubs didn't let their ol' ladies have any weapons. I knew Cam would be proud that I didn't let this fucker touch me. That by getting rid of him, I protected myself and the load. It was going to make him proud, right? I asked myself that repeatedly while I delayed undressing as much as possible, and the possible response I came up with was yes.

My plan was clear and simple. I would strip for him and get him on his knees, begging for me.

"Get on your knees," I told him while teasing the hem of my shirt.

"That's your job, bitch."

"I wanna watch your face when my tits come popping out. I promise it'll be worth it if you get on your knees." I bit my lip seductively. It was the first time I had used my body to get what I wanted, and it felt so good to be in control.

He was practically drooling and got to his knees faster than a motorcycle revving. Looking down at him, a spark ignited inside of me. A strength and glow I hadn't felt in a year roared in my chest.

I sensually moved my hips before tugging the hem of my shirt up. I wasn't wearing anything fancy or revealing, just a black lace bralette. I looked him in the eyes so he knew who the last person he would ever see was.

The gun was tucked into the back of my waistband, so it wasn't visible when I pulled up my shirt. His eyes were fixated on my chest.

In one swift motion, I pulled the revolver out and pressed it against his head.

"Give me the motherfucking keys." My voice was calm, and the words felt powerful on my tongue.

He sucked in air and tensed his body. The movement was subtle before attempting to call me on my bluff.

"Try again, lil lady," he barked back.

This time I held the weapon to his head. He frantically searched the ground to see if he could grab anything nearby. For the big bad biker that he was, he folded quickly under the cool metal gun.

"They're in the helmet. Didn't mean no disrespect."

"You meant no disrespect?"

That was enough for me. This fucker told me he was going to rape me, then kidnap me and make me his personal sex doll. The nerve to say he didn't mean to disrespect me was appalling. Venom leaked through my veins, and the spark I felt blazed to life.

Did men just fucking think that women would drop their panties for anyone? But when they took control of a situation, their fucking balls shriveled up. Cam would never appreciate someone talking to me like this, making me strip so they can violate me. I was doing the right thing.

In reality, seconds after I placed the gun at his head, I heard a noise from inside the woods and knew the tail was coming. My phone buzzed non-stop. I knew the tail had called Cam, and I had minutes before the crew got involved.

Seriously, though, no disrespect? I couldn't get those words out of my mind. Everything about this is wrong. I spent my entire life letting others control me, and use me as a doormat. Cam controlled where I lived, what I did, and my role in the club.

But I controlled this situation right now.

As the rusting from the trees got closer, I knew I only had moments to react.

"Someone's coming, aren't they? He'll tell ya it's a joke, girl. Say that guys like us, we joke all the time. It was an initiation."

"I see you've switched up from calling me a bitch," I said and simply pulled the trigger.

My body went numb, and I felt an incessant ring in my ears. I shakily dropped the gun and pulled my hands up to see them covered in blood. I watched as the blood dripped onto the grass and the ringing in my ears quieted. The grass turned from green to dark red, and the lifeless figure slumped.t. I walked away from him and put my bloodied shirt back on.

I should feel scared or disgusted with my actions or anxious. At that moment, though, watching this figure with shaking hands, I felt. . . fucking good. The power inside my body glowed so brightly. For once in my life, I had control over a sad sap of a man. I was a queen, and those who stepped before me heard me roar...or die.

My blooming excitement was cut short when I heard my tail, whatever his name was, screaming at me and into his phone as he ran toward me. He caught up to me and looked down at the body.

"You are totally screwed," he said as he dragged the body into the woods where he came from. I knew from the moment I heard the hum of the bikes, they were going to clean this mess up.

I saw and heard Cam speeding down the road toward the rest stop. I walked to the front of the building, where my helmet and the keys were on the ground. I was excited to tell him I did what he wanted. I protected the load and myself. Cam would murder anyone who touched me, so I knew he would be proud that I did that for myself. He had to be.

As the engine died, Cam dismounted and flung his helmet to the ground, his eyes avoiding me. He strode over to the drug-filled motorcycle and knelt down, running his hand over the fender and giving a gentle tap. He straightened up, and his crew arrived, switching off their engines. None of them moved until they got the signal from Cam. I looked at him and gasped as his eyes went dark. His hands clenched into fists as he advanced toward me. Every time he took a step, a high-pitched ringing filled my ears, overpowering any sense of accomplishment or confidence.

"What. The. Fuck. Did. You. Do?" He stood in front of me, and with each word, spit flew over my face.

"I killed him, Cam," I said breathlessly.

"I can see that, Tatum. Why the fuck did you do that?"

I looked behind him, and the crew still hadn't dismounted. This wasn't good. They should have been grabbing the drop and cleaning up behind the bathroom, but no one moved or looked at us. I quickly turned my attention back to Cam.

"He told me he was going to rape me and kidnap me. He was going to take me."

"Was the product compromised?"

"He told me he was going to take me and leave the bike with your stupid drugs here."

"Was the product compromised?" Cam repeated, this time a little louder.

"He threw the keys in my helmet. But he was going to take me, and if the drugs stayed here, who knows if a cop would come by or something? It would have been compromised."

He pounded his fists into the cement wall next to me.

"Goddamnit, Tatum. The product wasn't compromised. Luca would have grabbed the keys from your helmet and driven the bike back to Chicago."

"Are you listening to what I'm saying?" I asked, the excitement of the event draining out of me.

"I would have fucking found you, you dumb bitch"

I was suddenly transported back to childhood when I was told how worthless I was. I felt like a total idiot having pride for standing up for myself. Looking down at my arms covered in blood and splatter over my face, I felt like a toddler who got into markers and was now being told off. Everything I felt glowing inside me dimmed. My heart deflated.

"He was going to rape me." My voice came out barely above a whisper, and my eyes stared at the dirt on the ground. The same dirt I looked at when I was almost raped.

"I told you they were going to say shit. You needed to man the fuck up. Luca said he just dragged you out back and manhandled you a bit. He never said shit about him taking his dick out to fuck you. You're a fucking idiot. I knew I shouldn't have trusted you."

Tears streamed down my cheeks, mixing with the blood.

"I thought you would be proud," I said between sobs.

"Proud? You're pathetic. Do you know what a fucking mess this is gonna be to figure out?"

I shook my head, fearing what he would say next.

"This is gonna start a war. We killed one of the East Coast guys for no reason. Worse, word'll get out that my ol' lady did it. This'll be a freaking disaster. The drop was done, and no one got hurt, but then this guy ends up dead? They're gonna come for answers I don't have."

I could see him getting more upset as he spoke. His voice was yelling so loudly it was getting hoarse.

"You're gonna be the reason for war, little girl. You know what that means, right?"

His arm shot out and grabbed my chin, the same place the creepy man did, pressing into the sore spots. Shame and regret wrapped tightly around me.

"No," I squeaked out.

"You owe me. For the rest of your pathetic life. You're mine forever. I have to protect your worthless ass until you get killed, or I kill you myself. You will never leave me. I. Own. You," he snarled in my face.

"What?" His speech got my attention, and my eyes flew up to look at the person I thought would be so proud that I protected myself.

"They'll come for you until they feel their debt is erased. And they won't settle for anything less than a dead body. One for one. Fair is fair. You're gonna need me and my protection until we kill Orlando Agron, or you die along the way."

Orlando was the head of the Devil's Den, the motorcycle club on the East Coast. I knew about him because we had done a few deals with his club. His family had been running the club for decades and they passed it on to him. He was practically untouchable. He mainly managed different trade routes to deliver products in and out. While he was based in the East, his reputation was known around the country. In fact, the club was named after his known nickname, Devil, which his late-father was also known.

The likelihood of him being killed by some smaller Midwest club was unreasonable. So, what Cam said made sense. I would need protection. Otherwise, I was as good as dead. And they would make my death painful and torturous to prove their point. I always knew there wouldn't be an easy way out once I was in this world, but this moment solidified it for me.

"How can I help clean this up?"

"I'll clean up your mess. I'll clean up all your messes because you're mine now."

16

TATUM

Present

Oh my god. I can't believe that I said that out loud. I've kept that inside for nearly five years, and I don't even think about it most days. Even as the memory floods my brain, I think about how powerful I felt taking control and how quickly my ex shamed me.

That shame kept me in hell for over four years, stripping me of my freedoms and autonomy over my body. It left me paralyzed with fear, haunted by the possibility of Cam returning to drag me back. I couldn't even be sure Orlando was still searching for me after all these years.

I yearned for the power I felt holding that gun, especially now that this dance with Julian had taken a dark turn. My eyes darted toward the counter where he had carelessly tossed his gun. I could grab it quickly before he realized it. I couldn't guess his reaction, but his cock remained rock hard, and I may have created a stain where I sat on the countertop.

He stared at me as if processing my confession, and finally, he pushed away from me. I still couldn't read him, so I tucked my legs under me and pushed up against where I was standing. I was now kneeling on top of the counter.

"Mmm. Little bear, you just piqued my curiosity."

I shuddered at his confession and could almost feel the gun in my hand again. I was desperate to find the confident person I was when I pressed the barrel to that scumbag's head.

"You aren't scared?" I asked, still kneeling on his countertop. He was on edge like a lion stalking its prey, ready to pounce at any moment. I just couldn't determine if he wanted to kill me or fuck me.

"Scared?" He laughed, the sound echoing through the otherwise quiet home.

He finished and asked, "Me? Funny. I will never be scared of you. In fact, getting to know who you are has killed me in the best possible way." I looked down at his cock, engorged and pulsating through the fabric of his pants. I was desperate to release it and trace my hands over him. He was still at the edge of the large island and I was sitting a few feet from him.

"Get on all fours," he commanded. My heart pounded, and my core clenched at his voice and words.

Now was the time for listening and not thinking. I needed to feel something, and I craved him. I loved that he wasn't scared of me, that my confession seemed to turn him on more. I reveled in knowing it was me that made his dick so hard. I obeyed and got on my hands and knees on the countertop where his meals were probably prepared.

I still had on my work shirt and jeans, but he looked at me like I was completely nude.

"Pick up my gun." His hands gripped the side of the counter so tightly that his knuckles turned white.

I was wet with desire as my heart rate shot up. My brain couldn't think logically. If I picked up the gun, would it be to shoot myself? Or to give it to him to shoot me? But if I held that gun, I would feel that rush of power again.

I had control over how this played out. I didn't have to give it to him. I could also play whatever game he was playing.

"I can see your brain working. I am never going to hurt you, Tatum. Pick up the gun." His voice was commanding yet laced with a hint of truth.

The only logical way to get to the gun was to crawl. So that's what I did. I slowly moved my hands and legs to the gun. I didn't have to go far, and once I reached it, I looked up at Julian.

"Pick this up?" I asked, my voice laced with innocence.

A deep moan reverberated in the room from him, and he looked at me with an erotic need.

"Pick it up, little bear. Put it in your hands."

I looked at the innocent and innocuous weapon on the counter. It looked like freedom. It looked like power. It looked like the key to getting my glow back. I recognized its strength; the thought that I could get another taste of that tantalized me.

I reached out, hands shaking, toward the gun. My fingers hovered over it, and I glanced at Julian. I looked back at the gun, and this time felt different. This time I could hear it scream 'freedom' and 'safety.' It felt like I was regaining my confidence and putting the shame I had felt for years to bed.

I slowly picked it up by the barrel. Feeling its weight, I brought it to my face and held it against my cheek.

"How does it feel?" he asked, and every vivid instance of that rest stop came crashing down on me. The weight of those memories was suffocating, threatening to choke me as I struggled to keep my composure. My eyes burned with hot tears about to spill over, and the sense of sadness and nostalgia left me reeling.

I swallowed a sob and grabbed the gun. This weapon signified my freedom. I felt powerful and strong, and holding the pistol in my hand intensified the feelings dancing around my mind.

Power.

Freedom.

Strength.

I caressed myself, empowered by the symbols it carried.

"Good girl," Julian purred as I locked eyes with his deep emerald pools.

"Crawl to me, little bear."

With confidence flowing through me, I put it in my waistband and crawled to Julian. One hand in front of the other, I arched my back with each forward movement. My breasts bounced as I lunged forward.

When I reached him, he cradled my face and wiped my tears.

He spoke against my lips. "You are no killer, little bear."

Moving his lips over my jaw, he whispered, "And you look so delicious on your hands and knees for me."

This gave me the boost I needed. I pushed away, kneeled, and pulled the gun out with one hand, slowly unbuttoning my pants with the other.

Looking up at him for help, I nodded toward my hand, and he eagerly tore off my jeans with one swift movement.

Finally, I sat in my work shirt and lace thong, my legs over the counter and a Glock in my right hand. Julian and I locked eyes, his heavy-lidded stare pooling with desire.

"This is yours?" I murmured, my mouth watering in arousal. I lifted the gun to my mouth, my lips grazing the cold metal.

"It's mine." His hands collide with my hips, pulling me into his arousal. The friction quickening as our hips thrust into each other. We stayed there dry-humping each other for a few moments. I yanked away from him abruptly. With languid eyes, he pulled his hands onto my ankles as he tightened me into him.

I whispered, "No."

His hands immediately softened, and he spoke slowly and deliberately. "I'm not used to being told no." His lips turned up into a slight smile, and I knew I had him exactly where he needed to be.

Amusement crept in, and I grinned with satisfaction. I put the gun to my mouth. My hands held the handle as I brought the barrel toward my mouth. Satisfaction grew, and pride beamed brightly through my body. Liquid desire pooled in my panties. Imagining Julian's length going in, I shoved it to the back of my throat. The cool metal was a foreign feeling in my mouth. I carefully moved it in and out a few times, throwing my head back and moaning.

My free hand moved down my throat, imagining Julian's rough hands gliding toward my breasts. I switched off, lightly tugging on my nipples, and they perked up immediately.

When I took the cool metal beneath my hands out from the back of my throat, I watched Julian pull down his gray joggers. His cock protruded once they moved past his waist, and I gasped at the length. I thought it was large from the outline in his pants, but seeing it made me wonder how painful it might be. His hands moved to stroke his erection.

Up.

Down.

Up.

Down.

Up. Down. Faster. Faster.

He never once broke eye contact as his gun dripped with saliva.

"I can see how wet you are from here. You're practically sitting in it." His voice was low and gruff from lust. "You look like you are glowing."

His last phrase sent a thrill down my spine, and I could feel the ache inside me about to explode and I needed to cum.

I took the gun out of my mouth and ran my fingers over the wet and warmed metal, savoring its weight and the sensation of power it brought. With a shiver, I slowly glided the weapon down my chest, tracing my curves before letting it settle at my stomach. Leaning back on the counter, I arched my spine and lifted my chest, craving the touch of something more.

Julian's hands, slick with his pre-cum, slid over his length furiously. I brought the gun to my opening and circled the barrel around my clit. Each flick brought a wave of delirium and fever. A tiny moan slipped from my mouth as the top of the Glock thrust into my G-spot.

"Look what you're doing to me." An erotic voice interrupted my delirium, and I looked up to see the pre-cum dripping off of Julian.

I slowly took hold of the barrel, relishing the cool metal against my hot skin. As I pushed it in deeper, my body hummed with a primal desire. A deep moan escaped my lips as the tingling sensation intensified. The liquid that dripped from me mixed with my saliva, creating a delicious mess on the countertop beneath me. With each thrust, my pleasure heightened, and my body grew slick. The sharp edges of the metal sent jolts of pleasure coursing through me and made my body shudder with ecstasy.

"Oh, fuck," I moaned while we brought ourselves closer to our respective climaxes.

"You are so beautiful, little bear."

His voice groaned deeply. The sound sent shivers down my spine, as I watched him clench his jaw. He let out a guttural growl, a sound that made my body ache with desire. The way his voice dipped and rasped, each word spoken with a potent intensity, was a stark reminder of his masculinity. I could feel the heat radiating off him, and his breaths came in ragged bursts as he struggled to control himself. It was an agonizing sound that only heightened the intensity of the moment.

I yanked the gun out of me and replaced it with my hand, teasing my clit with a swirling motion. Using the gun was a wild idea that had never crossed my mind. Each stroke was more intense, and soon I was shuddering with pleasure.

With a final growl, Julian snatched the gun from my grasp. He fixated on the barrel, glistening with my wetness. My hand moved faster as I listened to his heavy breathing, and the anticipation of what was to come was almost too much to bear. I arched my back and used my left hand to support me while my right alternated between flicking and circling.

"I want you to cum with me," he moaned, his voice low and husky.

I couldn't hold back any longer. Molten heat surged through me, coiling tight in my stomach. A fierce, all-consuming need demanded release, and my body writhed with the intensity of it, begging.

"All mine." He groveled with the gun soaked in my saliva, my cum dripping down his cock.

"I need—" I watched my fingers work furiously as I thrust, grinding against my hand.

"Look at me," he demanded. I picked my head up and brought my eyes to his. I watched as he slowly picked up the Glock and moved it toward his face. My hands moved quicker. His tongue reached out and lapped up my juices. He licked the gun clean, swallowing and tasting every drop of me.

"You taste so fucking good." His voice was heavy with pleasure.

"I'm going to cum on you, dirty girl." He followed in anticipation, his hands working faster on his cock. A strangled moan escaped my mouth, and I knew I didn't have much longer until the intensity reached its peak.

"Please," I panted, my voice thick with longing. My body was on fire, aching for release, but I knew I couldn't do it without his permission. The anticipation was unbearable as I watched him, waiting for his response. Every moment felt like an eternity as I yearned for him to give me what I craved.

"Cum for me, little bear." I let out a low, toe-curling moan, my eyes rolling back in my head as I finally gave in to the pleasure building inside me.

Within moments, I felt a warmth on my stomach and heard him groaning as we unraveled.

It was an all-consuming release, and the arm holding me up weakened, making me flatten against the cool granite of the countertop. I melted from the most intensely beautiful orgasm I have ever felt, and my heart churned with some unidentifiable emotion.

His release dripped from my stomach as I turned to look for Julian. I saw him leaning against the opposite countertop, arms braced against the edges as he tried to catch his breath. His right hand still held the wet gun, and I could see spots where he had licked me up.

As I lay back and gazed at the ceiling, I couldn't help but think that if he was going to shoot me, at least I knew what heaven felt like.

17

JULIAN

Present

I had spent thirty-three years realizing I'd never had good sex. I brought countless women to my bed, but none of them were as absolutely beautiful as the woman on my kitchen counter, my cum dripping off her chest. The irony? We didn't even fuck.

The moment I laid eyes on her at Max's wedding, I knew I had to have her. She was the epitome of beauty and grace, with long, dark hair that flowed in the wind and piercing blue eyes that could stop a man in his tracks. Her body was nothing short of a Victoria's Secret model, and I couldn't help but feel drawn to her energy. She was a mysterious enigma.

For the past month, I followed her every move, learning her daily habits and favorite foods—even the scent of her damn perfume. I needed to know everything about her, and I wouldn't stop until she was mine. When James called to tell me her car had broken down and she had taken an Uber to work, I knew it was time to make my move. The days of gift-giving were over, and it was time to bring her to my place.

Growing up a Made man—my father part of the Cosa Nostra syndicate—I learned the value of power and respect early on. We were supposed to follow in his footsteps, but my father chose love over the mafia, and we left that life behind. Unfortunately, it wasn't long before my brother and I got back into it. Alex was the face of the company, but I took on the nitty gritty jobs. The ones where I had to deal with potential threats.

Our mother was the one who taught me about love and patience. The kind of person who baked cookies for the entire neighborhood just because it was a nice Friday night. She always wanted better for us, so we left the Mafia. My mamma wanted us to have a chance to live without fear of dying young, like so many in that world. But it was hard to resist the allure of money, sex, and drugs, especially when getting back in the game was so easy.

Officially, my job was wealth management. Unofficially, I laundered money from the Mafia to the US government. When the government had projects they couldn't fund from their own accounts, they came to me for a little extra. I took what the Mafia and other gangs gave me, and in turn, the cops, government inquiries, DEA, etc., turned a blind eye. The Mafia was initially interested in investing, and finding government projects was easy thanks to Alex's position as senator. It's a win all around.

Our mother may have been disappointed because we were involved in the Mafia again, but our blood ran thick. We were tight-knit, and it was hard not to want to be part of such an alluring world.

But today, all I could think about was Tatum. She was the one thing I wanted that money couldn't buy. And now that she was finally in my grasp, nothing would stop me from making her mine.

Staring at this woman, who just fell asleep on the counter after using my gun to get herself off, I can't help but want to know more about her. I had a rule, though. Once a woman got into my bed, I got her out quickly, never seeing the sheets change. But I hadn't been able to bring anyone else here since I met this woman. Not for lack of trying, of course, but because my dick didn't seem to want anyone but her.

She probably thought she was trying to frighten me, which was downright comical, with her confession, so I decided to give her a little test. I knew that if I asked a killer, someone like me who could take a life without flinching, to pick up a gun, their reaction would be as casual as me picking up a fork to eat dinner.

On the other hand, Tatum thinks she hides her emotions, but it's clear from her constant contemplation, questioning expressions, and bright smile that she wears her heart on her sleeve. I knew she would be scared of it when she picked it up. But what caught me off guard was her tearful reaction. It hit me deep, and I couldn't bear to watch her break down. Seeing tears stream down her face, I needed to distract and please her because I'd rather die than witness her in such pain. I hoped that by bringing her here and engaging in a passionate encounter, I could quell my curiosity about her. But it seems like it's had the opposite effect.

I watched her chest rise and fall as her whimpers filled the room. Part of me felt like I should call Christian to clean this shit up and bring her home, but the thought of another man touching her, let alone watching her naked while drenched in my cum filled me with a jealous rage.

The only thing to do is to clean her up and carry her to the bedroom. I dampened a cloth and wiped the mess from her stomach. This one's different, and I'd be damned if I didn't act like a proper gentleman. Touching her made my cock twitch.

"Calm down, you fucker. You just got a taste—we are one and done with this one," I whispered out loud, knowing it was a damn lie.

As I dried her off, I couldn't help but imagine the pain she went through. Whatever happened to her was beyond a bullet to someone's head. She spent the last month taking my gifts, and I heard nothing in return.

I picked her up bridal style, her head resting against my chest as I cradled her body and walked her to my bedroom. She was still in her underwear and work shirt, but her hard nipples were visible through her shirt as I watched her sprawl out on my bed.

As I made my way downstairs, I thought about the woman in my bed. She was a sight to behold, with curves in all the right places and a face that could stop a man dead in his tracks. It had been a long time since a woman slept in my bed, but something about her continued to draw me in. Whatever it was, I couldn't shake the feeling that I needed to protect her.

In the kitchen, my mind spun with thoughts of her. I grabbed a paper towel, cleaned the counter, and put the gun away. As soon as I was done, I practically sprinted upstairs.

She lay on the bed, so peaceful and vulnerable. My protective instincts kicked in, and I knew I'd keep her safe. I tucked the covers tightly around her, making sure she was warm and comfortable. I studied her face, admiring the way her lips curved up from a dreamy smile. For a moment, I was tempted to climb in next to her, wrap my arms around her and keep her close, but I quickly pushed the thought aside. I'm not the type to get attached, not when there's so much at stake.

With a deep breath, I tore my gaze away to return downstairs. I paused and looked at where she was sleeping, my heart heavy with longing. But I knew I couldn't let myself get caught up in her. I'm a Marchetti, and we don't fall in love anymore. It's just not in our blood.

A few hours passed while I worked, trying to close a few deals, when a crash sounded from upstairs. It sounded like a body hit the floor. I jumped from the desk, ready to attack whatever idiot decided to break in.

"Ah!" I hear a woman's voice groan from upstairs.

When I realized it was Tatum, I ran up the stairs, skipping every other step to get to her faster. I threw open the door and looked around frantically.

"What happened?" Keeping my voice as even as possible, I see her scrambling on the floor for who knows what.

"What are you doing? Inspecting my floors?" I half-joked.

"No, I'm trying to find my freaking pants." She's furious, looking at me with that gorgeous face, her lips pouty and begging to be on my—

No. Still one and done.

"Your pants are folded up on the nightstand. Also, you're welcome for not letting you stay passed out half-naked on my kitchen counter." I smirked, knowing it'd piss her off more.

"I need to go."

She scrambled to find her jeans, and I didn't move from the door frame. Instead, I leaned against it as she furiously put on her pants.

"You're missing something," I said as she moved toward the door.

"No, I don't think so. This," she replied, pointing between us, "was a huge mistake."

"Didn't seem like a mistake when your pussy was dripping on my gun and countertop." I stared at her, still blocking the door.

"I already told you." She huffed in exasperation. At this point, I knew I may have pushed one too many of her buttons. Her face morphed from mild frustration to the sadness that crept in occasionally.

"You told me what?" I asked softly.

"I don't mess around people involved in your world. I like to abide by the law, not live outside it." She looked so fucking sexy when she was lying to herself. Who messed this girl up? I knew when she finally figured her shit out, she would fuck that man up. Her power was just itching to come out.

"That's what you keep saying, little bear. But I don't see you pushing to get out of here. And you're staring."

I laughed when she realized her eyes were focused on the outline of my dick in my pants. Her cheeks turned pink, and she glared at me, her delicate hands pushing against my chest.

"You are infuriating." She tried harder to push past me. When I finally moved to the side, she stomped down the stairs.

"You're still missing something." I raised my voice slightly so she could hear and walked slowly down the stairs, taking my time and letting her realize what she still needed.

"My keys!" She finally exclaimed.

"I should make you beg for them," I said, staring into the deep blue of her eyes, not breaking eye contact.

"Let me go home." Her voice quivered, and I knew she was done with my shit. Hearing her sound so sullen made me want to throw her over my shoulder and go back to bed, but I'm not that kind of man. I was also done playing this game with her. It was fun while it lasted, but I needed to stop. The gifts, thoughts, and plotting to get her to see me consumed me the last month, and I needed to focus on work. If I got her out of my system, maybe I could reset and get back to my one-night rule. While part of me was desperate to know what world she was a part of, it wasn't enough to break my rules.

"Your keys are in the basket on the coffee table." I used my boardroom voice and cracked my neck to emphasize my annoyance with this conversation.

Was I annoyed? No. Anything but. I didn't want to break this façade I put on. A strong man didn't bend or snap, and he never molded to the enemy. I couldn't imagine Tatum as the enemy. . . ever. I shared my secret with her on our first date because she felt secure.

I got a waft of her sweet lavender scent as she quickly walked past me to pick them up and head out the front door.

When she got there, something possessed me to call out, "Thanks for the good time."

Her luscious ass came to a halt when she heard me.

Turning slowly, she looked at me with a glint in her eyes. "We didn't even fuck." Then she shot me the middle finger and walked out the door, where I heard the obnoxious engine of her car drive past my house.

Fuck. This girl would be the death of me. I looked outside and laughed.

"You have no idea what game you started, little bear."

I picked up my phone and called my brother, Alex, immediately.

"What's up?" he said quietly, which usually signified he was surrounded by people in the office and didn't want anyone to overhear.

"Hello to you too, little brother," I responded.

"Yeah, yeah. What do you need?"

"A favor."

"My favors are running a little low," he whispered.

I had tried connecting him with a motorcycle club on this coast, but the cops were cracking down on the drug tunnel from San Diego to the rest of the country. He was upset because he needed funding for an environmental project, and the only club willing to cough up cash was one he didn't want to work with.

"You need me, brother. I need you to look up everything you can on a Tatum Sloane. She lives in San Diego, works at Morning Goods Breakfast Restaurant, and moved here from Chicago. Double-check any syndicate associations."

"Guilio, what are you doing?" My brother's tone turned serious as he said my Italian name. When my parents left the Mafia, they changed our names to more 'American' versions. Alessandro became Alex, and I went from Giulio to Julian. We never changed our names because we didn't want any ties to the Cosa Nostra, even though we dabbled in business with them.

"Just some girl I fucked. I wanna know if I have to deal with her." I did my own background into her, but I was at an impasse. She worked at a shitty diner in the city five years ago but suddenly disappeared. Her bank accounts closed, the rent stopped being paid, and there were no phone records with her name. She stopped existing for those years until she came to San Diego. After today's confession, I had to find out more about the girl I was suddenly obsessed with.

18

TATUM

Present

After the encounter with Julian the other day, I didn't hear a peep from him. I woke up each day expecting one of his gifts. When they never came, I was disappointed. The first few days, I stayed home after work and busied myself with admin work from Lacey. And as the days turned into weeks and the holiday season approached, I chalked up the whole event to a life experience.

Despite my best efforts to push the memories of Julian to the back of my mind, I found myself pining for him, like a constant ache in my chest that refused to go away. Deep down, I knew I shouldn't be fixated on someone who had left such a brief imprint on my life. But, try as I might, I couldn't help but long for his touch, smile, and presence.

Why did I do that in front of him? It was erotic and exhilarating but also somewhat. . . dirty? It felt like the shame I had carried for so long no longer existed when I held that gun.

But I refused to give up hope. I knew I was meant for something more. Something greater than the pain and heartache that had been a part of me for too long.

I vowed to keep pushing forward and striving for greatness, even if it meant facing my deepest fears head-on. All to get my glow back. Because at the end of the day, I knew I was a fighter—a warrior with a heart of passion and a soul of fire. And no matter what the future held, I was ready to face it with all my strength and courage.

I also may or may not have set up a Google alert on my phone for him, so I knew where he was and what he was doing. I would admit that to anyone. Chels did some digging and found articles about Julian on various gossip sites and magazines. Most of them were about the model he was dating at the time.

The interesting thing was that he was never photographed with the same girl more than once. When I got sad, I realized I was just one of them. There was and would never be anything special about me. In fact, after all the models he dated, a murderer would probably be the last person he wanted to see again.

We also found out that his brother was a senator for our state. I didn't tell any of my friends about Julian's real work, so while my friends thought this was a bonus, it was just a reminder of the underworld Julian was connected to and how deep it ran. Julian was in charge of funding projects for his brother in the guise of being a wealth manager.

Admittedly, this made me feel better about the whole situation. Cam's world was about selling guns and drugs. In some twisted way, Julian was using dirty money to help his brother fund different projects that were helpful to the people of the state. It felt much more complex than outfitting motorcycles for drugs.

I was packing up after my shift when my phone pinged. I saw another article about Julian attending an art gala in Los Angeles. Sure enough, on his arm was a skinny blonde model, similar to the ones he had been photographed with before. It was the confirmation I needed to get over him. I just didn't know why it hurt so freaking much.

"What happened?" Maeve asked in concern, grabbing my phone to see what had me frozen.

After she read the article, she looked at me and immediately turned to the other girls coming in from their shifts.

"It's time for Plan C," Maeve said to Daphne and Chels.

"Fuck yes!" Chels yelled, shooting her fist into the air.

"Let's think this out a little more logically. Have we really brought plans A and B to fruition?" Daphne questioned.

Confused, I looked at my three friends and said, "Anyone wanna fill me in on what you're talking about?"

They laughed at their inside joke.

"She's clearly still in deep. I just caught her reading an article about him because she has a freaking G-alert on her phone," Maeve said to Daphne and Chels, ignoring my question and continuing as if I wasn't standing next to her.

"And he was just seen photographed with one of those LA types," she added for effect. Chels gasped, and Daphne looked over at me sympathetically.

"How are you doing?" she asked.

"I am fine. Really. Totally dandy."

I gave them a thumbs-up and plastered on a smile, which must have been what they were looking for.

"Oh, it's bad, bad. We gotta go. Do you still have some of your winter stuff from Chicago?" Chels asked me.

Little did they know I moved here with a backpack. I probably only had a long sleeve shirt and a light jacket for my winter clothes. They didn't need to know this, so I lied through my teeth.

"I can get some stuff, sure, but I am not going to Chicago."

They just laughed.

"No, silly. We're gonna take you on your first Cali-cation, also known as a place to get fucked up and look at hot snowboarders all day."

"What? I can't afford a trip, you guys. I'm so grateful for thinking of me, but it's just tough right now financially. . ." I trailed off, and Maeve looked at me with a smile.

"My parents have a house in Big Bear that they sometimes rent out as a vacation rental. I called, and they're letting us use it. We'll carpool and split gas and—" Daphne was interrupted by Chels screaming.

"And we already took the days off!" She started jumping up and down like a kid on Christmas. Between the glee on her face, the joy on Maeve's, and the sympathy on Daphne's, I knew that there was no way to get out of this trip.

"We figured it was time for the long overdue Plan C," Maeve added.

I took a shaking breath in and looked at the girls surrounding me. I finally had a group of friends who cared about me. For five years, I couldn't have a female friend outside of the shop. I lived in different worlds inside the books I read and envied the characters with groups of friends who put them first.

Now, I felt like I was part of something larger than my loneliness. I knew my three friends were solid pillars for me to lean on and that I needed to lean on them more. I was so used to doing everything for myself, including healing, that it was hard to ask for help.

I started to tear up, and my words came out as a blubbering mess. "I am so grateful for you three and so happy this random restaurant connected us. My heart is full. Thank you for being there for me."

We held hands and jumped up and down in a circle, matching Chel's earlier excitement.

"Wait," I interrupted. "When do we leave?"

The three girls said in unison, "Tonight!"

Shit, that meant I needed to grab some winter things. It wasn't freezing cold but I needed a few sweaters.

We said goodbye, and Maeve told me she would pick me up in a couple hours. It would take a few hours to drive up there, so we didn't want too late too start. I immediately went to the store and grabbed a few winter shirts and a coat.

I came across a tight red dress with long lace sleeves when I went through the racks. I tried it on, and without my curves, I would have looked like some of the models Julian was seen with. With my body, I looked like a damn pornstar. I laughed aloud.

It was a brief thought that ran through my head before I realized that I hadn't thought of him much today, aside from when I saw the article earlier, but in my world that was not a lot. Fuck it. I needed this dress to know I could pick up guys that weren't wealthy mafia-like billionaires.

"Get a grip," I whispered and rolled my eyes. He couldn't just let me have a good time with my friends. Even the mere thought of him dampened my mood.

I picked up the dress and the rest of my items and checked out before driving home to change. I threw on a pair of black leggings and an oversized hoodie. We were planning to drive there and check in to Daphne's parents' rental tonight, so I didn't need to get all fancy. By the time I threw my clothes in the same backpack I had used to move out here, my friends were honking in the carport.

I grabbed the bag with trembling hands, my heart racing like a wild horse as I locked the door. The fear of the unknown gripped me like a vice, and I scanned my surroundings to calm my nerves. The sweet scent of lavender that filled the air brought back memories of Julian. For a moment, I allowed myself to indulge in the warmth of that memory. But a sound from the bushes nearby jolted me back to reality, and my heart leaped into my throat. I strained my ears, trying to hear anything else, and my eyes darted around frantically, searching for any sign of danger. And then I heard the low rumble of a car leaving the alley. My breath caught in my chest as I recognized the sound. I knew whoever it was, they were following me.

"It's just the neighbors," I whispered, trying to push away the fear that threatened to consume me.

I went to Maeve's car, trying to appear calm and collected. But inside, I was shaking like a leaf.

"Hey, you didn't see anyone walking around the alley, did you?" I asked, my voice trembling slightly.

"No, should there be?" she replied, her expression a mix of confusion and concern.

"No, no. I'm being paranoid. I heard a noise, but it must be the neighbors," I said, trying to convince myself more than her.

"Do you want to go together to go check it out?" she asked, her voice filled with genuine concern.

"No, seriously. I'm being ridiculous," I said, but my mind raced with thoughts of who could be following me and why.

As we pulled out of the alleyway onto the main road, I felt relief wash over me. It was short-lived, though, as I saw a black car parked on the street ahead. My heart skipped a beat. *It couldn't be*, I thought. But as we got closer, I knew. The car looked familiar because it was the same one that had brought me to Julian's.

19

TATUM

Four years ago

It had been six long months since the incident at the rest stop. I couldn't recall the last time I had even stepped outside. My elderly neighbor who lived above me occasionally left a cup of coffee or tea at my door when she heard Cam leave in the mornings. I think she pitied me because when Cam returned, he would unleash his rage on me. While he never hit my face, he would violently throw me around, smashing every lamp we owned.

Every night, he blamed me for his actions, saying he was only trying to protect me from some unnamed danger. He screamed at me, claiming that keeping me locked up in our home was for my own good. I spent endless days reading and rereading books, grateful for the small collection I had gathered before the incident. On rainy days, I would sit by the window, gazing through the bars of our garden apartment, listening to the rain hit the pavement.

Would it be bad if Orlando somehow found me? This was not living. I finally found torture that was worse than waterboarding. Waiting all day until you got pulled, pushed, and fucked before it happened on repeat. At this point, a bullet to my head would be a welcomed escape from the hell I was in.

I tried to keep myself busy during the day and tried my hardest to cook and clean in hopes it would soften the blow. It never worked, but I was superstitious that things would worsen if I didn't keep doing this.

Today was all the same. I was stuck at home waiting for Cam to come to slam the front door open.

I heard a motorcycle engine as the clock hit noon, but it was far too early. I looked around at the books I was going through, and panic crept into my chest. This wasn't good. In no world would Cam coming home early mean anything good.

Instead of the boots slamming against the door and the pounding knocks, I heard a quiet tap on the door. I had to look through the peephole to confirm it was him because it was so silent and atypical. Hesitantly, I opened the door, my hands shaking the entire time.

I looked back again at the small mess in the front room and was paranoid. I attempted to put my body in front of it, but I had lost a lot of weight, so I didn't cover much.

"Hey, baby." My name slipped smoothly from his lips. He immediately reached for me, but out of instinct, I backed away.

"You're home early." My voice was shaky as his hands gripped my waist.

He walked past me to the kitchen and opened the fridge door for a beer.

"It's your lucky day, baby. I'm so sorry for keeping you here, but you get it's for your safety, right? It's time you step up and become my queen again. You want to be my queen still, right? Because you forgive me."

The last part should have been a question but was said as a statement. He didn't give me a chance to respond, and honestly, I was glad he didn't because I really wanted to growl out a 'fuck you.'

"We're gonna do something special today. Go get your shoes on, my queen."

I just nodded and pulled my sneakers from the closet. I quickly made the bed in case he said something about it being unmade. I found him in the kitchen texting someone.

When he finally looked up from his phone, I saw his eyes go straight to where my books were scattered by the couch. I was crouched by the closet looking for my shoes, but I stayed low momentarily to see how he would process the mess by the couch.

He looked over to where I was in our small studio apartment, and I quickly looked into the closet, moving away from his gaze. I had developed an instinct to flinch if he looked too hard, so I did my best to avoid looking him in the eyes.

"I'll clean up your mess, my queen. Today is such a special day." He simply walked over to my books and piled them together before putting them on the bookshelf.

This simple action made me panic, my heart racing and my palms sweating. Why was he being so nice? I couldn't shake off the feeling that something was wrong, that this was all a trap. I didn't understand, and not understanding only made me more scared.

"Thank you," I managed to force out. When he took my hand, I flinched and pulled away. The look on his face was unreadable and fueled my fear.

When we got outside, he thrust a helmet in my direction and ordered me to mount the bike. The sun's warmth peeking through the clouds felt like a cruel joke on my melancholy soul. I hesitated, but the thought of staying there, stuck in my thoughts, was unbearable. So, I straddled the bike, and the wind whipped my hair into a frenzied mess as we took off. The sensation was exhilarating; for a moment, I felt like I could escape my troubles. I clung to him, my fingers digging into his waist, as he recklessly swerved in and out of traffic, taking us to an unknown destination.

We finally parked, and he held his hand out to help me off the bike.

"Is it safe for me to be out here?" I asked before taking it.

"You're with me. It's my job to protect you. Just don't go making any mistakes today, queen." I gulped.

We walked a couple blocks, and I was so surprised that I was outside in public and it was just Cam and me. There was no additional security tailing us or any club. I couldn't help but look over my shoulder out of fear a few times.

"Here." He held the door to a blacked-out shop window open. There was no signage or mention of what this was. Maybe that's why he was being so nice to me. Because he brought me here to kill me or something. Blindly trusting him was better than being stuck underground in that tiny apartment, getting beat up, so I'd take a potential death to this.

I stepped inside hesitantly, my chest about to explode in anticipation. The darkness was suffocating, and I could barely see anything beyond the faint outline of objects. The door closed behind me with a loud thud, making me jump. Fear gripped me tightly as I imagined all the possible scenarios of what could happen next.

My hands shook like crazy as he guided me to some back room and flicked on a dim light. It took a while for my eyes to adjust, and then I saw a bunch of random tools and stuff laying around. The fear in my gut was getting worse and worse, like I was waiting for something terrible to happen. There was a loud buzzing sound all around us as we walked through the shop, and finally I noticed we were in a freaking tattoo place.

"Are you getting something done?" I asked him.

He just laughed, and his eyes darkened when he looked at me. In a low tone, he said, "Not me."

"So, why are we here if you aren't getting anything?"

"Because you are." His grip on my hand went from gentle and loving to tightening around my hands.

"Me?" I asked, feeling my heart pounding in my chest. I didn't have any tattoos and never thought about getting one. The idea of having a needle pierce my skin repeatedly made me sick.

"I don't need one, but thank you," I said, trying to keep the fear out of my voice.

"But you do need one, my queen." He pulled me into the back room, where a black tattoo chair was set up. A large man with face tattoos was prepping ink for the tattoo gun.

"I don't know what I want," I whispered, my hands trembling.

Cam looked at me, his hand still holding mine tightly. I felt like a trapped animal, desperate to escape. But where would I go? I had no one to turn to, nowhere to run. After a moment, he looked at the tattoo artist and back at me. He laughed, and the sound sent shivers down my spine.

Whatever he had planned, I knew it wouldn't be good. I wished with all my heart that I was back in the personal hell of my tiny apartment.

"It's time you got branded, girl. You'll get an eagle so everyone knows who you belong to. The Devil's Den won't take what's already been tainted." His lips turned up in a smirk.

"Sit down and turn over on your stomach," the tattoo artist said while looking at me. This guy had been paid off because there was no way a legit artist would force someone to get something they didn't want.

I just looked up at Cam with wide eyes.

"Do I at least get to pick where it goes?"

He laughed again, and I laid down, defeated. In the most demeaning way, Cam grabbed the waistband of my leggings and pulled them to my knees. My bare butt was exposed to the air, and Cam shoved my face into the tattoo chair so my eyes were fixated on the grooves of the textured leather. I had never gotten a tattoo before, but I assumed lying with your face into the leather wasn't normal. But none of this was normal, so it shouldn't surprise me.

I heard the buzzing of the machine start and knew I was being committed to a world I so desperately wanted to leave. And now I was being physically branded by that world too. I knew exactly what tattoo was going on me. Tears spilled from my eyes and pooled on the leather. I could feel the touch of the needle as it pierced the top of my hip.

"Put some on her hip. Doesn't need to be big just something she can wear proudly," Cam told the artist. It was at that moment I stopped listening. I couldn't do anything about it, so I tried to go to my faraway place that made me happy. Somewhere that was anywhere but here as I got branded.

My body trembled as I tried to contain my sobs. But the more I tried, the louder they escaped my lips. Cam pressed my head harder into the chair and yanked my hair back when I made a sound. He didn't bother to check if I was okay or offer to wipe my tears. I didn't expect him to be kind or gentle; his version of gentleness always came with a cost.

I escaped to a different world, imagining myself in one of my books each time he hurt me. It was my way of protecting myself from the pain and terror he inflicted on me. When I relived a favorite scene, the real world became more bearable. I knew the pain would end soon, and I would be able to escape to a happier place in my mind.

Eventually, the sound of the tattoo machine stopped, and Cam let go of my hair. He commanded me to walk over to the mirror, my pants still around my knees, my thong covering my modesty. I complied without question, hoping my suspicions about the tattoo were wrong.

Sure enough, as I turned my upper body to look at the mirror, I saw the same eagle Cam and everyone else at The Club had. Their eagle was tattooed on me. It was just a small outline; I was grateful it wasn't massive or colored in.

"Look closer, queen," Cam said, and I looked closer at the inside of the eagle's body.

I finally noticed what he was talking about. A big C was tattooed right inside the eagle outline. My heart sank. The tattoo was worse than I could have imagined. It symbolized ownership, a reminder that I belonged to Cam and his world of darkness.

I could feel my soul breaking as I stared at the design, the ink still fresh and sore. The pain of the tattoo was nothing compared to the emotional agony that filled me. I wanted to scream, to run away, but I knew there was nowhere to go. I was trapped, trapped in this cycle of abuse and fear.

"For me and The Club, baby. Now, you'll never forget who owns you. " His eyes narrowed on mine, void of any warm or loving emotion.

He looked at me and, without another glance, turned and walked out the shop's front door. The tattoo artist put some cream and some kind of plastic wrap on, and I pulled my leggings before leaving. My backside was sore, and we were so far from home that I hoped Cam hadn't left me to walk.

He was outside smoking a cigarette, leaning against the building. When he saw me, he looked over but returned to his smoke.

"I hope you like it, baby. It's all for you." He never once glanced over at where I was. I crossed my hands in front of my body and picked at my cuticles, not knowing what would happen next. I looked over my shoulder when I heard a car or two pass, almost begging someone to see me and rescue me from the hell of an existence I was in.

"Told you. You don't got to worry about anything. I'm gonna protect you. You're mine now. Always." He threw his smoke on the ground and crushed it with his foot.

Cam grabbed my hand again. The loving and caring man had returned and walked me to a car this time. I couldn't help but shake the feeling that there was something I was missing. How, after nearly half a year sitting inside the house because it was unsafe, was today the day it was safe enough for me to go outside? Why was it safe enough for me to go to a tattoo shop, of all places?

Regardless, my existence was now this cruel and brutal reality. The tattoo on my skin was a permanent reminder of my enslavement to a world that didn't care about my well-being or my freedom. No matter where I went, I would always bear the mark of how I allowed someone to control me.

As Cam revved the bike engine and we made our way back to our living hell, I knew that I had to find a way out, no matter the cost. Living like this was not living at all.

20

JULIAN

Present

One of the government contractors we worked with forced me to drive up to the mountain town in Southern California. Not only that but an epic winter storm was forecasted for this weekend. My brother wanted me to check out a few projects for his 'Save the Earth' campaign he was running in Big Bear, a few hours north of my San Diego home. He had a killer house overlooking the resort that I could crash at, so maybe a little change of scenery would be good.

My phone rang as I drove toward the mountain, and I answered it through the car speaker.

"Julian."

"Hey, baby," a voice whispered seductively through my speaker.

This fucking girl wouldn't get the hint. I had to go to some dumbass fundraiser earlier this week and made the mistake of calling one of the girls I used to fuck around with. She was the pretty model type, but I was a one-night man. I'd never lied about my intentions, and most of the time, the women I fucked appreciated the night and went about their day. But sometimes, you got clingy ones who couldn't or wouldn't take no for an answer.

"Georgia."

"Want to come to my place tonight? I can even come down and see you." She practically purred through the phone. It was gross. She tried to come onto me earlier at the event we attended, and honestly, I may have entertained breaking the one-night rule. But between her clinginess and a certain brunette who wouldn't leave my mind, there was absolutely no way it was physically going to happen.

"No, Georgia. Like I told you, I'm not interested."

"But did you see how good we looked in the tabloids, baby?" Her purring was becoming an incessant annoyance at this point.

I figured that's what this was about. She wanted to leverage me for whatever fame she was looking for. It was common, especially in LA, for women at functions to be photographed leaving the event with a rich dude. Again, I often allowed it because the favor was returned. But my cock wouldn't stop twitching over the complicated yet sweet taste of Tatum.

I put James on Tatum when she left my house. Something about her confession worried me that anything could go wrong at any time. The way tears rolled down her face at the first grasp of my gun made me think what or whoever had happened to her could still be out there. I didn't know what the fuck possessed me to care after she left my house, but the thought of someone hurting her made my heart clench.

"Baby." The girl's whiny voice broke me out of my thoughts.

"I said no, Georgia. Goodbye."

I hung up but got another alert for an incoming call.

"Handle it yourself," I gritted out. The GPS alerted me that I would arrive in the next twenty minutes.

"Boss." Christian had been my bodyguard for five years, and I trusted him entirely. He was a former Navy SEAL, and when he retired, he realized he could make a shitload more in private contracting. He could also take down a grown man in less than ten seconds. But beyond being my personal bodyguard, he also was a confidant. My father always shamed me for befriending my bodyguards. He said if he got too close, he could hurt me.

"Update," I demanded. There were two types of conversations we could have. If he called me by name, it would be a friendly conversation. But starting with Boss meant he needed to discuss business.

"I tailed her this morning, but I got too close to her house, and I think I may have spooked her. She was with the pretty friend."

"Are you on her now?" I was about to pull off this fucking mountain road and go find her myself if he lost her. I should have just done it myself.

"I lost her for a minute. But don't worry. The GPS tracker you put in her car will help."

"Are you on her?" I repeated myself.

"Yes, Boss. I'll find the pretty friend who'll lead me to her. They're all going somewhere together, the entire friend group."

"Christian. You need to ensure she's safe. Do nothing else until you find her."

"You got it."

Christian was watching her today because James came with me yesterday to collect a payment from a biker gang in the desert. While Christian was good at torture, James was our best spy. Pulling James from the watch would be risky, but Christian would ensure she was safe.

"Christian?" I asked after a few moments of silence.

"Yes, Boss?"

"The pretty one? Really?" I laughed and heard him mumble fuck off before the call ended.

For the rest of the ride up, I couldn't help but obsess over Tatum and whether she was safe. She was with her friends, which meant she was probably fine. I was also curious if she had seen Christian or not.

I smirked, knowing the shit show that would swirl in her brain if she did. I glanced at the obnoxiously large welcome sign as I pulled into the mountain community.

"Welcome to Big Bear, California," it said in a kitschy wood design with a family of bears playing.

If I thought I was obsessing over Tatum before, this town made me think of her harder. My little bear, where were you? I'm going to find you, precious girl.

I pulled into the large house on the biggest peak. Overlooking the double black diamond run, the house was understated elegance. The heat from the jacuzzi and pool in the back rose so high you could see it from the driveway. Alex bought this home when our mother was still alive many years ago. She spent most winters here, so her design remained untouched.

I parked in the garage and left it open so James could pull in behind me. Our father added a cabin on the back of the property that security stayed at during shift changes. I only brought one or two men with me at a time and often gave them nights off since this sleepy town hardly gave me any issues.

I opened the door and was welcomed by the familiar scent of Mamma. She died fifteen years ago from cancer. Alex and I were just teenagers. It wasn't surprising, as she'd been suffering for a while, but it hit Papa the worst. He gave up an entire world for her. Love was always disappointing was the lesson I had learned then. My mother died, people broke up, and women were always using me for fame or fortune. From then on, most of the Marchetti men vowed off romance of any sort, each with our own reasons.

Before shutting the door behind me, I waved to James and told him to take the night off. I wanted to spend the night finishing the work I had missed while driving. I walked further into the house and looked out the back. It was seven p.m., but lights were on from the ski run behind that ran behind the property. It illuminated the backyard, but between the steam of the jacuzzi, it was hard to distinguish the people coming down the mountain.

Papa loved that he could see anyone coming down the mountain, though, so we always left it open to the ski run and never put a privacy fence over the yard. I headed to the office, pulled out a bottle of whiskey from the mini bar, and opened my laptop to work, itching to hear from Christian and make sure he found Tatum. I looked at the clock and told myself if I hadn't heard from him by midnight, I was getting off this damned mountain and finding her myself.

Time passed by quickly when my phone interrupted me. The time was well past ten. After looking at the caller ID, I quickly picked up the call.

"Tell me you found her."

"I think so, Boss."

"All right, cut the shit. Where is she? Is she safe?"

There was silence on the other end. My heart was beating out of my chest, and I started to frantically gather my work. I moved toward the door, about to get my keys, when I heard some quiet chuckling from Christian.

"Spit it out," I demanded.

"I decided to find her by looking for the other girls first. I went to the tall girl's socials, and about five minutes ago, she posted something."

"Thank fucking god. I assume Tatum is there?"

Again, no response except for some muffled laughing.

"I have no fucking patience right now. Spit it out."

"Yeah, Boss, she's there and seems very safe."

"Where is she?" I practically seethed through the phone before adding, "Tail her."

"You see, that's the problem," Christian responded hesitantly.

"Why is that an issue? Christian, I'll send James if you've become incompetent at this job." That must have pissed him off because his amused tone shifted.

"She happens to be closer to you, and it would be much quicker for you to get to her and see what's happening than me."

"Where is she?"

"She's in Big Bear, sir. She actually happens to be getting tipsy at the Lazy Spoke in town."

I almost threw the phone across the room. Running my hands through my hair, I wanted to punch a hole in the fucking wall. This woman was going to be the death of me. Not only did she escape a highly trained individual to party with her girlfriends, but she was a five-minute drive from where I was. Beyond that, she was drinking without supervision at a bar.

I picked the phone back up and dialed Christian.

"Is she still there?" I barked at him.

"I'd bet on it. I can come, Boss, but it'll be an hour before I arrive."

"No," I snapped before lowering my voice, "I'll check on her."

"Show me where I can find this video."

A few seconds later, a text came through from Christian with a link to her friend's social. I clicked on it to view the story. I only had an Instagram because my publicist ran it for me, and it was mostly filled with the different projects I worked on with my brother and other government officials. While I wasn't tech savvy, viewing the story would notify the tall one. She could potentially tell Tatum, and they could run again, so I only viewed it right before grabbing my keys, wallet, and gun and leaving.

Sure enough, on a video from the middle of a town where people prefer beer and jeans to mini dresses and vodka sodas, there was Tatum and her friends in the middle of a large crowd. My initial intention was to make sure she got home safe and not interfere. When I looked closer at that video, I saw Tatum in the tightest fucking red dress known to man. Her tits were practically up to her neck and begging to come out with the slightest touch. The video panned to her other friends, who had a massive crowd around them as they took shots together.

My eyes didn't leave Tatum, who was cozied up to some fucker with a brown sweatshirt. His hands held the back of her thighs as he drunkenly tried to pull her in. I couldn't see her face, but the way she pulled against his hands to get some space, I knew there was no way I wasn't storming the fuck into that bar. That man was dead.

James threw his door open as I pulled out of the garage, but I didn't wait for him before screeching off. He knew better than to stop me, especially in times like this. I sped as fast as I could through town, probably waking the residents up as I revved the engine around each corner.

There was no way that brown sweatshirt asshole would leave the bar with two working hands, either. It would take everything in me not to shoot him point-blank when I stepped in.

Those thighs were *mine*. I pictured my cum dripping off of her and the sweet moans she gave me. But this guy? The fact that she was pulling away from him as he gripped on tighter was an absolute disgrace. My mind couldn't stop racing through all the scenarios that could happen in the time it took me to reach the town center and throw my car into park in front of the bar.

I was livid at her friends for not paying attention to her, consumed with the attention from other guys who would all be like the dead man. I hadn't changed out of my black pants and a button-up and was too busy to grab a coat before leaving the house.

As I slammed the car door shut, I tucked my Glock into the back of my waistband, hoping it blended in with my shirt but not giving a fuck if any of these fuckers saw it. They should all be scared right now because I am going to clean up this fucking mess.

For effect, I opened both doors simultaneously. Scanning the bar, I noticed her friends gathered around some guys at the front.

"Where. The. Fuck. Is. She."

The tall one looked up from the skinny dude she was flirting with, and fear widened her eyes when she recognized me.

"How—" she began to speak.

"I asked you a question. Do not make me ask again." I stared her down.

"I'll show you. Did something happen?" she asked as she walked through the crowded bar.

"Yes. This happened." I shoved my phone in her face, and she looked at the video. At first, I could see her start to devise an excuse about what she was doing. It finally clicked when she saw Tatum in the corner being manhandled by the almost-dead man.

"She's okay. I swear we've been with her the whole time. Wait, how did you know we were here?" She stopped moving and turned toward me.

"I happened to be in town and saw this stupid ass video. If you don't show me where she is in the next ten seconds, I will burn this place down. We both know she'll hate this attention on her."

She pointed down the bar where the brown sweatshirt guy was still talking to her. His hands were now on her waist, and she was anxiously twisting her hair around her finger.

I saw red.

The only thought in my head was to get her out of this situation.

I practically ran toward her. When I got there, I ripped the man's hands off her, throwing her behind me.

"What the—" She squealed before realizing I was standing before her.

I created a barrier between her and this asshole. I could feel her eyes burning through my shirt.

"Who are you?" I asked to give him a chance to dig his way out of the hole he didn't know he was in.

"Hey, chill, man. I was just talking to the pretty lady. What are you? Her boyfriend?" He laughed, his obnoxious surfer-boy accent piercing my brain.

I reached back for my gun as I stared at him.

He must have been coherent enough to know what that meant. "Yo, bro. It's all good. She's too weak for me anyway. I like 'em a little spicier."

What the fuck?

My deep laugh resonated over the loud bar music, coming from a place of protecting the woman that had a hold on my heart.

This dude had no idea how incredibly strong Tatum was. And he'd never get the chance to know. She was reserved for my touch and taste alone.

I stopped laughing and turned around to look into her eyes. She looked scared. The thought that this man caused her a second of fear made me want to put my hands around his neck and squeeze the life out of him.

"Are you sure about that?" I turned back to him. He must have sensed that this was not going his way because he shot up from his barstool and stepped back.

"Bro." I towered over his small frame, making him crane his neck to look up at me.

"You deserve a fucking bullet through both hands for putting them where they don't belong," I growled. I leaned down to get right in his face when I spoke.

"Then, maybe your kneecaps to make it a little...spicier, as you said."

I reached for my waistband again when a small voice whispered behind me.

"Please don't do this."

I looked back. She was crying, tears coursing down her face as she looked at what my hand was about to grab. Then it clicked. She wasn't scared enough of this douche to cry. I was the reason for her tears.

Oh god.

I needed to make this up to her. I looked at the man again before turning around to focus on Tatum.

"Come with me," I murmured, my hand reaching for hers and pulling her close, my anger disappearing.

"Do I have a choice?" she asked, swiping her tears away.

"You always have a choice," I whispered. Her question broke me. I was an asshole to everyone else in my life but to her? I would never let her think she had no choice, just like when she walked away after dinner. I gave her the freedom to leave when she found out about my world. Did I want her to walk away? Abso-fucking-lutely not. But what we want in life and what we need are two different concepts.

She sighed in exasperation, her tears still falling in a mixture of a sadness and anger, and ripped her hand from mine to storm toward the door. She was infuriating, but her anger only made me want to get to know her more. I followed her and waved at the tall friend watching the situation unfold. She simply nodded and returned to where the others were sitting.

I went to open the door for her, but she pushed ahead of me. She started to shiver as soon as we hit the winter air. I tried to wrap my arm around her to warm her up, but she pulled away.

"Why did you do that? Why are you even here? How did you even find me?" She clenched her fists and turned away. "I knew you were following me. I saw Christian in my freaking bushes today. I'm a big girl; I don't need you around. I begged you not to be involved in your world but following me was because you had told me about your business, wasn't it?" She huffed, the cold air coming out as she spoke. I nodded.

"I wanted to make sure you were safe. I've been worried since you left my house." The next words got stuck in my throat, so I blurted them out. "I promised to keep you safe."

"You don't need to worry. That whole thing inside"—she pointed at the bar—"is why I left your house. I don't want to be forced to leave a bar that I'm at with my friends or have someone I was just talking to threatened."

Her hands wrapped around her body; the fact that it was my fault for angering her made me want to comfort her in some way. I didn't want her upset. I wanted to help her. I wanted to protect her.

"I just wanted—" I began.

"That's the problem; it's all about you. *You* just wanted to make sure I was safe. *You* wanted to protect me. *You* wanted to have me followed. I had no say in it."

Now I was angry. Of course she had a fucking say in it. Maybe I was an ass for not listening to what she had to say but apologizing for giving a shit? No.

"You wanna go back to the bar with your friends? Fine. You want to figure out how to protect yourself? By all means, I'll pull James from your detail. Need to scream and yell at me in the cold outside a shitty bar? Absolutely. Wear the tightest, sexiest dress I've ever seen and flaunt it in front of my face? I'll beg you to."

I leaned down toward her, my hands slowly gripping her waist to pull her into my arms. Partially because I was tired of watching her shiver while making her point. But also because I was desperate to touch her again. It was an addiction that I had no need to quit.

I dropped my mouth to her ear and whispered, "What you will *not* do is let another man put their hands on you when you don't want it. And if I see it? I will take them out to protect what belongs to me."

She pulled back to look into my eyes. She was nothing like the other girls I slept with. The smell of lavender and vanilla enveloped me when she was wrapped in my hands, and I never wanted to let her go. She was taking over my every thought and desire.

"I don't belong to you," she said breathlessly.

She was infuriating. She had no idea how much she fucked me up when she came all over my countertop. My dick only responded when I thought about her long brown hair flowing out behind her and the moans from her sweet lips.

I just laughed.

"You wanna be like this, little bear? Okay. Go back with your friends and be on your own."

I walked to my car, leaving her standing on the snow-covered sidewalk. I stood next to the opened door and looked back at her, my chest heaving from the cold air and being so close to her again.

"But if you want to find out how I treat what's mine? Come for a ride with me."

Without waiting for her response, I ducked into the car and pressed the ignition. She was still standing there, face showing her shock at my words. Her mouth was agape, and I revved the engine. Putting the car in drive, I pulled forward and lowered the passenger side window.

"Get in the car, Tatum," I said and reached over to push open the door.

I leaned back in my seat and rested my hand on the wheel, waiting to hear her get in.

Within a second, I heard her huff and the shuffle of her boots against the snowy sidewalk. She leaned down before getting in, and I looked over at her. Truthfully, the first thing I saw was her chest spilling out of her dress. It took all my willpower to force my eyes back to hers. Her lips quirked into a smirk.

"I'm the one asking the questions tonight."

She climbed in, slammed the door behind her, and refused to look at me as she buckled her seatbelt. A smile spread on my face, knowing she was close enough to taste again.

21

TATUM

Present

If I was being honest, I was only sitting in this car because it was so scorchingly hot how he stood up for me. When we arrived at the bar, I got separated from my friends, and some slimeball had his hands all over me. I froze. My brain was stuck in the past, and I couldn't move my body away from him.

When Julian showed up, I was beyond grateful. Even though threatening that guy wasn't something I wanted. Ugh, why couldn't I have a normal relationship? And how had I managed to move from one underworld to another?

I acted surprised when I saw him, but I knew he was always nearby after I caught Christian spying on me. Did I like it? No. Did it make me feel safe? Well, yes, but I wouldn't admit that to him either.

I was a goner when I saw him in all black with the first three buttons of his shirt undone and his dark hair flopped to the side. Now I was sitting in his car, watching his large and dominating body spread across the small seat of the Corvette. His thighs barely fit, and his hand almost covered the entire wheel. His free hand repeatedly switched from resting on the gear shift to running through his hair. It wasn't long until we pulled up to what might be the largest house in town. It had to be. It was a giant log-cabin-like house that, while inviting, screamed opulence. I looked toward the back and saw the ski run. I wasn't a winter sports person, but seeing all these people going down the mountain was cool.

He parked in the garage and got out of the car. Part of me was disappointed he didn't say anything, and I was just expected to follow him. I ran my hands down my dress before I was startled. Julian had opened the door and stood there, his hand reaching out to mine.

"It's warmer inside for you to ask your questions." His face turned up into the smile I remember from our dinner together.

I grabbed his hand and let him guide me out of the Corvette. I ran my hand over the red trim. We never dealt with new cars like this when I was with Cam. He worked on some restorations of older models, but it was fun to drive in a sporty car.

I followed him into the cabin, and if I thought the outside was winter-cabin chic, the inside was even cozier. Instead of a candle-lit fireplace this one had a real roaring fire, but the vibes were immaculate.

"Wow. You need to thank your interior designer," I said as I walked to the fireplace.

He laughed.

"This was all the work of my mamma."

Was? He used the past tense, which meant she was no longer here. I looked back at him. He stood behind the couch, hands shoved into his pockets and a sad smile on his face.

"She passed away when my brother and I were teenagers. My brother actually bought this house from my dad. While it may seem like I was stalking you, it just so happened that I was up here checking up on a few environmental projects for my brother."

"Or kill some people who fucked up," I mumbled.

I felt his presence behind me as I faced the fire. He gently put his hands at my waist, but his touch had no sexual intentions.

"Contrary to popular belief, I didn't have to kill anyone. . . today."

He kissed the spot above my ear and took a deep breath. I could practically feel the tension leave his body. I tilted my head against his and rested it there, feeling his skin against mine, before I remembered why I was there. Quickly, I pulled away and stepped back, not trusting myself to get too close.

"I want to ask you questions."

"I know. Can I get you something to drink? Please, sit." He gestured to one of the couches. I sat down before he returned with two glasses of a favorite cab I requested.

"You seem like more of a whiskey guy. I was surprised when you had wine at the restaurant."

He laughed, and I took the glass from his hand.

"I am, but I'm trying to impress you with my sophistication. Is it working?" I shook my head and took a sip.

He sat down sideways next to me against the arm of the couch so he could see me. He took up nearly half of the oversized couch, even sitting that way.

"Should we play a game?" he asked.

"What game?"

"A question for a question. You go first." He gestured toward me, and I shifted to face him. I hated sitting in these dresses. I liked to sit cross-legged on the couch, but I'd be completely exposed if I did.

I was a jeans or sweatpants kind of girl, another reason Julian wasn't a good fit. He lived a mobster lifestyle far from who I was and wanted to be. Curiosity got the best of me, though, and I wanted to play the game.

"Fine. I'll play." I tried to find a comfortable way to relax in this dress. He looked at me curiously.

"How many siblings do you have? I know you have your brother, but anyone else?"

"Starting on an easy one, I see." He laughed and sipped his wine.

"It's just me, my brother, and my dad. Like I mentioned, my mom passed away when we were teenagers. She was the one who actually designed this place." He gestured around the room.

"It reminds me of your place in San Diego."

"I guess it does, doesn't it? I never put that together." He rubbed his hand along his jaw.

"My turn." He adjusted his shirt and pulled it out from his pants. I knew exactly what he was doing. He was slowly trying to get me all hot and heavy.

"Just ask it," I gritted.

"I had my brother look into you. Where were you during the five years before you got here? After you left that diner in Chicago, you stopped existing. Who did you become?"

Of course he looked into me. Another indication that the world he belonged to could find anything out.

"I was involved with some shitty people, well, person, who was involved with various other shitty people. He took everything from me."

My foot started to tap anxiously against the couch. The roar of the fire and the tapping were the only sounds after my confession.

"What did he do?" Julian glanced at my foot before looking back into my eyes, his face completely unreadable.

"Nuh-uh. It's my turn." I tried to change the mood by teasing a little. I looked at his hand and saw that he was squeezing the stem of the glass. Any more pressure, and he was going to crack it.

"Have you ever been in love?"

This time he smiled, and the pressure eased from the wine glass.

"Never. And honestly, I never want to. My papa left the Cosa Nostra to get out of an arranged marriage because he fell in love with my mamma. When she was diagnosed with cancer, I saw his heartache. Then she passed, and the three of us decided that love wasn't kind to Marchetti men. So we vowed to stay away from love in any form."

His answer took me aback. I knew he had connections to a darker world, but I didn't realize he came from a Mafia family. When I was with Cam, he often met with different capos of the Cosa Nostra. They dealt more with money than dirty drugs, but sometimes their business meetings overlapped. The Mafia was known more for their dirty money business versus moving crack or heroine around like The Club was.

"Except you sleep with a lot of women," I retorted, not knowing what else to say.

"Fucking women and falling in love are very different, my little romantic. Plus, I only fuck a woman once."

"Including me?" I shot back.

"We haven't fucked yet," he said with a wink and I chuckled

Somehow his confession weighed on me. I felt terrible for him and his family. At the same time, I understood where he was coming from. I could honestly say that while I thought I was in love at one point in my life, I didn't really know what love was. It's probably just a figment of our imagination that we hold onto to escape our crappy realities.

Julian took a long sip and crossed one leg over the other. He focused on me, staring deep into my soul. I knew the question that was about to come out of his mouth.

"What did he do?"

Even though I anticipated the question, there was no preparing for it. I felt it deep within my core and wasn't ready to answer. I honestly had no idea where to begin or what he might be referring to.

He waited for me to speak but kept his eyes locked with mine, his body rigid in anticipation. I tried to find the words inside my head but couldn't string a sentence together. I thought I offered him as much vulnerability as I could at this point. I had trusted him the last time, but maybe what little alcohol was still coursing through my veins could give me the same confidence to share something else personal and profound.

I got off the couch and stood in front of him. I tried to shore up and strengthen the walls I used to protect myself from getting hurt. He watched me intently, then placed his wine on the table beside the couch.

I reached behind me and tugged the zipper on my dress, slowly pulling it down and keeping eye contact. My chest felt tight as the zipper got lower. If he even began to talk, I don't think I could get my vocal cords to work.

I slid my hands down my sides, my fingertips trailing over my scars. Memories flooded back with the fear and pain inflicted upon me. But I pushed it all away when I saw the desire in Julian's eyes. His gaze flickered between my scars and red-lace underwear, and I felt a surge of power wash over me.

I stepped closer to him, my heels clicking on the floor. My body trembled with nerves, and I could feel the wetness between my legs. I knew I wanted him, and I wanted him to see every inch of me, flaws and all. He brushed his fingertips over my scars, tracing the marks with a gentleness that made me ache. I let out a shaky breath as he leaned in to kiss them, his lips soft and warm against my skin. The pain and shame melted away, replaced by pure need. He abruptly stood up, pressing my body against his as our mouths collided in a fierce and hungry kiss. His taste, mixed with the sweetness of my desire mixed with the wine, was intoxicating. As his hands roamed over my bare skin, I knew I had never felt more alive.

But I couldn't take the silence anymore.

"Say something," I whispered, gazing deeply into his eyes as I ran my fingers through his hair. Every strand felt like silk between my fingertips, igniting a fire that only he could quench. As I pulled away, my body ached for his touch, but my heart raced, anticipating what he might say.

He dragged his hands to the back of my thighs and pulled me onto his lap. He looked at me with eyes full of concern.

Instead of speaking, he kissed each scar gently as I arched backward for him to allow him space to continue to trail his mouth down. He moved slowly between scars, kissing each one. I threw my head back in pleasure.

I had never been taken care of like this. The fact that he was trying to take away my pain had me holding back tears. I wasn't much of a crier, and since coming to San Diego, I don't remember crying at all, trying to protect myself from the years of unshed tears. But this man had me crying like a freaking baby every time I was with him. I hated how vulnerable he made me feel.

"Please." I brought my head back down and watched him continue. The way he treated me with care ignited a dark part of me.

When he had reached every scar, he looked up at me. He pulled me closer and wrapped his hands around my waist.

"Your turn."

"Did you sleep with her?" I hoped he understood who I was talking about. The girl in the magazine from the event he went to.

"No." He brought his face to my neck.

As he traced up to my ear with his lips, he growled, "I cannot stop thinking about you. Day in and day out, you possess my every thought. It's dumb because I knew it would be in the tabloids. Those girls liked to leave an event attached to some man to boost their popularity. I made a mistake. You've been my sole focus since you left my house."

"Why did you stop sending me gifts?" The question came out shakier than I wanted. I didn't want to be vulnerable with him. And what he did in his free time wasn't my business. "I thought you forgot about me."

He growled deep in his chest and pulled me in tighter. I was so close I could feel his erection. Only the fabric of my thong kept me from thrusting my dampness onto him.

194

"I thought you wanted nothing to do with me after you walked out. But I swear I haven't stopped thinking about you, little bear. I want to know what you eat for breakfast or if you thought about me when you touched yourself at night." I blushed because I knew he had now seen me when I spent every night masturbating to him, well, either him or James if he was creeping at all, and I sure as fuck hoped it was him.

"I was, you know. Thinking about you."

"Ugh." He pulled back and ran his hands through his hair. His eyes filled with darkness and desire.

"I just hope James didn't report on it." I laughed.

"I spent every night sitting outside your house and just watching you. I loved the mundane things you did to the way you took a shower and walked around without a towel." I shivered, and a chill went down my spine. "We really need to get you better curtains than the sheer ones you have." I couldn't help but laugh at creepy as he sounded.

"Are you cold?" he asked.

I looked outside and saw the condensation from the jacuzzi forming in the air. I looked back at him, and he didn't even ask before standing up and hoisting me over his shoulder.

I smacked his back and squealed, "Put me down!"

His only response was to slap my ass and throw his tie onto one of the lounge chairs. The cold breeze blew over me when we stepped outside, and something wet touched my cheek. I craned my neck to see snowflakes falling from the sky. A rush of water surprised me and for a moment I thought I was drowning. When I surfaced, I realized he had thrown me in the pool.

"I hate you," I muttered.

He just laughed and stood in the falling snow, slowly unbuttoning his shirt. I watched lustfully, and when he got to the last button, I bit my lip in pleasure.

He pulled off the black button-down, his broad and muscled chest covered in ink. In one swift movement, he dropped his pants.

"My turn." His green eyes looked at me intensely.

"On or off?" he asked as nonchalantly as one would ask for change at a grocery store.

"Off." Knowing what he was asking and what I wanted didn't require any explanation.

His hands pulled down on his gray boxer briefs, exposing his broad firmness.

"Come here," I murmured in the warm bubbles.

He walked in and sat on the opposite side of the hot tub from me.

"It's my turn," I whispered as I moved toward him.

The warm water flowed around me as I reached him. He stretched out his hands and pulled me onto his lap, the water lapping at our bodies. The sensation was exquisite, and he held my waist as we swayed together with the water's gentle movements.

My underwear and bra were soaked and clung to my skin. I leaned into his neck, tasting the saltiness of the water as I licked up to his ear. His response was immediate, a deep guttural groan that echoed in the night air. I couldn't help but let out my own half-moan in response.

Curiosity got the better of me, and I pulled back to look him in the eyes.

"Why do you call me little bear?" I asked, wanting to understand the meaning behind those words.

For a moment, his eyelids fluttered. Then, his gaze met mine, and he spoke with conviction, making my heart twist in my chest.

"I sensed your energy when I met you at the wedding. You were a little fearful, but you were powerful when you came out of your shell. A force to be reckoned with. Like a bear, you're protective of yourself and don't let anyone in unless they've shown they're worthy of being in your inner world. However, bears are also capable of joy and fear. Their strength is so different than their soft interior. Just like you." His words left me speechless as I struggled with the emotions churning inside me.

"I used to call someone very special to me something similar. You remind me of her."

He leaned in, and I could feel the heat rising between us as our bodies inched closer, our breaths syncing. His lips hovered over mine, teasing and tempting, and my heart raced excitedly. Our eyes remained locked, the moment suspended in time as if nothing else existed but the electricity between us.

"My little bear," he whispered huskily. The anticipation was unbearable. Our lips finally met, and I melted into his arms. The taste of him was intoxicating, his lips soft and pliant against mine. I couldn't get enough of him, my body yearning for his touch. The heat and passion between us grew with each kiss. It was as if nothing else existed but him and me, lost in our lust and desire.

Our bodies fought to get even closer than we were. His mouth met mine with fierce hunger, his tongue thrusting urgently.

My body's core temperature rose as we pushed each other into a frenzy. I arched my back just as his hand unclasped my bra. I threw it into the snow, and my breasts bobbed in the water.

"So pink and perfect." He made me arch my back so he could roll my nipple over his tongue, moving back and forth between my breasts. A cry escaped my mouth, encouraging him to also use his teeth. His hands grabbed my hips, moving and grinding them over him.

Our gluttony for each other was insatiable. At this moment, I felt like I would do anything to satisfy my thirst for him.

As I looked around the jacuzzi, I couldn't help but notice the intricate details. The wood slats that lined the pool's edge were cool to the touch, their rough texture contrasting with the silky smoothness of the glass interior. The steam rising from the water enveloped us in a warm, sensual haze, heightening the sensations of his lips and tongue on my sensitive nipples.

"Off," he instructed and ripped my underwear from me in one swift movement.

As his hands gripped my shoulders, I stood in front of him.

"Tap my knee three times if you need to." I twisted my lip in question. "Do you understand?"

I nodded hesitantly, not knowing what was coming.

Without warning, he pushed me under the water, and the world above vanished instantly. The rush of water filled my ears, and I couldn't see anything as the cloudy liquid enveloped me.

Panic threatened to overwhelm me as I struggled to catch my breath. But then, Julian's hands found their way to me, steadying me and bringing me back to myself. I clung to him, feeling his knees against my skin like a safe haven. His touch on my back was electric, sending shivers down my spine and causing me to arch towards him. His fingers brushed against the top of my core, and I moaned softly, my body already responding to his touch.

In that moment, I realized that I was completely at his mercy. But I didn't care. I trusted him completely. Despite the danger of being underwater and the threat of drowning, I felt secure in his embrace. He had promised to protect me, and I believed him. The vulnerability I felt was tempered by the knowledge that he was there to keep me safe. It was a heady mix of sensations that made me want to surrender to him completely.

The longer he kept my head down, the faster his fingers worked, flicking at my clit. Just as I was about to sink into an unconscious abyss of bliss and lust, he hoisted me up. Water sputtered out of my mouth as the cold air burned my skin. I tried steadying my breath but had no time to spare before he lifted me up and raised my legs onto the wooden planks so I was straddling his neck.

I wanted to break boundaries. I was blissfully sinking deeper into a state of bliss when his voice broke me out of my delirium.

He growled in pleasure. My flesh was in front of his face as I threaded my fingers through the curls of his hair. My legs were pointed in the cold snow, and my backside was warm from the water lapping through me.

"You are so wet for me," he murmured, using one hand to hold my ass up while the other circled the top of my opening.

I was consumed with the need for him to touch me. My feet had become numb, and I pressed my clit into his finger in desperation.

"Say please," he teased, smirking at me.

"Never," I whimpered. I couldn't bear to give in to his teasing, even though every fiber of my being was screaming for him. The tension between us was feverish, and my body responded to his every move.

But still, I refused to give him the satisfaction of hearing me beg. He pulled my hips away from him, and the building pressure suddenly halted.

He leaned in closer, his breath hot against my skin, and whispered, "Just say the word, and I'll give you everything you want."

"Please," I begged finally, the words coming out in a needy moan.

He lifted me and immediately dove into my core. His tongue explored my mouth, moving from the top to the bottom, savoring every taste. One of my ankles was pushed into the snowbank, and I couldn't feel my toes, but the heat radiating from between my legs was so intense that it didn't faze me as I rocked against the hand holding me up. My chest heaved in satisfaction as I let out a sob. His tongue circled my clit, and my eyes rolled back in ecstasy. I was on the verge any second, and I knew I was going to explode.

"My legs are frozen," I whimpered, suddenly aware of the cold around us.

"Focus on me," he commanded, directing my attention back to the pleasure inside me.

My heel lifted and pressed into his back, surprising him. But he didn't stop, and I felt his thumb circle my back entrance. I whispered a breathy yes, permitting him, and he pushed his finger into my ass.

A sob escaped me, and I arched deeper into his mouth. If this was how this man fucked all the time, I knew why he had a revolving door of women.

His finger pushed deeper inside me, and his mouth flicked quickly. I felt the build-up inside me on the brink of exploding into his mouth.

"I need—" I tried to speak, but he interrupted me by removing his finger and throwing my body back into the hot pool. The shock to my system of hot and cold was only adding to the growing erotic hunger.

"Not until I feel the inside of your pretty pink pussy, little bear," he growled.

I groaned, and he cupped my jaw with his wet hands and kissed me fiercely. We moved feverishly, trying to take more of each other until our lips felt rough and raw.

He pushed me to the other side of the large pool, and I stood atop one of the corner seats. The water dripped down my naked body as I rang out my cold hair. I looked at him sitting inside the pool, watching my every move. The bitter wind changed from the heat radiating from my core.

"You mean this?" I took two fingers and stuck them deep inside me.

I left them there, feeling the pleasure, before pulling them out and dropping back into the warm water.

"Swim to me," I commanded, looking up at the black sky above and lifting my hands over my head before bringing my fingers into my mouth. My tongue swirled around them as I brought them in and out, mixing them furiously with the hot liquid inside my mouth. Snow covered my lips as I finger-fucked my mouth, watching him swim toward the edge where I was sitting and sit on steps like a truly made man on his throne. Before bringing my fingers out, I glided over to him in the pool's steam.

"Don't ever tease me again," I growled and pushed my fingers into his mouth.

"You taste like heaven, little bear," he groaned, his words sending shivers down my spine. I felt his rough hands grip my waist, pulling me closer to him. His voice was raw and guttural, his words dripping with a primal, feral energy that sent shivers down my spine. I was his prey, and he was the predator, taking what he wanted with a brutal force that left me breathless and trembling.

His eyes locked onto mine, gleaming with savage intensity as he claimed me as his own. I was helpless to resist, completely at the mercy of his wild, untamed desire.

I threw my hands into his hair, reveling in the sensations he evoked with each touch. He brought my fingers into his mouth again, savoring every taste, and my body was consumed with elation and delirium. When he stood up, water cascaded around us, but my focus was solely on him as he lifted me to straddle his waist. In that moment, I was transported to a state of pure ecstasy and rapture. Faint sounds in the background only added to the thrill of being in his arms, and I felt blissful.

I scanned the area, feeling paranoid that someone might see us.

"What if someone sees us?" I whispered nervously to Julian. We were a perfect show for every skier coming down the mountain behind us.

But he just chuckled as his hands explored my body. "That's the thrill. Anyone could walk by and catch us."

As the skiers whizzed by, I couldn't help but feel a rush of adrenaline. The danger only heightened my senses, intensifying the electricity between us. He must have sensed my excitement because he pulled me closer, his breath hot against my ear. He brought me toward the house and stopped to hoist me up against the door where the glass door framed the house.

"Are you getting turned on, little bear?" Julian teased, lifting me so I was straddling his waist. I let my lips brush against his neck.

"Fuck me," was all I could muster.

"As you wish." He pushed my body flush with the side of the house. My ass smushed into the floor-to-ceiling glass, and the wind whipped around me. If he dropped me, I would be stepping in a heaping pile of snow. He stood on the wooden slats of the pool's edge, which seemed to be heated because there was no snow under him.

"Tell me, how many times have you touched yourself thinking about my cock?" His eyes stared into mine.

"Every night since I left your house."

That must have been enough for him. He pushed his rock-hard cock into me. I cried out in painful pleasure as his entire length thrust inside.

"You're so big." I let out a breathy moan as he lowered himself deeper onto me.

"Breathe, Tatum."

As he pushed deeper, following his instructions, I felt a new sensation. His length explored parts of me that I didn't know existed, awakening my senses to a pleasure I had never experienced before. The moans that escaped my lips were guttural. He took control of my hips, guiding them up and down to the rhythm of his thrusts. Our breaths became shallow, and our bodies moved in perfect sync.

As I gazed out at the skiers in the distance, I couldn't help but wonder who among them was watching us. The thought of them witnessing the possessive way Julian looked at me made my skin tingle with anticipation. It was as if he was unraveling me, breaking down every wall I had ever built.

"I am going to try something again. If you're uncomfortable at any point, your safe word is ice." I nodded almost too quickly.

He put my feet on the warmed wooden slats of the deck. Only a few feet of snow separated the slats and the glass wall. He pulled my hips toward him and lifted my hands above my head against the glass wall with his other hand.

"Mine," he groaned and then playfully teased the opening of my entrance by circling the tip of his cock around my dripping opening.

"Oh," was all I could get out between gasps of icy cold air. I was freezing and his teasing was the only thing warming me up.

"Say please," he murmured. I was getting wetter as he teased me with the very tip of him.

"Please," I croaked as the cool air circulated through my lungs.

"Julian," I implored.

As Julian pressed his body against mine, his hands manipulated my curves, caressing and fondling every inch of me. With each stroke and squeeze, I felt a powerful impulsion and momentum building inside of me.

"Not yet."

I turned my head, unable to use my hands and not wanting to move my feet from the warm slats. He growled, but looked quite amused. As I watched, he pulled out of me. My body was left slack and bent in half, my hands falling to my ankles and my ass in the air as he went to get something.

When he came back, something was in his hand.

"What—" His finger quieted my sentence.

"Turn around." I faced the glass, and through the reflection, I saw the tie he had left on the lounge chair when we came out here. He placed it over my eyes and tied it in the back. All I could see was darkness, but I realized I trusted him implicitly, just like earlier in the jacuzzi.

"Remember, ice is your safeword."

"Mmm," was all I could say.

"I need you to say yes." His tone was serious.

"Yes. The safeword is ice."

He gently placed each foot inside the snowbank, and a chill immediately went down my spine. I wanted to stretch them quickly to the warmed planks but stayed there, breathing through the cold.

Suddenly, a sharp slap on my ass jolted me out of my thoughts. I yelped, but the cold snow numbed the pain. Then he threw a handful of slush at me, mixing with my arousal, creating a hot liquid that dripped down my thighs.

As I shivered, he teased me with a giant icicle, running it up and down my thigh. It was long and pointed on one end, smooth and palm-sized on the other. The icy touch made my teeth chatter more, and I felt a surge of both pleasure and pain. I couldn't see what he was doing, but I could feel him melting the icicle with his warmth, tracing lines of fire along my skin.

"Such a beautiful girl." His voice was barely above a whisper.

As soon as the icicle touched my clit, a jolt of pain and pleasure shot through me. My body was alive with sensation, every nerve ending on edge as he slowly pushed the smoother end inside me. I melted around it, the warmth of my insides enveloping the cold ice. His hand held mine against the wall while the other pumped the icicle in and out, driving me to new heights. I was completely lost in sensation, unable to focus on anything except the intense pleasure radiating through my body.

He knew exactly what he was doing to me, holding me against the wall, my ass high in the air, while he worked the icicle in and out of me. My groans grew louder with each thrust, my body aching for release. The thought of someone watching us from the ski run below only made it hotter, the voyeuristic thrill of the idea sending shivers down my spine.

"Let me," I begged, unable to hold back any longer.

In an instant, he pulled out the icicle and set me back on my feet. The sudden warmth of the slats beneath me sent a wave of pleasure through my body, but it was short-lived as he lifted me against the wall again.

"You're going to be my demise," he growled, thrusting into me with wild passion.

My breasts pressed against the cold glass as he took me, his hands gripping my hair and pushing against my lower back. I could feel him getting closer, his chest heaving with each breath.

"I want you to see what you do to me," he said, ripping the tie off my face. I looked back at him as he poured himself into me, taking me to new heights of pleasure.

"Please," I begged, unable to hold back any longer.

"Don't stop." My body exploded with pleasure as he thrust into me, the pressure building until I could no longer hold back. I shuddered and gasped for air as he held me close, his arms wrapped tightly around me.

"Such a good girl," he murmured, pulling me up by my hair.

I leaned into his embrace, basking in the warmth of his arms as he carried me inside. The cozy and crackling fire added to the warmth as he carried me upstairs to the shower. He held me close and washed me clean, never letting me leave his arms.

After he wrapped me in a towel, he brought me into a dark room and laid me on what felt like a fluffy cloud. Lost in a haze, I felt Julian's arms pull me tight against his burly figure.

I looked at him dreamily and mumbled, "I'm on the pill." It was the last thing I said before a wall of darkness welcomed me.

22

TATUM

Present

The smell of coffee wafting through the house wakes me. This bed was softer than anything I'd felt, and I almost forgot I wasn't in my house until my eyes finally opened.

"Ugh." I held my head as the effects of alcohol rang through my brain.

I looked over and saw two Tylenol and a large glass of water which I assumed was for me. The small snowflakes falling against the windows reminded me I was still in Big Bear. I pulled the covers off and saw I was in an oversized black T-shirt. I inhaled and smelled the same musky leather that I associated with Julian.

I walked down to the kitchen and stopped to take in the sight of him. I couldn't help but notice how the light danced off his skin. His jawline was sharp, and I could see his Adam's apple as he swallowed.

There was something magnetic about him, something that made it hard to look away. My gaze drifted to his arms, where more ink adorned his skin. I noticed a tattoo with "famiglia" written across his back. There were other various designs I couldn't make out, and the ink seemed to wrap around, accentuating the definition in his muscles.

He turned around and caught me staring, and I was caught off guard. I quickly averted my gaze, feeling my cheeks flush with embarrassment. But as he walked towards me, I couldn't help but feel drawn to him.

When I told Maeve's daughter about wanting lollipops, I thought I was addicted to this flavor. In fact, I think this particular flavor of candy is the only one I could ever need.

"I need to go check up on some projects for my brother before I head to Sacramento for a few days." His whole demeanor was softer than usual as he set a cup of coffee in front of me.

"I wasn't planning on staying," I said defensively.

"That's not what I'm saying. But you are staying. I'll have James bring you to your friends to grab the stuff you have here." He looked at me, amusement growing on his face.

"What are you talking about? We're going home tomorrow."

His hands fingered his floppy jet-black hair while he picked up his coffee cup.

He said before bringing it to his lips, "I don't know your plans for the holiday, but they'll now be with me in Sacramento. Call whoever you need to, I assume your tall friend, to let them know you won't be staying with them."

He took a sip before adding, "I protect what's mine; I told you this. "

"And I told you that I don't need protection. Plus I told you how important it was to me not to be forced into doing things I didn't want." I crossed my arms over my chest.

This time his face turned softer and he walked toward where I was. "You are right, little bear. Would you *please* come? "

I hated how much I loved when he begged.

"Fine," I huffed.

"You look so good in my shirt." He winked at me, and I tried to ignore the tingly sensation that vibrated through my body at his compliment. When I lifted my hooded eyes to him, I knew he felt the same.

He set down the cup before going upstairs.

"You won't be making a casserole this year." I could hear the walls vibrate from his laughter.

I totally forgot Christmas was in a couple of days. The restaurant was closed for the week, so I would only be missing a couple of days of work if I went with him. Wait, why was I even entertaining this idea?

Probably because last night was the most addictive thing I've experienced. If I was honest, the way he took care of me was just as addicting. The sex didn't feel like a punishment for me but an experience we enjoyed together.

I was being absurd. He flat-out said he only slept with a girl once, so going with him was pointless. But going to Maeve's ex-husband's Christmas wasn't the top on my list either. I appreciated that she had invited me and I had no other plans, so I would have gone.

I padded up the stairs to follow and found him slipping on another pair of black pants and a black button-down.

"Do you always wear black?" I laughed from the doorframe.

"Do you always wear so much color?" he retorted.

"Wait, I came up here for a reason."

He was buttoning his sleeves as he spoke and raised an eyebrow at me to continue.

"I'm not coming with you. You don't sleep with the same person more than once. Last night was our one time, so why would I come?"

I leaned against the door frame. He stopped what he was doing immediately, his shirt still half-buttoned.

He stalked toward me and said, "I've decided to break that rule. You have the most addicting pussy, little bear." He rolled his tongue up my face before kissing my cheek. He fucking licked me.

"Any more objections?" He smirked, and I wanted to melt into a puddle.

"Let me," I offered, gesturing to his shirt.

I tugged on the sleeves and slowly fixed his shirt, feeling the heat of his gaze during this seemingly intimate act. I plucked some lint off before looking at him.

He pushed me against the frame and grabbed my waist with one hand, placing his arm on the frame above me and leaning into my body.

"Touch me again and I will come undone."

His hand slid down to my throat, applying a small amount of pressure and making a small groan slip out. His other hand slid under the hem of the oversized shirt.

"Wanna play a game?" he murmured.

"Hmmm." His hand caressed the scars under my breasts before reaching my nipples which were hard in anticipation of his touch.

He closed the gap between us and gently tugged on my pebbled nipples. A strangled moan escaped as I gripped his arms, fingernails clawing into him.

"If you're wet right now like I think you are, you'll come home with me."

In that instant, I knew he was going to win this bet. I wasn't sure there had been a moment in the last twelve hours that I wasn't drenched thinking about him.

"That's not fair," I cried as his fingers traced down the center of my body.

"Any last words?"

"You're an asshole," I spat out.

He chuckled darkly and slipped two fingers inside of me. He was right. I was completely and utterly soaked for him. He pushed deeper, and my body jolted from the quick sensation.

His hand left my throat and wrapped around my back, cushioning me so I didn't slam into the wall. He pressed inside me for a few pumps. It was just enough to get me growling.

As quick as he slid in, he pulled away aggressively. His fingers traveled up to his lips, where his tongue slowly licked them from bottom to top.

"You taste so sweet." He lapped up my taste until his fingers were clean. It was so casual, like he was sitting down for dinner, which only made me desperate for more.

Fixing my shirt, he went into the bathroom, where I heard him wash his hands.

"James will bring you to the rental and you can grab your stuff," he said from the other room.

I stomped toward him, sexually frustrated and annoyed that he had won.

"What about your stupid rule?" I gritted.

"I told you, I'm not done with you." He looked at me in the mirror, then turned to the closet for a tie.

I put my hands against his chest to prevent him from leaving, knowing he could thrust me aside if he wanted.

"Wait, please," I said, and he obliged me by stopping.

I wasn't used to talking back to men or even stopping them from doing something. I knew he could sense that it was taking a lot of courage for me to vocalize what I wanted to share with him. I had to figure out how to say what I wanted, but I struggled with this sudden burst of confidence.

Once he realized I was struggling, he dragged his fingers through my hair and then stroked my cheek with his thumb. With his touch, I felt the glow in my chest pulse.

"I'm not coming with you to your. . . business meetings."

I needed to make it clear that I wouldn't be part of his world. His business was just that, his.

Before opening the bedroom door, he looked at me and said, "I'm not a monster. I would never want you to be a part of it. Business is business. You are mine," With that, he shut the door.

Little did he know, I was well acquainted with a monster. I felt a salty liquid on my lips and wiped it away. Words spiraled through my mind, but I couldn't string together a sentence. It was in this moment I knew I could be safe.

I dressed quickly in my red dress so I could do the walk of shame and went outside to see James sitting in the car. I hated the silence in the house without Julian there.

"Hey. I heard you've had a front-row seat to the Tatum show the last few weeks. Hope it wasn't too boring for you," I joked when I got in the car.

I watched James smile as our eyes connected in the rearview mirror.

"I enjoyed with Tony and Samuel on the front porch."

"They knew?" I screeched from the backseat.

"Of course they did. I didn't want to look like a creep sitting in my car outside their house."

"Oh, I see. Only around me."

I slumped back and watched the snow fall on the short ride to Daphne's parents' house. I got out, and James promised to wait while I collected my things. I took a deep breath of the cold mountain air and braced myself to be barraged with questions.

From the moment I opened the door, the girls ran toward me. Maeve jumped in first.

"I am so incredibly sorry. I didn't see that guy putting his hands on you. I'm a shit friend, and I understand if you don't want anything to do with me."

"It's fine. I'm fine. Nothing happened, so please don't beat yourself up."

"How many times did you have sex? I can smell the glow on you." Chels walked over to sniff around me for effect.

"Chels, leave her alone. She'll tell us if she wants to," Daphne chimed in. She was always the reasonable one looking out for everyone's mental state. I slumped onto the couch.

"You guys, it was everything. We had the best sex ever. Honestly, I'm not even sure I can call it sex. It was an. . . experience." I sighed, thinking about what happened last night.

"Yes, girl!" Chels screamed and jumped up and down.

"I just can't get it out of my head that he said he only sleeps with a girl once."

Maeve's face was the first to fall. The three of them looked at me sympathetically, knowing if we had sex yesterday, then it was over for us.

"The weird part, though," I continued, "is he wants to take me home for Christmas."

"He wants to what now?" Daphne asked.

I turned to Maeve.

"And I think I said yes. I'm so sorry, but I won't be able to come to your ex's."

"What? I don't even want to be there. You have to go. You're going to meet his family. This is a big deal. He definitely wants to be with you more than once."

"Yeah, maybe you're the exception to the rule," Chels added.

"His driver is waiting outside for me to go to Northern California."

"Where are you gonna catch a plane around here? There isn't an airport for miles," Daphne questioned.

"He has a private plane," I said shamelessly and put my head in my hands, waiting for the squeals.

And five, four, three, two. . .

"Ah!" the three screamed in unison.

"A private plane!"

"Oh, he is like rich, rich."

"Ugh, am I making the worst decision of my life? His family has connections to the underworld too." I casually dropped the last line in.

"The what?" Chels' eyes bugged out of her head. "They're like bad news then? You have to be careful." Chels was the fun-loving one that pushed us to go on adventures, so seeing her be serious about something was concerning.

"You know what you're doing. He really seemed worried about you yesterday. Sure, maybe a little overbearing too, but I saw the look on his face at the bar when he couldn't find you. He was really worried," Maeve said.

"Go and suss it out," Chels responded.

"I think I will. I'll go and just see. It's one holiday."

The one good thing about being with Julian is that I felt safe. If Orlando or Cam were looking for me, being around Julian was the safest option.

I went upstairs and packed my backpack of stuff. I didn't have much, but I certainly didn't have something modest enough for a holiday. I walked to Daphne and Maeve's room.

"Do you have something I can borrow? I only have jeans, T-shirts and a skimpy dress that I've already worn. I'd bring something from home, but. . ." I rambled on.

The girls smiled at me. Daphne handed me a few blouses and sweaters she had brought, while Chels gave me a bohemian-patterned maxi dress.

I thanked my friends and said goodbye before returning to the car with James.

"Private plane, huh?" I mused out loud. He just grunted back. Not a talker, then. My hands needed something to do as anxiety coursed through me. I picked at my nails as I stared outside. I had one chance to make this right.

23

JULIAN

Present

It was the longest meeting I've ever had. I obsessively checked my phone to make sure James had her and was going to the airport. I held up a hand when the director started droning on about saving the trees.

"Gentlemen. Thank you so much for showing me the property. I'll happily report to Alexander that the project is well on its way and funded appropriately." I shook their hands, got in my car, and headed to the airport.

I dialed my brother's number.

"You're calling to say you're not coming for the holidays."

Since our mamma died, it's been the three of us. Italian families are known for their large holiday gatherings, but when my papa left the Cosa

Nostra, the rest of our family ostracized us. Over the past few years, we've tried to contact because of my brother's and my business ventures. It didn't matter that Christmas was a holiday we chose to spend the three of us. It was never a big party but once of year time we spent together as a family. Most of the time we talked about memories of Mamma and the crazy holiday decorations she went all out for.

"Thank you for sitting through a three-hour lecture about trees instead of being at the house with a girl I want to lick from head to toe," I sarcastically retorted back at him.

"Get on with it."

"All is well, and I'll send you an update later. What did you find on the girl I asked you to look into?" I asked.

"Ah. The same girl I assume you had in your bed?"

"Yes, and might I say my new favorite flavor."

"You're gross. Anyway, yes, her name is Tatum Sloane. According to the DMV, she's twenty-five and stands at five foot three. She was born in Chicago, and her mother spent most of her childhood in a rehab facility for a mental health illness. Afterward, the family ran in a wealthy social circle in the city. She worked at a diner after high school and then vanished. Then there's no trace of her for almost five years."

That has to have been when she got involved in the underworld. Most gangs knew how to make a person vanish physically or from government knowledge.

"What is it about this woman that you have me looking into her?" he asked.

"Well, brother, you and Papa will find out yourself. She's about to board the plane with me. See you all in an hour. Be on your best behavior and tell Papa."

"Julian Marchetti—" I laughed and hung up on him midsentence.

I pulled up to the tarmac and watched her after parking the Corvette. She was getting out of the car with a simple black backpack. One of the things that drew me to her was that she wasn't fussy like most of the women I'd been with. She was wearing a freaking bright pink sweater with tassels on the sleeve and jeans and boots, for God's sake. Against the white backdrop of the snow, she glowed. Her long brown hair—that I couldn't wait to pull—was in a high ponytail.

"I'm so glad you came," I murmured as I closed the gap between us and guided her onto the plane with my hand on her lower back. She looked at me, and her nose did that scrunching thing when she was about to tell me off. It warmed my heart immediately but made me feel like such a pussy.

That's exactly what this woman did to me. She had me craving her taste, smell, and her time. After spending the better half of the day with businessmen, she warmed my cool exterior. God, even a small touch of her body made me dizzy.

This woman was different.

She looked around the plane and marveled at the luxurious interior. Her mouth agape at the jet yet all I could think about was her plush lips around my cock as they opened to stare.

Fuck, I was pussy-whipped. I made a commitment to my brother and father to swear off women after Mamma died, but something about her made me want to break that promise.

Tatum sat across from me and was silent most of the flight after I had told her that we were going to see my family. Occasionally, she would test herself by moving her knee closer to mine but quickly took it away. By the time we arrived, she was picking at her fingers.

"Nervous?" I asked as I grabbed her hand to help her off the plane.

"Am I nervous? There are so many things right now. I barely know you. I'm meeting your family. The holidays are usually a very private time for people. I don't know what to say to you, and you just keep staring at me." She huffed out her words.

"And to top it all off, I don't even have a gift to bring to your dad for his hospitality!" She exasperatedly threw her hands in the air and walked down the plane. We were greeted by one of my dad's drivers.

I held the car door open for her and nodded at the driver before getting in. She was back to her anxious self, staring out the window. I wasn't sure what possessed me, but I reached out to grab her fingers, interlacing them with mine. She glanced at me, a look of surprise on her face. I was worried she'd pull away, but she kept her delicate hand in mine.

"We can get some flowers if you want to bring something." I smiled at her softly.

She nodded in agreement and looked back out the window. The whole time, her hand never left mine.

24

TATUM

Present

After stopping by a florist and picking up a bouquet, we pulled up to one of the largest houses I had ever seen. Between Julian's house and some of the venues I worked, nothing seemed to top this. It looked like a smaller White House with big white pillars and Italian statues in the front roundabout driveway. As we approached, I couldn't help but be struck by its sheer opulence. The sprawling estate was surrounded by lush gardens and perfectly manicured lawns, with the scent of blooming flowers permeating the air. The mansion's facade was just as breathtaking, with its gleaming white exterior and towering pillars that seemed to stretch up to the sky. The intricate Italian statues that adorned the roundabout driveway were a sight to behold.

As we drove toward the entrance, two men were outside waiting for us as we finally pulled to the front.

I immediately recognized the familiar features.

One was older, but his salt-and-pepper hair couldn't hide his youthful face. He had the same green eyes as Julian, but his face was softer. He wore a button-down and jeans and radiated the same power as Julian.

The man standing next to him was younger-looking. He was much cleaner than Julian's raw, primal power. His hair was cut shorter but still the same dark black. He was standing in khakis and a white button-down. I knew immediately he was the politician by the way he stood.

"Are you okay?" Julian asked before we left the car. I gripped the flowers tight. Family was a strange concept to me. I wasn't often involved in my family gatherings, usually left with a babysitter.

"I'm fine." My hand was laced with his, and I gave it a little squeeze of affirmation.

"If it helps, I'm right here."

Julian opened his door and never let go of my hand, pulling me out of the vehicle to approach the men. They looked at our hands clasped together and had to conceal the shock on their faces.

"Son." The older man stepped forward and gave Julian a double-cheek kiss.

"Papa. Buon Natale. This is Tatum Sloane."

I snapped my head at him, not realizing he knew my last name. I swear I didn't tell him, but I guess he knew everything.

The older man touched my shoulders and kissed me on both cheeks before pulling away.

"It is a pleasure. My name is Elio. I have to say, it will be nice to have a feminine presence for the holidays. It has been a while."

"Giulio, you son of a bitch." The younger brother pulled Julian in for a hug.

"Giulio?" I asked.

Elio laughed and said, "Before we left our old home, the boys changed their names to blend in here. This one's name is Alessandro, and he is Giulio."

He held his arm out to me. "Please do me the honor, and let me show you around."

I took his elbow and looked at the two brothers ahead of us. They were yin and yang. One clean-cut and the other brash.

After a tour of the home, which was adorned in ornate Italian style, everything was antique and large with red and gold accents around it. A few workers were buzzing about, including a grounds taker, butler and chef. Julian and Elio walked me around and I gasped at every new corner we saw. Between the movie theater, indoor shooting range, pool, steam room, and different living wings, the house was expansive, to say the least.

"I put you in the guest room across the hall from my son. Should you need anything, please let me know. I'll let you settle in." Elio leaned into me for a brief hug.

"My son has never brought someone home. Thank you for coming," he whispered before leaving me shell-shocked in the hall with Julian behind me.

I slowly turned to face him after his father left.

"I'm going to stay in here." I wasn't sure if the statement was for him or me.

"I told my dad you might want your own space." He turned into his room and closed the door, leaving me in the hallway with my Jansport backpack, feeling quite out of place.

I went into the room, and of course it was luxurious. There was a red satin duvet cover on a bed littered with gold pillows.

I texted my friends to let them know I had arrived and rifled through my bag to pull out the maxi dress for the holiday dinner. I began getting ready and curled my hair with the iron Chels let me borrow.

A few hours must have passed and I had decided to go sit out by the pool with a book and a sweater. It was a beautiful cool day and I wanted to watch the sunset. I must have been engrossed in the book when I looked up and Alex was on the lounge chair next to me.

"Good book?"

"Oh, yes. I didn't see you there. I didn't mean to be rude and ignore you."

"No, no. I haven't been here long."

I put the book down, and we sat in comfortable silence, staring at the disappearing sun.

"Do you live nearby?" I asked, finally breaking the quiet.

"Yes. I have an apartment in the city. It's easier to be there for meetings and when we're in session."

"Right. You're a senator."

"What do you do, Tatum?" he asked in the same cool tone as Julian.

"Nothing exciting. I work at a brunch place and occasionally assist a wedding photographer on the weekends."

"Ah, a small business owner." He looked over at me. His eyes were dark brown and full of questions.

"Maybe one day. I'm just an assistant now."

"You know, I've never seen my brother with a woman before. He isn't the. . . type." I raised my eyebrow at him, knowing he was often at the same events Julian's been at.

He looked at me and laughed, his chest heaving.

"You're right. I take that back. I have seen him with women but never serious enough to bring them home. In fact, never serious enough to bring anywhere. He usually meets girls at events, but you're different."

"I don't know about that. I just think we have something fun." I closed my eyes to the darkening sky and took a deep breath.

"Keep thinking that, and you won't be able to see the truth in front of you." I felt him stand and grab my hand to lift me up and guide me to the living room.

After a gleeful holiday dinner where we all must have had over three glasses of wine and endless plates of dinner, I leaned back in my chair, watching the three men jovially poke fun at each other and share inside jokes. Elio looked between his sons.

"Your mother would be so happy you are both here." He reached a hand over to me before saying, "She would also be so happy you have joined us."

A heavy sadness blanketed the table for a minute.

I said quietly, "She must have been pretty amazing to raise such a kind son."

A ridiculously loud laugh cut through the room, and Alex banged the table, tears rolling down his face in amusement.

"If that ain't the first time I've ever heard anyone say Julian and kind in the same sentence."

"Get the fuck out." Julian punched his brother's arm. "I can be nice!" Just like that, the atmosphere turned back to being happy and loving. After retiring to the sitting room, we spent time drinking more wine and laughing.

"I better get to bed," Elio finally spoke up, and I glanced over at the clock realizing we had been up all night.

"Boys, it's always a pleasure to have you home. Even for a short time."

He turned toward me, "Tatum. Please come back soon. Don't let my son run you off so fast."

We were leaving tomorrow morning so I could work a wedding in the afternoon with Lacey. Part of me wished we could stay for another day or so.

Alex hugged his brother and reached out to give me a peck on the cheek before heading off to bed. Julian grabbed my hand, and we walked to our wing of the house.

"Your dad is so young," I admitted.

Julian looked amused. "He is. My parents had me when they were eighteen. He's fifty."

With some quick math, I realized Julian was thirty-two. Only seven years older than me, which wasn't a terrible age gap.

"I'm younger than you." I looked at him before we got to our doors.

"I know. You're twenty-five." Of course, he knew.

I leaned back against my door, and he stood in the center of the hallway.

"Thank you for coming here. It was much nicer than having to deal with them myself."

"Thank you for having me. It's been a while since I was with a family for Christmas. Most of mine were spent with a nanny or friends." I smiled sadly.

He walked over and lifted my chin so my eyes met his gaze. His eyes flicked down to my lips and then back up. He lowered his mouth to mine for a slight kiss before pulling away.

"Good night, Tatum."

I walked into my room and noticed a small silver package on my bed. My heart raced. I didn't put that there. It wasn't mine. How would anyone have penetrated these walls? But what if this was from Cam or Orlando? I picked it up hesitantly and saw the small note.

Little Bear,
Merry Christmas.
-J

I honestly forgot we were here celebrating a holiday. No gifts had been exchanged, and Christmas Day was technically tomorrow, so I hadn't even thought about gifts. Wait, I guess it was today since it was well past midnight. It wasn't like the run-downstairs-to-your-mom but it was so much better surrounded by lots of wine and laughter.

I opened the package and pulled out a dainty silver chain. At the bottom of the chair was a charm of a bear. On the back of the charm was an inscription that I held up to the light to read.

"Little bear," I whispered.

It was so beautiful and thoughtful. I wondered when he got it because we'd been together for the last few days. I held the chain and opened my door to walk across the hallway.

I rapped quietly on his door.

I didn't hear anyone respond, so I turned the knob and stepped inside when I heard the shower. Something bold awakened inside me. Maybe it was the thoughtfulness of the gift, the evening with his family and the wine, or a combination of both, but I desperately wanted to show him how much I appreciated him.

I took my dress off and walked slowly to the connected bathroom. I saw the steam on the glass shower door and pulled off my underwear before I slipped inside with the necklace in my hand.

He quickly turned, water beading down his body. His broad shoulders looked massive inside the small shower, and the swirls of gray and black were all over his body. As the water washed over him, I carefully stepped into the shower.

"I didn't get you anything," I said, clenching my hand.

He was amused.

"It's just something small." But it wasn't small. The fact that he had it engraved said a lot.

"Put it on me?" I asked.

He turned me around and gently moved my hair to the side as the water soaked it. Once it was clasped, he pulled me back against him and wrapped an arm around my waist. I could feel his hard erection pressed tightly against my butt. He kissed me softly down my neck, whispering soothing words against my body.

I turned around and bit his lower lip.

"You're my present." His voice was low and husky as he spoke, sending shivers down my spine.

His words were possessive and filled with desire, and I couldn't help but feel excited at the thought of being his.

I wrapped my arms around him, the hot water cascading down our intertwined bodies. He lifted me by my thighs and turned off the water, steam billowing out as we stepped out of the shower.

After a very quick rub down with a towel, we moved toward the bed, where he sat down, his strong arms supporting me as I straddled him. We melted into one another, lips meeting passionately as we explored each other with reckless abandon.

"Let me give you more."

I slid off him and stood between his knees. I watched the veins in his engorged cock pulsate.

"Get on your knees." His carnal need reverberated in the otherwise quiet bedroom.

I dropped down and turned my attention to his swollen cock. I slowly ran my tongue over the head, teasing him with a few circles.

I looked up at him, eyes wide, as his hands tangled in my hair.

"Take me inside you, little bear." He lifted so his erection thrust to the back of my throat.

"Now, suck." The sudden movement made me gag, but he kept going. He pushed in and out relentlessly as I used my hands to guide him. Half frustrated he was taking control, I reached under with one hand and gave his balls a slight squeeze and tug.

"You look so good on your knees." His voice deepened as I tugged on him.

He continued to slam toward the back of my throat. He had an insatiable thirst for the warmth of my mouth, and I allowed him to slake that need. I used my teeth gently against him, and he groaned some more.

Feeling confident, I matched his repetitive thrusts by taking him deeper. My lips swelled as I opened as wide as possible for his girth. Finally, a warm liquid filled my throat.

"Swallow." His command was dominating, and when I looked up at him wide-eyed, he had a devilish fire in his eyes.

I sat back on my heels, hands on my thighs, and exaggerated swallowing his cum.

"Such a good girl."

He lifted me from the floor and threw me onto the bed.

"I need you." I could barely say the words, my need taking over my voice.

"Use your words. Tell me what you need."

"I want your mouth on me."

"As you wish." He licked his lips and looked toward my center.

He dove into me, lapping up my juices in languid strokes. I cursed at the pleasure burning through my veins. His mouth ate me like I was the best meal he'd eaten.

His tongue caressed my lips, parting them as he brought his thumb up to circle my clit. I clenched his face between my thighs as an eruption burst through me.

I sobbed softly as he pulled away, his eyes locked on mine.

"You taste like candy," he whispered, his voice thick with desire. We were lost in each other's gaze, but it didn't last long.

"Hands on the headboard, little bear." The anticipation sent shivers down my spine as I eagerly complied with his command. I felt his fingers dance around the opening of my backside.

"Do you remember your safeword?" he asked.

I nodded, my eyes half-open with need.

"I need you to tell me with your words. What is your safeword?"

"Yes. Yes. It's ice."

He dipped his fingers into my wetness and used it to circle my backside. Without hesitation, he pushed two fingers in, and I screamed.

"Deep, slow breaths." A hiss of pain and pleasure escaped my swollen lips.

I attempted to slow my breathing, but Julian's fingers stretched me, scissoring and moving in and out.

"Remember, you always have a choice."

"You," I begged.

I bit my lip, trying to hold back a moan as he flipped me around and positioned himself behind me. His hands traced the curve of my waist, sending shivers through my body.

He moved his fingers and pushed his throbbing cock against my backside, slowly penetrating my tight ring of muscle. The sensation was overwhelming, pleasure and pain I couldn't quite describe.

But I was so turned on, already craving more of him. With his strong hands on my hips, he set a steady rhythm, pulling back and thrusting forward with increasing force. The sound of our skin slapping together echoed through the room, adding to my gasps and moans.

I arched my back, pushing against him, wanting him deeper inside me. The intensity of our movements increased, and I knew I was approaching my release. He pulled out before I could reach my peak, leaving me empty and desperate for more, when I felt a rush of warmth on my back and heard him groan. He reached back around to finger my clit, and I exploded.

Dazed, I felt him step away and then come back to wipe my back with a cool towel. I lay there panting, my body trembling with the aftershocks of pleasure. He moved next to me, his fingers tracing slow, lazy circles along my skin, and I couldn't help but smile in satisfaction.

"What's this?" He stopped before he reached my butt cheek, and I froze.

I knew what he was referring to, and suddenly, I felt vulnerable. Shame exploded inside of me, and I thought of how I could get out of having this conversation with him.

"Just something from my past." I tried to sound nonchalant and not give anything away, so I shifted onto the hip with the offensive tattoo to face him. I knew he could sense my discomfort, and he pulled me into a tight hug. I inhaled the sweet smell of our sex and his lingering body wash.

"I thought you didn't have sex more than once with the same person," I mumbled.

He chuckled and placed a gentle kiss on my hair.

"I guess I like breaking the rules when you're around."

"Hmm," was all I could say before sleep beckoned me.

The warmth of his embrace and the intoxicating scent of his skin lulled me into a peaceful slumber. I couldn't help but feel a sense of contentment wash over me, knowing that I was safe and loved here. For the first time in a long time, I felt truly at peace and knew I was exactly where I was meant to be.

25

JULIAN

Present

I woke up before she did. She splayed across my bed with the sheets bundled up around her. I was totally and utterly fucked when it came to her. After last night, I knew there was no way I could let her out of my sight. And while she was a delicate, breakable doll, she had this inner strength and courage that just did it for me.

I dressed and packed my suitcase, knowing we would be leaving soon. I went downstairs and saw my brother at the dining room table.

"Papa sleeping?" I asked, grabbing a coffee and sitting across from him.

"Yeah, seems like no one could sleep with the zoo noises that were happening even though you guys were in another wing."

"Jealousy is not a good look for you, brother," I said slyly.

"What're you going to do?" he asked after a moment.

I knew he was referring to the brunette sleeping in my bed. A girl whose past was a mystery and whose touch was absolutely addicting.

"I'm going to enjoy tasting her a while longer." I winked.

We were always crude with each other. Only a few years separated us, and we spent most of our twenties after our mamma died in clubs sharing too much pussy.

"You're breaking your own rule. Our rule too."

He knew about my one-and-done rule and referred to us having vowed off women after Mamma died. We thought it would bring us closer as a family, as a Marchetti force.

"I think she is worth breaking," Papa said from the door.

"I like her too," Alex said. "The elephant in the room is the world we live in. Bringing her into a world like ours makes her a part of it."

Elio chimed in. "Alessandro has a point. Your mamma was born into this world and knew what it was to be connected to the Mafia. Does she know what kissing the darkness means?"

I knew Tatum had some connection to a dark world, but mine was deeper. It was full of death and fear.

"I think she has an idea of my world."

"I like her, though. She has a tough exterior but can hang with family." Elio smiled.

"Yeah, I think I'll keep her a little longer," I confessed. The words surprised even me coming out.

I hugged them and promised I would visit soon. When I got to the room, I found Tatum sitting on the chair, reading a book.

"Do you always have a book with you?" I asked from the doorframe.

"Always," she murmured and tucked her book into her backpack.

"It's something I picked up from my past. When I had to sit through things I didn't want to hear, it was easier to bury myself in a book and escape. Now, it's nice to read about modern-day fairytales." She looked out the window, and my heart pulled toward her, wondering if she felt like me.

"You'll drop me off at my house when we get back? I can also Uber—"

I stopped her. "You will go to work then come back to my house. I have no intention of dropping you off and spending the night without you." I reached out and threaded her necklace through my fingers.

I dropped to my knees in front of her. "You are worth breaking every rule for. I will not spend another moment until I know what every inch of you tastes like. Then I'll go back and start all over again."

She pulled herself against me, her body fitting perfectly, and pressed her full, soft lips to mine. A deep, guttural moan escaped my throat, a sound I couldn't hold back if I tried.

"If you stay on your knees, we may never make our flight." She pulled back, and I pressed our foreheads together.

When did I become so weak? From the moment I tasted her, I couldn't resist her pull. I took her hand and led her to the car.

We drove in silence until we reached the airport, where Christian and James were waiting for us at the airport. She sat close to me on the plane, and her fingers played with mine. Her touch meant everything to me, and she was holding my world together. When we got in the air, she looked at me, her tiny fingers drawing circles on my palm.

"Tell me about your mom," she whispered.

I sighed and pulled her closer so she was nestled against my chest and under my arm. I felt her breathe out as if she had been holding it in since we got on the plane.

I hated talking about Mamma. It made me feel. . . raw and exposed. It wasn't something I shared with anyone outside my brother and Papa. Her sacrifice to leave the only life she knew, her death, and then the guilt I felt turning around and doing exactly what she moved us all away from weighed heavy on my heart.

"She was beautiful. Her smile could outshine everyone in the room. She lived boldly and loudly, just like you." I winked, and Tatum's cheeks flushed. My cock twitched. Stupid thing, wrong timing.

"She was born into a Made family like my papa."

"A Made family?"

"Yeah, a Mafia family. It was arranged that every woman in the family married an older man, but Mamma fell in love with Papa. They grew up in the same town. Their families were not on the best terms when they fell in love, but their parents brokered a deal for peace between the two families." I looked down at Tatum; her beautiful blue eyes stared intently back. I thought I was boring her, but her body language encouraged me to continue.

"In my culture, the bride must remain a virgin; otherwise, she must marry the man she loses her virginity to. After one night of passion with my papa. . ." I cringe at this part because who likes talking about their parents having sex? "They were forced to marry. I was conceived that day, and Alex came along a year later."

"Ah, that makes sense why you have a hot dad." Tatum teased and I laughed at her, then pressed a possessive kiss to her lips.

"Wait, so how did your family actually leave then?"

"When my mamma found out she was pregnant, she knew she didn't want to raise a family in that culture. It was hard to leave the family, but they had to pay their dues—"

"Dues?"

"That's a story my papa can tell one day."

She nodded, and I continued, "Anyway, the families agreed to let them go, and they both moved into a small house on the beach in Northern California. My papa worked at a nightclub as an owner most weekends. Honestly, I think he was still dabbling in the family business, but I didn't know. All I knew was that my mother was present for every school field trip and forced us to take hour-long walks on the beach in all types of weather. She cooked pasta dinners for the neighborhood kids and tucked us in every night.

One day when I was in high school, she just got sick. It was a week max before she passed away from the illness. Today, with doctors around the country looking into her autopsy, nobody knows what the cause was other than a progressive disease that killed her quickly."

I squeezed my chest as I spoke about Mamma's death. I'd never said this out loud and almost felt physical pain through my body. As if Tatum could sense my pain and discomfort, she slung her legs over mine and looked up at me with her beautiful eyes.

"She sounds like an amazing person. You miss her a lot." She looked at me sadly and then clasped our hands tighter. I was choked up. I missed my mother more than I could ever say. She was beautiful and gone so quickly.

"She was like me a little then?" she asked, thinking she was joking, but little did she know it wasn't a joke. They were so much alike, their souls innocent yet full of fire and power.

My mom was like the mother bear of our town, and Tatum? She was my little bear. From the moment I met her, she was the strongest person I had ever met, yet she kept such a mask of fear and nervousness.

"I know you were trying to make a joke," I replied, my eyes tender against hers, "but you remind me so much of her."

"Julian," Tatum murmured, pressing kisses against my hand.

"I don't know what to say." She pushed up to her knees and threw her arms around me, pressing her plush pink lips to my head.

"Just say you'll stay with me tonight after you get off work. Say you won't let go." I practically begged, feeling like a idiot but desperate for her to stay. The thought of losing her was too much, even for a night.

"Of course." Her mouth was on mine, and I lifted her onto my lap.

I ducked down to look into her eyes.

"Should we join the mile-high club?" I asked as I yanked at the hem of her shirt and threw her over my shoulder, heading to the back room of the plane.

The flight was only an hour, but I instructed James to collect Tatum's camera gear because of the weather. We were a little delayed, and I didn't want her to be late.

Christian stopped me before we exited.

"Boss," he said. Using that name meant this conversation was business-related.

"James went over to grab her cameras earlier and said the door was kicked down and the house ransacked. He didn't find anything obviously missing, but someone had been there."

I heard Tatum gasp as she clung to my arm. Her grip grew tighter, and I could practically taste the fear emanating from her in waves. The thought of someone breaking into her home and wreaking havoc—violating her safe space—made my blood boil. Knowing her safety had been compromised was enough to ignite a raging inferno inside me. I wanted to hunt down those responsible and make them pay with everything in me. For now, all I could do was hold Tatum close, providing shelter and safety from her fear and panic.

"Tatum?" I glanced at her and saw wetness pool in her wide eyes.

"I need to go there."

The fury boiling inside me made me want to hunt down whoever had upset her and make them suffer.

As soon as she started down the stairs, a large noise erupted. Christian and I reached for our weapons, and I pushed her behind me back into the plane. I could see her peering out the closest window.

"Who are they?" A large crowd quickly gathered on the tarmac. Fuck. How did they get past airport security? I made a mental note to tighten checkpoints around the private airport.

"Little bear, I need you to hold my hand and stay close. And put your jacket over your head. We're just going to walk to the car. Christian is going to clear a path for us."

"Is it paparazzi?" Her eyes were big with questions.

"Yeah. Someone must have tipped them off, and now they're here." Someone must have shared that I was seeing someone knew and sure enough they came in droves wanting to be the first to capture our photo together.

"Will you be okay?"

"I don't know," she gritted out. "I'm so damn angry right now, I could scream. How could someone do this to me? It's not just about the things they took, it's about the violation, the feeling of being unsafe in my own home…" Her words trailed off as she looked up at me, her eyes brimming with tears. I could see the sadness etched into her face, a deep ache that seemed to run through every inch of her body. She was frustrated, sad, and angry. I could tell that the emotions were all-consuming.

"But if you're talking about being okay with the paps, then, yes I'll be fine."

I looked at Christian before exiting the plane to follow her. My fists clenched at my sides as I felt a surge of fury coursing through me.

"Find him. I want to be the one to kill him."

"Got it, Boss."

We grabbed hands, and I led her down the stairs. The flashes of cameras blinded us, and the shouts from the paparazzi deafened us as we made our way to the car. Their intrusive presence was suffocating, making it difficult to breathe. I could feel Tatum's fear radiating off of her, and I tightened my grip on her hand, shielding her as much as I could from the invading lenses.

"Julian Marchetti! Who is this woman who went home with you for the holidays? Is it true?"

"Mr. Marchetti, does she have a name?"

"Is this going to be the woman that tames you?"

The questions blurred together, and my only concern was keeping hold of her hand and getting her to the car. This was yet another example of a world she didn't belong in.

James was waiting to open the door, but I stopped and looked at her. She moved the jacket for a second and caught my gaze. There was so much suffering there, yet a depth that had me yearning to explore.

I couldn't help but feel a wave of sadness wash over me, realizing how much I was dragging her into my world. The weight of that was suddenly crushing. I never wanted to cause her pain or suffering, but it seemed like every step I took brought her further and further into the darkness. As James ushered us into the car and closed the door, I couldn't shake the feeling that I had failed her, and it was a heavy burden to bear.

With the questions and noise muffled inside the car, she reached toward me and touched my knee, noticing my discomfort. It was a silent acknowledgment that we didn't have to suffer alone. She looked out the window, and I grabbed her fingers, clutching them with mine. I could have sworn I heard her exhale.

The drive to the house was quiet, and someone was already replacing the door as we arrived. Tatum went to the main house to tell them what had happened.

I walked into her house. I had never been inside, but everything felt like Tatum—bright and full of color. Even though the items were strewn around, it still felt like her, a little chaotic and beautiful.

"It's so small and obnoxious," I heard from the door as Tatum started frantically picking up her things and putting them in place.

I placed a hand on her to stop.

"It's just like you." I leaned down to give her a comforting kiss, but she turned away, and I realized she had tears forming.

"This is too much." She ran into the bathroom and slammed the door.

I picked up her clothes, folded them, and put them away in the drawers for her. I had no idea where things went, but I figured cleaning some of the mess may help her feel better.

"The day I see Julian Marchetti folding women's underwear." James whistled in amusement.

"Get the fuck outta here. While you're at it, take the man incessantly hammering with you."

After they left, I walked to the locked door. After a few knocks, I heard sobs through the wood.

"Tatum. Let me in." I added a little command to my words, hoping she'd listen. After a few moments, I heard the click of the lock. I squeezed into the small bathroom and found Tatum sitting in the bathtub, her head resting against bent knees and her hands pulling at her hair. Her eyes were red and swollen.

I leaned down and sat on the edge of the tub, placing a hand on hers to stop the pulling.

"The world is terrifying," she mumbled.

"Certain parts of it. Though, the world isn't always just black and white. There are those of us who live in between, in the shadows of gray. But the man who did this? He lives in the dark part."

"He is the darkness. A living devil." She looked up at me, and my heart lurched, wanting to pull her out of the tub and hold her in my lap.

"I like the shades in between." She looked up at the ceiling. I knew she was talking about me. How could something this delicate and small could ruin me?

I didn't know how long we sat there in silence. I wanted so badly to fix the problem and make it all the better for her.

"You look ridiculous in this bathroom." She laughed. The sound of her voice embedded itself into my brain.

She leaned her head against the side of the tub where my hand rested and dropped her cheek on top of it.

"He used to hurt me." Her words came out low and rough. I reached my other hand out to cup her cheek. So much of my past wanted me to seek revenge, kill, and torture this person. She was folding into the protective barrier she kept up, and I so badly wanted to protect her from whatever inner turmoil was happening in her mind.

"What do you need from me?" I whispered, my heart heavy with sorrow.

"I don't know. I don't think I need you to do anything," she replied, her voice filled with pain.

My eyebrows furrowed in concern. "I'm not leaving," I said firmly, trying to reassure her.

"That's not what I meant," she said, rubbing her temples. "I don't need you to fix anything. I just need...you."

Her words hit me hard. I knew I would do anything for her. Anything to help her heal.

"Can you just listen? You're about to be the only person who knows this part of me, and I think I just need a friend," she said, and I scoffed inwardly.

Friends didn't do the things we did together. But then again, what were we, if not friends?

She sobbed in the bathtub and told me the horrific story of her abusive ex, and I felt a fierce anger building inside me. I wanted to start a war, to make him pay for what he had done to her.

But as her tears slowed and she leaned into me, I felt a sense of powerlessness. I was always in control, but in that moment, I had nothing. I was just a man and a flawed one at that.

"Come." I stood up, my back hitting the sink, and lifted her out of the tub.

"You folded my clothes?" she questioned when she saw the cleaned bedroom. "Do you even know how to do that?"

"No. Don't open your drawers." My lips turned up at the corners. She laughed at my confession and put some broken plates into the trashcan.

"Grab your things, and let's go. You can call Lacey from the car and tell her you won't be in today. You're sick."

"I can't do that." She looked so sad. I didn't know how else to make her happy, but my heart yearned to make her feel better. I wanted so desperately to bring the brightness back.

"I will not let you go to this wedding alone. Not with whoever is out there, and you not giving me a name."

"I'm going. It's my job, and I committed to it." She went over to make sure her camera gear was still there. "Plus, it'll be a welcome distraction."

"Can you please come with me after? Please," I begged.

"Is the powerful Julian Marchetti begging for me?" she joked, her little glow of brightness sparking.

"Don't make me get on my hands and knees."

"That would be interesting. . . But fine. I'll come over when I'm done."

"Okay, and you'll take James with you."

I saw a moment where she wanted to argue with me, but she quickly shut her mouth, only nodding in agreement.

"I'll see you later then, little bear." I leaned in and pressed my lips against her forehead before turning to leave.

As I walked out the door, I couldn't help but think of all the women who would beg me to ask them out on a date. In fact, I couldn't remember ever taking someone on a date and inviting them to stay at my house. This woman was changing my heart, and I didn't want to disappoint her with the darkness surrounding my life.

26

TATUM

Present

A weight lifted off my chest, and I could finally breathe again. The state of my apartment didn't matter anymore. It was as if a missing puzzle piece had found its place, and I felt whole. Julian had listened intently without trying to fix me or judge me. He let me be vulnerable and share my darkest secrets. I poured out every detail of the abuse I had endured—every punch, kick, and bite. The words flowed out of me, uncontrollable and raw.

I didn't reveal Cam's name or the club he belonged to, and Julian didn't push me to. I shared my story because I needed to feel safe again. Knowing that someone was hunting me left me vulnerable and exposed, and I needed to feel secure some other way. It wasn't easy to ask for help, but when Julian told me James would come with me to the wedding, I didn't refuse. I knew I needed a sense of safety, and Julian offered it without hesitation.

At first, this felt too messy to be Cam's doing. Nothing was stolen or felt out of place. It felt like someone came in and messed things up to scare me. Maybe Orlando finally caught up to me, and this was his way of getting my attention.

I grabbed my cameras and an overnight bag when something slipped off my nightstand. I picked it up and unfolded it. When I saw what was on it, I gasped.

A small eagle and The Club insignia stared up at me. I guess this answered my question of who did this. It was Cam. Cam was in San Diego. Suddenly, I couldn't get enough air into my lungs, and my legs felt weak.

James came in just as I thudded to the hardwood floor.

"Miss Tatum. Are you okay? Do you need a doctor?" He grabbed his phone.

"No. Don't call him. I'm okay. Just tripped." I looked up at him, hoping he didn't catch my lie.

He stared at me. "I still think I should call the boss."

"I'm late for this wedding, so let's just go."

He helped me to my feet, and we walked to the car. I glanced back at the house and knew everything I had feared was coming true.

It was an uneventful evening of Lacey barking orders at me. I let her because my brain was fried from the earlier events. It was the day after Christmas too, and I was generally grumpy around this time because it reminded me that I didn't have a family to celebrate with.

Sensing that I was distracted—and in a rare show of feelings—Lacey let me leave early. James and I drove back to Julian's. When I was with Cam, I numbed the pain by disassociating, like watching your life move in slow motion. That same feeling of numbness washed through me.

We pulled up to a house lit up outside. I loved how coastal the house felt.

"Miss. Tatum." James held the door open for me, and I scooted out to the front door.

Words escaped me when I was greeted by a house wrapped in the comfort of darkness. The heavy door closed with a soft thud, sealing me off from the outside world. The dark was broken by the flickering of countless white candles, filling the air with a rich and comforting aroma. I was drawn to the exquisite flower arrangement on the polished wooden coffee table, its vibrant colors standing out against the subdued lighting. The air was still, and for a moment, I felt like I was standing in the center of a peaceful sanctuary, protected from chaos.

I let the peace of the room wash over me, but I knew I wasn't alone. His scent mingled with the fragrance of the white candles, creating a warm and welcoming atmosphere.

My attention was finally drawn to the figure by the fireplace. He wore his usual attire of black pants and a black button-down shirt. The top button was undone, revealing a hint of tanned skin. His curly black hair was tousled and framed his handsome face. He looked even more beautiful in the soft glow of the tealights that illuminated his features.

I was struck by the depth in his eyes. They held a hint of sadness but also warmth that immediately put me at ease. He smiled shyly, a hint of vulnerability in his expression, and gestured for me to come closer. I moved toward him, drawn to his calm and reassuring presence.

"What is this?" I whispered, knowing he could hear me.

He picked up a glass of wine and an old-fashioned from the coffee table.

"I wanted to do something special for you. I can't say I didn't have help."

"Who helped?" I asked inquisitively.

"A tall blonde who claims to be your best friend?" His grin grew.

"Maeve? Wow." I walked around and admired everything. A cool sea breeze wafted through the doors, and even the pool was illuminated with candles. "This is so. . ."

He came up behind me and wrapped me in his arms, handing me the wine.

"I didn't know you had this in you if I am being honest," I confessed.

"I actually didn't know I had this in me either." He gave me a small squeeze. "I wanted to show you that the darkness can have light too. My world isn't just full of death. And add your light to my darkness, making me glow."

My heart squeezed inside my chest, and any words I wanted to say wouldn't form. I took a deep breath and noticed a familiar scent.

"Lavender?"

"I had the gardeners plant a few outside so I could always be reminded of you."

The gesture was too much. I sat on the leather couch and tilted my head away.

"Why?" I asked without looking at him.

He came over and sat next to me. His hand burned hot on my knee.

"I'm at a loss," he admitted, his voice heavy with emotion. "You've completely consumed me. It kills me to know that you've been hurt, and I couldn't do a damn thing about it. You've become everything to me, someone who truly understands my pain and embraces my world. No one else could ever come close to taking your place. No matter what the future holds for us, I can't deny what I feel."

"Julian." I breathed, my eyes searching for his. His fingers played with my necklace.

"Please. Let me get this out."

I nodded.

"I want you to be my exception to every rule. I want you here with me all the time." He gestured to one side of the room.

It took me a moment to realize he had set up a bookshelf for me.

"For me?" I walked over and touched the wooden shelves. He had even put my favorite, *Pride & Prejeduice,* on the top shelf.

"I may have taken those from your apartment. But I want you here, Tatum. With me."

"You built this for me?" I turned toward him as he walked to me.

"It was a bitch to build." He laughed and looked at his hands. "Christian may have lent me a hand."

"Folding clothes and building shelves. Some may say you've become quite domesticated." I poked at his waistband, where I knew he kept his handgun.

"Only for you."

He pressed his lips to mine. It was slow and sensual at first, but his tongue pushed in further, deepening the kiss. With one push, the coffee table was pushed aside, and he pulled me down to the closest couch.

My hips arched, pushing against his erection. We lay there, grinding into each other, while I unbuttoned his shirt. He looked like a dark shadow in the warm candlelight. He placed his Glock on the floor somewhere, and I began leisurely undoing his belt.

"I missed you." He ripped his shirt off, buttons scattering. His body was tantalizing, his ink making him look primal. He ran his hands over me, and an insatiable hunger grew between us.

"Take it off," he commanded and tugged on my blouse. I whipped it off and pulled my bra off with it. The moment my breasts were free, he groaned.

"Your skin is so sweet." He licked around my nipples.

"Lay back."

He left me vulnerable on the ground and returned with a candelabra, three large candlesticks on top.

"Remember your safe word." I nodded in anticipation.

"Use your words, Tatum," he demanded.

"Ice. Yes," I grumbled. He picked up a candle and slowly poured wax onto my abdomen.

The heat stung, and I let out a startled cry.

"These are low-heat candles but can still get warm. If it gets to be too much, use your safeword."

The wax dripped slowly, and each sent a ripple to my core. My desire craved more. I let out a needy whine.

"I bet you're soaked." He pushed my thighs apart and drove two fingers into my core. He thrust his fingers in and out while moving the wax to the top of my center. The closer he got to my needy pussy, the more I writhed beneath him.

"I am so fucking horny," I wailed.

The wax filled me with an afflicted pleasure that had me begging for more of Julian. I needed him inside of me as the pressure built.

"It's so hot." I just screamed as he dripped the wax up my torso. His fingers continued to thrust.

He laughed diabolically, knowing the half-pleasure half-pain wasn't stopping but pushing my boundaries further. He slowed his fingers and dripped the wax on my nipples. They pebbled, and I cried in bliss. I was covered in the hardening substance, but he put the candle down and pulled out his fingers. His teeth grabbed my nipples and tugged.

"You get my cunt so wet," I moaned. This twisted version of pleasure and pain suffocated me.

He pulled my legs apart and drove his length deep inside me. His hands worked my clit as he pushed into me, carnal and unrestrained. His mouth dropped to mine, and I bit his bottom lip. He growled.

"You're such a dirty little bear. Tell me what you need." He slowed, but my hips shot up to meet his.

"Need. You." A fevered desire burned through my blue eyes and I needed to feel more of his warmth on my skin.

He drove back into me in quick succession. My heart was warming in the heat of his half-hooded eyes. His insatiable appetite grew with each moment, and I knew I wasn't going to last long. I straddled him, and he grabbed me by the waist and pulled me tight into him.

"I want to watch you take me deep and scream my name when you come."

God, that phrase fed my need. I let him pull me onto him. He was so big that I could feel his length pulsing as he entered me. I lifted my hips back up and lowered them slowly to get used to his size. With each movement, our bodies were synced.

Julian's hand gripped my neck, and his teeth ran down my throat. I groaned and burrowed my hands into his hair.

"I need to—"

I pushed down on him again, and it sent me over the edge at the same time he exploded inside. Heat erupted throughout my body, making me shiver. I fell onto his chest, and he hugged me tightly.

"You are *mine*," he whispered.

He pulled out of me and carried me up to his room. He turned on the shower and held me as the water ran down us. I nuzzled into his chest, relishing the warmth of the water and his body.

His touch was gentle, which contrasted with his primal nature. He took care of me, washing every crevice and whispering sweet nothings in my ear.

"I am an addict, and you, little bear, are my drug."

Our bodies came together in the shower, and something shifted between us. The air was charged with electricity; our eyes locked, and my heart raced.

His touch was slow and deliberate, exploring with a reverence that left me breathless. His fingers trailed over my body, sending shivers down my spine, and when he pressed his lips to mine, it felt like the world stopped. I opened my eyes and gazed at him, watching the moonlight cast shadows on his chiseled features. His jawline was sharp, and I couldn't resist tracing it with my fingertips.

"I don't want this moment to end," I whispered.

"Neither do I," he replied, pulling me closer. "Let's stay like this forever."

I knew I was his completely, and he was mine. Our connection was unlike anything I had ever experienced, and I couldn't wait to explore it further.

After a half hour in the shower, he wrapped me in a warm fluffy towel.

"Wait, how is this warm?" I questioned.

"Heated towel rack," he said, laughing as he placed me on the bed.

The aftercare made our connection stronger. The level of intimacy between us was opposite to the savage experiences we shared in bed. His weight dropped on the bed next to me, so I turned to face him.

I looked into his eyes, and they darkened for me. My heart clenched looking at him and all the different ways I had never felt like this before.

"I hate cooking," I said, referring to him asking me to move in.

He nuzzled my nose. "We'll get a chef. Now shush."

He pulled me tighter, and my eyes fluttered as I sank into the darkness of sleep.

The next week was that weird time between Christmas and New Year's when no one worked, and things were slow. The restaurant was still closed, and I didn't have any weddings to assist. Julian occasionally tapped away on his laptop, but I spent the entire week with him. We didn't cook, just ordered in, and after the new year, he promised to find someone to cook for us since we were both atrocious in the kitchen.

We fell deeper into each other's embrace as the days went on. We spent lazy afternoons wrapped up in each other's arms, basking in the warmth of the candle-lit fireplace. In the mornings, we would sit together on the couch, the gentle sea breeze wafting through the windows as I read my romance novels. He always asked for a summary, his eyes sparkling with interest and curiosity. I never felt embarrassed or ashamed by the reading material, and he always treated me with the utmost respect and never made me feel inferior.

We talked and laughed, and the outside world faded away, leaving us as we discovered love. In those moments, I knew I had found my home, my sanctuary, and my safe haven. And even though I couldn't predict the future, I knew with every fiber of my being that I wanted to spend it by his side.

We also fucked everywhere: the pool, the bed, the kitchen counter, the couch, and the car. Anywhere with a surface, we dirtied with our bodies.

Occasionally, he would leave with Christian or James on 'business.' I even got bold enough to prod for more answers to the uncomfortable questions about his job.

Apparently, he worked to provide government protection to different gangs, motorcycle clubs, and other underworld groups. They needed his help to broker their deals without getting the feds involved. Yet dealing with those folks didn't always go smoothly, so he was an enforcer and a money launderer.

He was involved in a seedier side of the law, but I was just his partner. He kept me safe and comforted at home and never involved me, although I knew if we got more serious, that would be something we discussed. And if I became his girlfriend, it would be public knowledge, and his enemies would become mine.

It was late, and I had to work tomorrow with Lacey, but we sat on the couch eating sushi.

"I found us a chef, little bear." His fingers traced up and down my legs. I was just wearing one of his shirts that was so oversized it looked like a dress on me.

"I need to go back home eventually, Julian." I shoved a piece of sushi in my mouth so I didn't have to answer whatever he would return with.

"No, you don't. It's not safe for you." He put down my plate and turned to face me, his eyes concerned.

"I'm a big girl. Before I knew you existed, I managed to take care of myself." I stood up.

The little shit only splayed his body wider so he took out more of the couch. He looked like he was at a business meeting—cool, calm, and collected.

"I understand that, Tatum." He emphasized my name, something he never typically called me. "But, now I am here. Let me help you, please."

"You can't fix all of my problems," I huffed, walking away.

He reached out and grabbed my hand. I looked down at where he held me, and something inside me snapped. I was triggered and lashed out to protect myself.

"Get. Your. Hands. Off. Me. Now," I demanded, shaking with fear and anger.

He immediately released me and let me step back to get some space. He shot up off the couch and poured himself a whiskey, staring out the window. His hand shook as he raised the glass to swallow the contents in one gulp. My chest tightened, thinking I had overreacted.

I approached him tentatively and put a hand on his back. His muscles tensed, and I hesitated before speaking.

"I don't like being grabbed like that," I said softly.

He turned to face me, his voice calm but cold. "You're right. I shouldn't have touched you without your permission. I can't promise I'll be Prince Charming like in your fairytales, but I will never hurt you. Ever."

I felt a lump form in my throat. I knew he wasn't perfect, but I had always seen him as a protector. The thought of him being capable of causing harm was terrifying.

"But you are," I whispered. "I just need you to let me continue to find myself."

He turned away, his body still tense. "And I need to protect you. There will be a time when my enemies become yours, Tatum," he repeated.

"I know," I interjected, sounding more confident than I felt.

"Let your enemies become mine," he growled in my ear.

"You know this morning, when you just sat and listened to me?" He nodded. "Sometimes, that's exactly what I need. There are some problems you won't be able to fix, like this one. I just need you to listen."

He looked at me for a second before setting his drink down. The cool indifference formed through his stoic face.

"No, I can't do that. There are moments in this world when I'll need to protect you. I can't promise I won't step in to help, even if it displeases you. In this situation, I *want* to protect you. I need you to accept that a crazy man is hunting you, and I will hurt him if he finds you."

He turned and walked up the stairs, leaving me looking at him. The bedroom door slammed shut.

"Asshole," I muttered under my breath.

"I heard that." A voice shouted down the stairs.

I wish it was easier for me to accept help. If I had support from my family, it would have been easier to accept help from others. I hated not sleeping with him, but I also wasn't going to cave and go up to our bedroom. Ugh. I needed to escape and quickly. I grabbed a book from the bookshelf he made me and cracked open the spine. I read on the couch until my eyes grew heavy, and I fell asleep.

I awoke a few hours later to large hands gently shaking me.

"Little bear." I heard through half-opened eyes.

"Mmm."

"I can't sleep without you. I'm sorry." I stretched and sat up, looking into Julian's distressed face.

His body heat warmed me instantly as he pulled me onto his lap.

"If you go to the wedding, will you take my car?" he asked.

"Take your Corvette? No. How dare I?" I said sarcastically. He laughed and brought my face to his so our noses brushed.

"Can you promise to call when you arrive and come home right after?"

"Yes, Daddy." I winked at him.

"Keep calling me Daddy, and I'll show you who Daddy is" He lifted me bridal style and walked upstairs.

"Mmmm, Daddy, is that you?" I shifted beneath his hands so my hip was grinding against his hard-on.

He threw me onto the bed, and we spent the rest of the night showing him just how much he could trust me.

I woke the next morning to the smell of eggs and bacon. I stretched out to Julian, but the sheets next to me were cold, so I knew he was downstairs.

I padded downstairs and saw a friendly older woman in her late sixties. She wore an apron, and her mousy hair was pulled on top of her head.

"Little Bear, this is Lola, our new chef." Julian looked like a kid on Christmas. I shuffled over to him and climbed onto his lap.

"For someone so rich, seeing you so excited about a chef is strange," I whispered so Lola couldn't hear us. He chuckled.

I got up. "Hi, my name is Tatum. It's nice to meet you." The woman shook my hand, and we indulged in breakfast.

"Please, no more!" I pleaded. "Thank you so much, Lola. This was all absolutely amazing."

"You are quite welcome. I'll be back this evening." She smiled, washing the last dish and leaving out the back.

"Has anyone told you how absolutely breathtaking you look in the morning?" I giggled and when he came close, I breathed on him.

"Well, after you brush your teeth." I laughed at him. I lived for this kind of slow morning where we just teased each other.

We bound upstairs, where I got ready for the wedding. While Julian was in the shower, I took the photo of him from the wedding we first met. He looked beautifully carnal in his black tux. He stared into the camera, the corners of his lips turned up in a slight smile. Everything I loved about him was in this photo. It might have been a bit presumptuous, but I had it framed.

I finished getting ready in another bathroom and heard his footsteps head down the hallway.

"Did you take this?" he asked, holding up the frame. I nodded.

"Thank you. It was the moment you took my breath away. The moment I realized you would break every single rule I ever had." He kissed me on my forehead, and I hooked my arms behind his neck.

"It's the moment I realized I would be obsessed with you too," I managed to whisper.

He deepened the kiss, and a moan escaped.

"No. We can't. I have to go. Save it for later."

"Ugh. You're going to be the death of me."

An hour later, I threw my camera gear into Julian's car and walked back in to see Julian leaning against the doorframe.

"Everything will be okay. He hasn't even tried to come to find me in a week. He probably went back to Chicago." I reached up on my tip-toes and kissed him. I don't know if I believed it myself, but I had to convince myself that he wasn't here. I was safe.

"I don't like this, Tatum." He gripped my waist.

"I know," I reassured him. "Thank you for letting me do this on my own. I like my freedom, and I know you're here to protect me too."

He grumbled, "I know you can take care of yourself."

I looked at him and knew this was different. I knew the words to describe how I felt, but I just couldn't say them out loud yet. If I whispered it, it would change us. It would bind me to yet another underworld. It would connect me to him forever. I just. . . couldn't yet.

"I'll see you later."

He fixed my necklace, rubbing his thumb over the charm. There was a pregnant pause in the air, filled with a sense of heaviness.

He kissed me gently.

"I'll see you later."

"This isn't a goodbye, silly. It's just a few hours." I laughed, got in the Corvette, and headed down the highway toward the wedding venue.

Lacey was even grumpier than usual, barking her orders extra harshly today.

She asked if I could take over as we sat down to dinner and then disappeared. "Don't fuck this up. I think I ate something weird. You need to take over for me."

I looked at my watch, knowing this would make me much later than anticipated. Julian would be worried, but there wasn't much I could do if she was sick. Someone had to stay and finish.

"Oh geez. I hope you're okay." I had never worked a wedding alone, so my anxiety bubbled. "Don't worry, I can handle it. Just go home and take care of yourself, Lacey."

She gave me her memory cards, and right before dinner ended, I texted Julian.

Tatum: *Hey. Lacey is sick. I have to stay until ten to finish up the wedding. Don't wait up.*

Julian: *Of course I'll wait for you. I can send James to pick you up and get the car up tomorrow. It's late.*

Tatum: *Julian. . . we talked about this. I'm okay. Nothing's happened. It's only a couple more hours. There are a lot of people around here.*

The three bubbles appeared and disappeared a couple times before his response came through.

Julian: *Fine. Be safe, little bear. I have eight letters here waiting for you.*

My heart felt heavy, and the beat throbbed in my ears. Eight letters. God, eight was actually my lucky number. It took eight tries to get out from under Cam's hold, it was my mother's OCD number, and now Julian had eight letters waiting for me.

I hurried through the next few hours of the reception, but Julian's text replayed in the back of my mind. It was dark when we finished, and most of the vendors and guests had already left by the time I finished packing my gear. I walked to the car and pulled out my phone to look at Julian's message again. Those eight letters were at the tips of my fingers.

I love you.

27

TATUM

Present

I felt the presence of someone come up behind me as I reached for the keys to my car in my camera bag. I turned around, half expecting to see James or Christian.

"I told you—"

"Don't say a single fucking word."

The figure standing in front of me was shrouded in darkness except for the street lamp above. I could see deep bags under his eyes that hinted he might be using yet again. His hair was slicked back, and I couldn't help but notice a few new tattoos on his face. Dressed entirely in black, he tightly gripped the keys in his hands. As he smiled at me, my heart raced, and a chilling realization washed over me. In that moment, I knew he had triumphed. If I hadn't known who he was, I would have mistaken him for the devil himself. He was the embodiment of my worst nightmare—the person I had desperately tried to avoid and had gone to great lengths to evade, now standing right in front of me.

"Please," I pleaded and reached for my keys, trying to keep my voice calm. I knew not to rile him up.

"Shut your fucking mouth, bitch," He brought a hand up to my lips and held them together with his thumb and forefinger.

"He's going to find you. Don't do this, Cam," I mumbled through his fingers.

His eyes darkened, and he chuckled darkly while applying more pressure on my lips. He leaned down, his repulsive breath washing over my face.

"Don't mock me, Tatum. You're mine. I branded you and protected you for five years for a mistake that should have cost you your life. Running away was an embarrassment to The Club and me. You're pathetic. Always have been and always will be."

His spittle hit my face, the rank drops making me gag. I looked around the dark parking lot, hoping to see Christian or James. I kicked myself for running out on Julian today. If I had just listened to and stayed with him, this exhausting day would have never been like this.

I wish I could say I was shocked too. I wanted to run away, screaming and crying, hoping it would change the inevitable outcome. But deep down, I knew better. The life I had built out here, the happiness I had finally discovered after a year of self-growth, was just temporary. I had a gut feeling that someone would eventually find me, and it would either be him or a bullet from Orlando's crew.

A wave of frustration washed over me, like a heavy weight in my chest, and the spark of joy I had nurtured inside was fading away with each passing moment. I could sense the icy veil of protection descending over me, accepting that these were my last precious moments in San Diego.

I looked up at the starry sky and breathed the cool winter air. My eyes flicked to Julian's, my last little reminder that this fantasy was real. Tears welled in my eyes, filling my vision with a blurry haze.

"I wrote you a note. I begged you to let me go."

Cam looked at me and laughed maniacally. The quiet parking lot echoed with the sound.

"Are you kidding me, Tatum? That damn note was a fucking joke. Do you have any idea what you've put me through? The Club thinks I'm an asshole, pathetic even, because it took me over six months to track you down. I've searched high and low, turning the world upside down. My leadership has been questioned, and they forced me to step down. Tommy is now running everything, all so I could spend the past year with one focus—figuring out where the fuck you disappeared to."

His voice lowered, and he pressed his lips to my ear.

"You sat in on every single meeting I held at The Club. You have all of my secrets. You know the organization and the ranks. You don't seem to understand that you cannot just run off with that information. Someone will kill you before you are allowed just to have it."

"I promise I haven't said anything. I haven't told anyone your name, who you're with, or where I came from."

"Yeah, right. Your pathetic boyfriend has ties with us, you know. I dug into his life. Thanks to your stupid friend's social media nonsense, I tracked you down and found your little love nest. Your boyfriend was an easy target to figure out. And guess what? After reaching out to Tommy, I realized why his face seemed so damn familiar. He had helped The Club when the police seized a bunch of our stuff at the border."

My mouth was agape. I didn't know what else to say. He saw the photo of us when we got caught coming home from the holidays. I knew the exact photo he was referring to. We were walking out of the plane and I was staring at him. It was a moment frozen in time. He stood there just smiling at me right before I pushed the jacket over my head to cover my face. We were holding hands and looked like we were in love. Probably because I did love him. I do love him.

I loved everything about Julian. I loved the way he kept me separate but informed about his business. I loved how sexually adventurous he was. I loved the way he took care of me after. I loved that being with him was full of experiences, even if we just sat at home in sweats.

Home... His home was a place I had come to love and cherish. A place where he and I existed together.

"He's not my boyfriend." It was the truth. We never defined what we were. Yes, he took me home to meet his family, and we fucked often, but he could have some weird pity kink for me...

More laughter echoed in the dark lot.

"Tell that to the tabloids, then. You look like a lovesick puppy. To him, you're just a number. You always knew I was yours first."

Cam violently pushed me against the car, and I couldn't help but slip back into the submissive role I used to survive during those torturous five years with him. As his grip tightened around my throat, my body instinctively responded, yielding to his dominance. The fear that had once consumed me returned in full force.

He yanked at my clothes, pulling my black midi skirt down, leaving me exposed and humiliated. My body pressed against his, and he delivered a harsh smack just above the eagle tattoo on my ass—a permanent mark of his ownership.

"You see, my queen," he sneered, his voice dripping with venom. "This C and The Club's insignia on your skin means you belong to me. I'm gonna reclaim what's rightfully mine and erase any trace of that sleazy man's touch. You're gonna regret ever letting someone else touch you."

His grip on my throat intensified, cutting off my breath. There was no desire or consent in his touch—only a cruel attempt to assert control. I struggled to swallow, but his tight hold on my vocal cords suffocated me, leaving me gasping for air. My skirt remained pulled down, exposing me in a way that made me feel utterly vulnerable and filled with shame.

"Let's go," Cam demanded. A new level of derangement had consumed him. He glanced around frantically, searching for any sign of cameras or witnesses, desperate to ensure he was alone with me. "MY fucking queen," he murmured as he pressed closer.

I thrashed in his hold, flailing my hands against his body and hoping he would stop.

"Orlando's been looking for you. He wants your head on a stake still. Needs to punish you for being a very bad little girl. The dirty little whore who's all tainted now."

Spots formed in my vision, and I knew my oxygen was running out.

"See, you're so sweet when you can't talk." He licked my face, making me flashback to the man at the rest stop. This was it for him. All of the terrible things I've done in life are the real reason I am here today. In an instant, the spots grew around my eyes and the next thing I remember was a haze of darkness seeping through my skin.

***

I woke to the sound of waves. I tried to move, but the bed underneath me was anything from what I'd been used to sleeping on. I felt like I was on a hard cold surface, but the air was humid and damp. I peeked through half-lidded eyes, and that is when the memory of what happened, or rather didn't happen, spilled through my mind. My stomach churned. I needed to confirm what I could have sworn was just a really bad dream.

I jumped up and noticed I was in some beach house. It was nothing more than a few walls made of hardened mud and bamboo. There were no glass windows, but a large door opened to the sea air. If I squinted enough, the sand was a deep yellow color different from our San Diego beaches, but the color of the ocean remained the same deep blue.

The walls were a rust orange and the bed was just a platform made from wooden slats, dirtied mattresses without anything covering it and a light top sheet.

I grabbed my neck, desperate for a reminder of home, of Julian. I breathed a sigh of relief when I felt the necklace still around my neck. The little bear reminded me who gave it to me, and tears welled in my eyes. I needed to figure out a plan.

I could smell eggs, so I padded into the other room and continued to look around. One small bathroom off the corner of the room smelled like it hadn't been cleaned in a decade, so I couldn't imagine what it looked like inside. The main room had a small couch, stove, and fridge made for an RV camper van. It was so small. That was it.

Was this what the rest of my life would look like? Trapped in a shitty beach shack with a man who would hurt me until I died? I closed my eyes and wished I could tap my heels to go home. Home, where Julian lived. I ran into the dingy bathroom and threw up in the toilet, thinking about the events that had transpired over the last twelve hours.

"No," I whispered, the tears spilling from my eyes again.

The floodgates opened, and I was consumed with memories of us together. He must be so worried. I wondered if he had sent Christian or James to find me and how he reacted when he saw my empty casita. At this point, he had to be using every clue to find me, but I hoped Cam was too drunk or high to cover up all his tracks. Even though I knew Julian had the connections, I just couldn't imagine a possibility where he would find me in a remote shack in Mexico. There was absolutely no way out of this.

"You seem chipper."

I looked at the stove to where Cam stood talking and wiped the puke from my mouth. He stood in nothing but his briefs with a beer in his hand. He was downright terrifying. This person was even more twisted than the man I met at the diner five years ago.

I should be scared. I should be crying. I should be clawing at his back and screaming at him. I should be doing absolutely everything to get away from here. I should feel anything other than the eerie calm and emptiness in my chest. I should, but I didn't.

What if Cam was right? What if I was just a pathetic little girl who knew nothing? I didn't deserve happiness. I deserved what was coming to me.

"Where are we?" I ignored his comment and looked at the ocean.

"Mexico, my queen." His lips turned up at the corners in amusement.

"What happened to Orlando?" I asked. Before Cam choked me out, the last thing I remember was him saying Orlando was on my tail.

"You're safe here. No one knows where we are. In fact, the main town is a couple hours away by car."

I glanced at the keys on the counter next to the kitchen sink.

"Don't even think about it." He stalked over to me. His menacing eyes beat into mine, making me feel smaller the closer he got.

"You are not to leave this house without me. Ever. Not even to walk out and get some air. You are mine, and I am the only one who can keep you protected."

"It's totally unreasonable for you to expect me to stay in this scorching heat with no relief. We both need to be closer to the shore to catch a breeze. Can't you just let me go down to the shoreline and take a swim? You can literally see me the whole time." I pointed to the door that overlooked the shoreline when it was open. "If I have to stay cooped up in this stuffy, hot house, I swear I'll suffocate. I need some kind of break if I'm going to survive these end-of-days conditions."

"Fine." He huffed and threw a plate of hard scrambled eggs at me.

They tasted like leather. Leather. Oh god.

The smell of leather and whiskey wafted into my nose like a gentle reminder of the life I could have had. The life I did have. The worst part was that I didn't get the chance to tell him I loved him. I wanted so badly to say it when I left before the wedding. Instead, we lingered in the doorway. I sensed he wanted to say something too, but he rushed me off and promised he would see me when I was done.

He promised. Promises are like pomegranates. On the outside, they look plain, but when you crack them open, they're full of seeds and holes.

I took a few bites of the eggs and tried to swallow them. What time was it, and how many beers had he had? He'd definitely had more than one by the way he was swaying. He flipped open his phone and started tapping away.

"I see the rules only apply to one person," I mumbled under my breath as he flipped through his cell and started thinking about how I could steal it.

I sensed him as he stumbled behind me. His hand pulled my hair. If he yanked an inch further, I would be toppling off the stool I was sitting on at the kitchen counter.

"Say that again."

"I just wanted to see if I had any clothes to change into. I need a swimsuit and a few different shirts and pants. And I really need underwear."

"I'm going to town. I'll get you those things."

"Are you sober enough to go?" I questioned. I didn't want to push it, but I figured if he let me go with, I could somehow alert someone that I had been kidnapped.

He was never much of a drinker when we were together. He had a few beers with the boys after work but always said he needed a clear mind to track inventory and payments. I assume he didn't cope when Tommy took over.

"I'll be fine." He huffed and let go of my hair, my head jerking forward into the mess of eggs on the counter.

This was an all-time low.

My relationship with Cam never had love. Love was so much more than that. It was being taken home to meet the family, feeling included and accepted. It was the intimacy of the post-coital shower, the tenderness after sex, the stolen kisses. It was curling up with a good book and making love under the covers. Love was compassion and kindness, a sanctuary of safety and security.

As my fingers instinctively reached for my necklace, I knew I had found my true home with Julian.

This was my shot at real life, a chance to taste the true essence of existence. If I were to die having savored even a hint of what it meant to be alive with Julian, I wouldn't have any regrets. Anything was better than being trapped with an abusive man, stuck in a vicious cycle of agony and torment. I wanted to thrive alongside Julian. Deep in my heart, I knew I was secure with him, and that he would shield me from any harm. In my mind's eye, I could envision us living on the cliffs in La Jolla, our sanctuary illuminated by flickering candlelight and the crashing waves beneath us our symphony. Cam could never breach that sacred place, and I would be truly, unequivocally safe.

My hunger had vanished, so I absentmindedly cleared my plate and stowed it away. It was the same routine I had in our apartment five years ago. Glancing down at my clothes, I noticed I was only in an oversized T-shirt.

No, no, no. This would be the death of me. Being touched when I wasn't even conscious? I wanted to puke. I looked down, and my hands were shaking uncontrollably. My legs threatened to collapse.

"Did we have sex, Cameron?" I asked him timidly.

"I wanted to, but your dumbass must be on your period. I got you some of those girlie things before we crossed the border. And I'll grab more at the store now."

Cameron has killed many people, but the one thing that grossed him out more than anything was periods. He thought it was strange that women bled every month. Blood was a symbol of death, so it felt wrong to have sex. This was always the best week of the month for me. It meant I owed him nothing. I silently thanked my body for saving my life.

"I'm going. Don't even think about leaving," he growled and left the house.

I went back to the bedroom area and collapsed on the bed. On the wall behind the bedpost, with my fingernails, I scratched a single mark on it. I wanted to use it to count the days I would be here. I rolled over on my back at stared at the ceiling as I let the heat bask into my bones.

28

JULIAN

Present

She was gone. It felt like my soul was ripped from my body. Christian called to tell me she never made it to her car after the wedding. I did everything right. I respected her wishes by not following her to the wedding, but I knew something was wrong when the GPS never ticked on the Corvette. Christian's call only confirmed what I felt.

"Boss, we're gonna find her," Christian said over the phone.

"She's gone. He took her!" I yelled.

"We're going to find them." His tone was calm, but I was frantic. I was used to being under pressure, but this was different. This was Tatum.

I wish I had said what I felt when she walked out the door. It was right there.

"Fuck!" I punched at the wooden desk I stood in front of in my office. I had been watching the GPS obsessively on the camera in my office. When the clocked turn ten and it hadn't turned on, I wish I had just driven over there and gotten her.

"Julian." Christian's tone was soft and friendly. "You need to stop and think of a plan. You have a plan for everyone and everything, and your cousins are in the goddamn biggest crime syndicate in the entire country. You will find her."

"What if I find her and she's. . ." I couldn't say it. I couldn't bear to think of the worst possible scenario, but I knew it was a strong possibility.

"She survived with him for years. She'll make it out. It's not even a possibility."

Goddamnit. He was right. I needed to get my head on straight. I was going to find her, and when I did, the motherfucker that took her was dead.

"What's the plan, Boss?" Christian asked, sensing that I had gotten myself together.

"I need to call my brother. I'll call back when I have any updates. In the meantime, go through her house. Find clues. Call the photographer. Find any fucking clue."

"Roger."

The phone line went dead. I was going to find her. I was so pissed at her for not telling me anything else about him. That even with his abuse, she protected him and his organization.

But the rage pumping through my bones was misdirected. I was pissed that I never said anything to her when I should have. She needed to hear from me the three simple words that could have changed us both, but I was too much of a coward to tell her.

Wasted minutes were ticking away when I needed to stop thinking and start doing. I picked up the phone to text my brother, but he didn't answer immediately. I shot him an SOS text.

Me: *NOW!*

The time for pleasantries was gone. I paced my office before venturing into the main room. Her books were piled next to the fireplace, and the blankets were strewn across the couches. I moved toward them, desperate to touch something she did.

I lifted one of the books and inhaled deeply, the scent of lavender enveloping my senses. I had instructed the gardeners to plant lavender bushes by the pool so that the fragrance would linger on her skin after she went for a swim or when she sat outside reading, using a sprig as a bookmark. Holding her possession felt like holding a part of her, and the weight of her absence felt heavy on my chest. The coldness that had once consumed me began to seep back in, and the man who had once been gentle and warm was replaced by the one who used women for pleasure.

My phone rang, and I picked it up immediately.

"What's the issue, brother?"

"They took her." It was all I could get out, my voice shaking with fury.

"Hold on." I could hear my brother moving away from whoever he was with. He brought his voice down to a whisper.

"Who took who?" he asked.

"Tatum. Her ex-boyfriend is a gangster from Chicago, and he found her and took her. When we got home from Christmas, her house had been vandalized, so she was staying with me. We thought it could have been her ex, but she never confirmed it. I let her go to this wedding she was scheduled to work, but she insisted she didn't want security. I let her go, Alex. Me."

"Shit. I didn't realize she meant this much to you. Papa and I suspected it after you brought her home, but this. . ." he trailed off.

"I had one chance to do something right in my life. One chance to be with someone I loved. She was like Mamma was to Papa. She's the one." My voice cracked.

"Okay. Then you will find her. *We* will find her."

"I need everything you can find on her or any known gang affiliates. Look into the mafia, bikers, gangsters, petty theft, and sex traffickers. Look at everyone."

"I'll do the best I can, brother. I tried before, but I'll comb through every database I missed. Tell me about her."

"What can I tell? When she reads her books, she sits with a hooked finger around her nose. She loves her friends. She works for a shitty boss. She is mine. . ." I trailed off thinking of the times we had spent together.

"While I appreciate the ballad, I meant, does she have any identifiable markers on her? Scars? Bruises? Tattoos?"

I thought for a second. I knew I should tell my brother about her scars. But I would do anything to find her.

"She has quite a few scars underneath her chest and breasts. Almost look like scratches and teeth marks."

"Shit. From this dude?"

"Yes." It was all I could say without wanting to throw the fucking couch at the window.

"Tattoos?" he asked.

Tatum's skin was a milky golden color. It was feather soft and plush in all the right places.

"Wait." She had an eagle by her left hip. When her back was pressed to my chest at Papa's house, I remember running my hand down the length of her. I stopped on a small, fine-line tattoo that was clearly an eagle with a C in the middle of the body.

"Yes. She has an eagle tattoo. Left hip, by her butt, with a C inside the body."

"That has to be something. . ."

"I'm on it. I'll call a colleague in Chicago and see what I can figure out." The line clicked as he hung up.

God save anything that stood in my way today because I would rip them in half.

A few hours later, I had exhausted every possible search on my computer. I reached out to all of Tatum's friends, but none of them had any idea where she could have disappeared to. Even her boss, Lacey, hadn't heard anything since last night. Lacey had to leave early due to food poisoning, but she didn't know if anyone else's car would be in the parking lot.

I started making frantic calls to the valet, venue owner, florist, bride, and groom, pleading with them to remember my girlfriend. Hell, I was on the verge of dialing every single person on the four hundred-person guest list. I didn't care how insane I seemed to these people; all I wanted was to find what was mine.

Girlfriend. Fuck. I never thought I'd say that word. We never labeled anything because I never thought I could sustain a relationship long enough for labels. Right now, she was so much more than a girlfriend. She was mine and losing Tatum was more unbearable than the idea of committing to her.

Alex:*Found some associates.*

I furiously dialed him.

"Do not send me some inconspicuous text message!" I roared.

"You're welcome, *brother*. But I get it. You're a little testy."

"What did you find, Alex?"

"I called one of my buddies who works as the right-hand man of Chicago's mayor. He told me he knew exactly what the tattoo meant. It's a motorcycle club called The Club. They're primarily in the Midwest but sometimes deal with the West Coast Den out here."

A motorcycle club. That's who she was involved with.

"She must have been an ol' lady."

"That was my thought too. Rumor has it there have been some problems with whoever's in charge. I guess the former leader had some sort of a mental breakdown and was pushed out of the position."

"That's him. It has to be," my tone was low and filled with rage.

"Give me a name."

"Cameron DeSalle."

"I gotta meet with Bobby." He was the head of the West Coast Den, the primary club out here. They worked with our organization often. We helped them figure out when the shift changes were happening with the US/Mexico border patrol. During those shift changes, the border was 'accidentally' left wide open so they could import their drugs. They paid the price to us to move their drugs with minimal police interaction and in turn, they funded some anti-drug policies in the government. It was all an ironic give and take.

Once I hung up with Alex, I texted Christian to meet me in LA and set up a meeting with Bobby. It was a two-hour drive north, and I sped the whole way. Tatum was with this Cameron. I wondered if she was safe.

I arrived at a run-down mechanic shop on the outskirts of Los Angeles. It was dingy, in a shitty area, and contained one of the biggest imports of heroin and crack. Bobby was in his forties, a big guy covered with tattoos who wore his club's vest everywhere. When I stood next to him, I looked tall and official, but we were all crooks the same.

He sauntered out of the shop after I parked the Corvette, which I had gotten from the venue where Tatum was taken. I had to drive it. It smelled like Tatum.

"Julian Marchetti," the old man said as he walked out of the shop. He was with a younger guy I didn't recognize. Christian noticed the new guy too.

"To what do we owe this pleasure?"

I stalked toward him, my boots hitting the cement pavement hard.

"One of your clubs has someone very important to me. I'm not fucking around. I need her back."

"Ah, this is exactly what I thought it was." He gestured to the guy next to him. "Lemme introduce you to Tommy O'Rourke. He runs the Chicago chapter of The Club."

My fucking brother actually came through. There had been an exchange of power, and the last guy in charge had Tatum.

"Let's go inside and talk." Bobby walked to the small side door. I had been there plenty, but I needed this information now.

"No. Tell me what you know. And you"—I looked at Tommy— "Tell me where he took her."

Christian pulled out his gun and held it at his side.

"Come on, Julian. Let's not be rude to our guest." Bobby laughed at me.

"Rude." I stalked over so I stood in his face. He had to tilt his head slightly to look me in the eyes.

"Rude is taking something that isn't yours. Do you know what we do to little fuckers who have information and don't share it? I will bleed you dry. All those dollar signs coming in from the border will no longer exist. I will have every one of your men arrested with every single export you attempt to make," I growled.

"Anytime you drive on the street, I will have my men arrest you. I will seize your product and you'll be shit out of luck, owing more debts," I stared him down.

"I may not kill you, but I promise you will never be able to do business on US soil again. That is what will kill you because either your men are going to revolt, or this will be disintegrated." For effect, I waved around to the shop.

I looked over at Tommy and said, "You will have the same experience as him. As a new head too, don't you want to make a good first impression?" My eyes could pierce inside of his brain.

"His name is Cameron DeSalle. He was our boss for a decade. He met some chick five years ago and made her his ol' lady. She left him six months ago and he lost it." I cracked my knuckles as he continued.

"He's a drunk now. He took her to a safe house we have in Rosarito Beach. A few of our associates saw him in the town and reported back. We sent someone to confirm he's got her there. She isn't harmed."

"She better not be, or it's your head."

"The girl is alive. I don't know for how long."

"Send me the coordinates," I barked and turned back to the car.

"One more thing." I heard Tommy call out behind me.

"What?"

"She killed a known associate of Orlando Agron about five years back."

Ah. That explained her and the gun.

"What happened? Tell me everything."

"We never put our ladies in charge of drops, but Cam said he wanted her on. She claimed the guy tried to touch her, and when he didn't stop, she pulled the trigger. Orlando wanted revenge and spent six months trying to find her. Cam killed him in a drive-by while he was visiting a drop in Chicago. We were ordered not to tell her he was dead. She must still think he's alive."

Motherfucker. This guy was so messed up. Abusive isn't a strong enough word. I'll be the last person he sees alive. I ball up my fist and punch Tommy in his jaw.

"What the fuck was that for?" he said, cradling his broken nose.

"For saying my woman "claimed" he touched her. If she said he did, he did."

I turned to Bobby.

"A pleasure as always."

When I got in the car, Christian told me the plane was ready and waiting to go to Tijuana. With the coordinates, we knew where to find the safe house. She was so close.

"I'm coming, baby," I whispered.

29

TATUM

Present

I ran a finger down the walls and felt the six little marks. I'd been here almost a week. I was grateful to still be on my period and hoped to stretch it as long as I could before Cam noticed and demanded something I wasn't ready to give. I spent as many daylight hours floating in the ocean as I could, wondering how long it would take me to float away.

I slipped back into the familiar patterns he had imposed on me with alarming ease. The evenings became a repetitive cycle of scrubbing away the grime in the bathroom, preparing rice and beans, and keeping myself occupied with mundane chores. I used everything in my power to suppress the relentless thoughts racing through my mind, desperately seeking solace in thoughts of Julian and the cherished memories we had created together.

Cam spent the days drinking, and by the time my chores were done in the evening, he had passed out. He kept his hands mostly to himself, only throwing items, which was how the abuse started in Chicago. I knew the worst was coming. The scariest part was that I didn't know how to prepare myself for the physical pain.

After spending the entire afternoon in the ocean, Cam said he was hungry. I grabbed a towel and looked toward each end of the beach. Every day I hoped to see someone I could call out to for help, but no one came.

"Heat up some soup. Stop being such a lazy bitch," he barked from the couch. He was watching something on his phone, and five empty beer cans were scattered underneath him. Two more, and he'd be passed out. Thank god.

I grabbed a pot under the sink and poured in the soup.

I heard empty cans being kicked around and felt Cam behind me.

He grabbed my waist and pressed himself into my back.

"I can't wait 'til you're done with your bleedin', and I can taste you." His breath reeked of beer as he pressed his mouth to my cheek.

"Can't wait." I sarcastically retorted.

I poured the soup into two bowls and sat outside while he ate inside. I watched the sun hit the ocean. While living with my family, I wished to be taken far away from them. My parents rejected me so much that I was so desperate to know what obsession felt like. Now that I have it, I crave freedom and independence. I craved comfort and mutual love. I craved Julian.

I heard a large noise from the house and knew Cam had finally passed out just as the sun dipped past the horizon. I gathered my things when I heard a noise at the shoreline. It was too dark to see that far now. It was so tiny I swore I was hallucinating.

"One chance," I said to the ocean. I only had one chance at a life worth living so I needed to make the best out of it.

I closed the door behind me and nestled into the bed beside the snoring ogre, well aware that our room lacked windows or curtains to shield us from the outside world. I attempted to create a barrier between us by wedging my pillow against his form, ensuring there was no physical contact. As I succumbed to the clutches of a deep, unsettling sleep, I knew that tomorrow held the ominous promise of repeating the same harrowing experience.

I could have sworn I heard something at the front door and jolted out of bed. I hadn't seen another soul for over six days or heard anything so I wondered what it was.

"Tatum," I swore I heard my name whispered.

I was hallucinating. Cam must have drugged my food. Which wasn't even logical since he was passed out.

Curiosity got the best of me, and I walked out to the front room. I carefully walked up to the open window. I leaned my head out tepidly to see what sort of animal was out there.

A gloved hand covered my mouth, muffling my scream. It was complete darkness, and I couldn't see anything. Shit, was this Orlando? Had he found us?

"Tatum." I recognized the voice this time.

"Christian?" I whispered behind the glove. The hand on my mouth came down, knowing I wouldn't scream again.

The figure came moved in front of me and illuminated his face. As I watched, he pulled the ski mask off his head.

"Oh my god. Where is he?" Nothing else mattered.

And then I heard his voice. It had that deep, husky timbre that reverberated through my body and sent shivers down my spine. It was warm and comforting, like a soft blanket.

I had spent all week yearning for this moment, and now that it was here, my heart felt like it might burst with joy. Two strong arms pulled me out of the window, I jumped into his arms. Quickly straddled him and pressed my forehead against his, savoring the sound and feel of his voice as it filled my soul.

"Little bear."

"You found me."

"I will always find you. I'd go to the ends of the earth for you. And I'll never spend a single living day without you."

He pressed his lips to mine, and I felt my glow spark back to life, and the cold dissociative layer slowly fading.

"Let's go, Tatum." Julian put me down on the cool sand. It would have been so easy just to follow him out and never look back. The taste of freedom was right there at the very tips of my fingers.

"Don't fucking move."

I felt the cool barrel of a gun against my head before I recognized who it was. The hand that pulled me back was Cam's who was suddenly awake and sober behind me.

"Your entire club will be fucking pissed at you if you press that trigger." I heard Christian's voice say from the corner.

"You think I give a fuck about them? I spent the last year trying to find her and now that I have her, you're not going to kill me without going through her first."

He pushed me so I was out of Julian's reach and standing in front of his body.

"You're outnumbered." Julian's cool tone bit through the air. It was still pitch dark aside from the hint of moonlight, so I couldn't figure out how far away he was from me.

"She's coming inside." Cam tugged on me, and he kept me in front of him as we walked back to the house.

The warmth that engulfed me upon seeing Julian was fueled by a protective instinct. Every thought in my mind shifted into survival mode. While I couldn't envision a way out of this situation without risking my life, I had to trust that Julian knew what he was doing. I also had the unsettling feeling that James was lurking somewhere nearby, possibly accompanied by other unknown individuals. His hidden presence only intensified my unease.

Once we entered the house, Cam switched on the light, and I swiftly turned to catch a glimpse of Julian stepping through the doorway. My heart longed to reach out to him, to seek solace in his arms. Yet, as I met his gaze, I saw anguish etched in his eyes. Dark circles lay heavy beneath them, and his typically composed demeanor appeared disheveled, indicating the depth of his distress.

"Put your gun down," Cam demanded from behind me. He pushed the barrel against my neck harder.

"Don't harm her, and we won't harm you." Julain was deadly calm. His tone matched the severity of the situation.

"I knew about you, you know?" Cam said, pointing the gun around the room. Christian remained in the corner of the room with his weapon up.

"The little boyfriend she has. We're like Eskimo brothers, then, aren't we?" Cam's breath reeked of alcohol.

"Anything but." Julian stood there.

I looked him in the eyes while he watched me with a gun pointed at my back. I stared into his eyes as they conveyed a sense of safety. He never moved his gaze, and I knew he was trying to comfort me without drawing attention to the situation.

"Tell me, *brother*. Does her food still taste like leather?"

Julian cut him off, "No because we have a chef." He rubbed the bottom of his chin and the sides of his lips curled up, knowing he had won this fight.

"You know you're not coming out of this alive. I'm just giving you a few moments not to sound like a total shithead."

"What decision is that? I will die either way, so may as well take your little bitch with me."

A snarl came from Julian, and he attempted to step forward, but Cam pushed the gun harder against my head.

Through gritted teeth, Julian growled, "You're right about one thing. You are going to die here tonight. I'm just trying to decide how much torture to put you through before I end your miserable life."

Julian's eyes looked right at me. His right eye glinted with something that I couldn't recognize. His face was stoic, but his eyes were always his tell. He quickly looked down at the floor and then back up at me. Within an instant, I heard a noise behind me.

I sensed James' presence when I heard a small creak from the front door. My heart made the decision for me as I dropped to my knees.

"DOWN," Julian screamed.

I fell flat to the floor. Cam's gun went off. I looked at my hands before I moved and didn't see any blood, but a ringing buzzed through my heart. I couldn't make out the voices in the background.

"No!" I screamed, scrambling to figure out what happened.

"On your knees." I heard James' voice from the front door as he walked in and slowly turned around to inspect the scene.

Cam was on his knees, and Julian was now pointing two guns at him, with James pointing one from behind. Christian was still cooly propped up over by the window. A ripple from the house's mud fell and I noticed the bullet lodged into the corner.

Julian gestured to Christian, who jumped from where he was crouching and took his place. He approached me and tucked his two weapons into his waistband before kneeling on his haunches.

"Look at me, little bear."

Without another thought, I threw myself into his arms, sobs erupting from me.

"Shh." Julian gently caressed my back while standing up.

"I've told you before. 'No' is not an option for me. We were always meant to be. Always," he declared, his voice laced with determination. Finally, I locked eyes with him, wanting him to truly understand my words. "Right now, you don't seem to grasp the depth of my feelings. I simply cannot envision a world without you in it. Without your vibrant presence, your soothing lavender scent, your taste that lingers on my lips."

My hands gently traveled up to his jawline, lightly brushing against the stubble. His confession ignited a fervent warmth within me. Little did he know, I couldn't fathom a reality where he didn't exist either. The mere thought of living without the freedom to openly love him was unbearable. He leaned in, his lips close to my ear, as if to convey his deepest secrets.

"I need you to make a decision," he whispered.

"Do you want to stay or go?"

I understood his implications, and I trusted Julian's honesty. Cam wouldn't leave this place alive, and he asked me if I wanted to be a part of it. He knew it was crucial for me to keep my distance from his affairs, but this was personal. This was the man who had inflicted years of torment upon me. In the dead of night, with a fire coursing through my veins, I could taste the sweet essence of freedom.

The choice presented to me opened up my heart. This was what a healthy obsession felt like. This was what genuine love felt like, even if our version of it was twisted. I yearned to throw myself into Julian's arms and express my remorse for not uttering those three words to him before I departed for the wedding.

"Stay," I whispered back.

"Good girl," Julian purred.

"He's not going to be able to protect you from Orlando." I heard from behind me.

"What?" I asked, looking over at Cam on his knees.

"He still wants you dead. You won't be safe with him." I glanced back and forth between Julian and Cam, my heart pounding. Julian's face twisted with confusion, and he recoiled from me.

"Wait, you believe him?" Julian questioned, while I nodded, afraid that speaking Orlando's name aloud would summon his presence from the shadows.

Julian gripped my cheeks tightly, his eyes searching mine with a mix of concern and anguish.

"He died four years ago. Cameron killed him. He's already dead. Is that what you were scared of?"

The confession shocked me. Orlando's been dead for four years? I lived in fear because of him. My hands began to tremble with anger. I suffered for years because of this man. Now knowing it was all a lie?

"You. . . you killed him? When?"

Cam's face lit with the evilest fire in his eyes.

"The day I brought you to get your tattoo. I killed him that morning while he was doing a drop in Chicago. So I officially made you mine. . . forever."

"She can get it covered up. Your ink means nothing."

"I... I can't believe it," I stammered, each word escaping my lips slowly and filled with uncertainty.

"You were too stupid to understand anything." Cam spit in my direction.

Christian took his gun and hit Cam across the face with it.

"Do not dare speak to her like that ever again. It's taking every ounce of strength within me not to pull the trigger myself," He warned, his voice seething with anger and determination.

As my eyes met Christian's, a grin spread across my face. It was a sensation I had yearned for since childhood—the feeling of belonging to a family. These people were more than just associates; they had become my family. They treated me with the same care and support one would expect from their own blood. And Julian. . . He was the center of my world, the missing piece that completed me. He was the comforting sweatpants on a lazy day, the reassuring presence in a storm. He was the perfect complement to my existence—the darkness to my light, the yin to my yang. He was my made man, my possession, my everything.

"Tell me," Cam's voice dripped with venom, blood spilling from his mouth as he spoke, "does she still squirm and moan when she comes, or did the pathetic little bitch save that for me?" He let out a sickening laugh.

Without thinking, I reached for one of the guns tucked in Julian's waistband. The chaos within my chest churned with primal anger. I existed in a fractured world of compromised freedom as long as Cam continued to breathe. I knew I would always be bound to him in some way, and the mere thought of him finding me and taking me again pushed me over the edge.

I thirsted for vengeance. I yearned for him to experience the agony I had endured for years, and I wanted to be the one to inflict that pain upon him.

"Little bear." Julian's voice interrupted my thoughts.

Julian was right. The world wasn't black and white. It was a twisted mess of gray, and I reveled in it. The darkness called to me, and I answered eagerly. I needed to make him suffer, to inflict the same pain on him that he had inflicted on me.

I turned, and Julian's lips curled in anticipation. Christian had backed away, leaving me to face Cam alone. The roles had been reversed, and it was my turn to stand over him. The power I felt was indescribable, and I knew I couldn't let it go to waste.

"Did you ever love me?" I looked at Cam in the eyes. Hoping maybe a flicker of light would come through. Something I could use to save him from the dark.

"You were just a dirty whore I liked to use. You want to know what I loved?"

I could hear the crack of Julian's knuckles, but he stood firmly next to me.

"What?" I saw nothing but a black hole of pain and suffering. Not a single glow.

"I loved when you screamed like a dirty little whore when I sunk my teeth into your skin."

I choked on my breath, his words cutting deep into my core. How the hell did I let this bastard into my life for five goddamn years? The pain he inflicted was unbearable, and it filled me with self-pity.

"We all got one shot at this crazy life? And in the past year, I've learned what it means to really live, even if it's not always black and white. I found real friends, people who have my back no matter what. And I found love," I said, my eyes shining with fierce determination as I locked eyes with Julian, seeing the pride shining in his gaze.

With a trembling yet determined hand, I raised the gun to Cam's face. A sinister smile twisted across his lips. He didn't beg for forgiveness or plead for his life. He wanted to depart this world, knowing that the last thing he had was me. Little did he know, he never truly possessed me.

My index finger pulled the trigger, and the sound reverberated through the air. The recoil sent me sprawling backward, and I landed in Christian's arms. He swiftly carried me out of the house, the world around me spinning in a disorienting haze. As Julian reached for the gun in my hand, muffled voices reached my ears from inside. I heard another gunshot followed by Julian's impassioned shouts directed at James, but the words remained indistinguishable.

Blinded by darkness as we emerged outside, the night enveloped me. I felt myself being gently laid in a car, and I surrendered to the fatigue, closing my eyes. It was finally over. I was safe. "It's over," I whispered.

The warmth of large muscles was the next thing I remember feeling. I was on a couch. A couch?

I blinked a few times, seeing a hotel room. Everything was in colors of neutral beiges. Luxurious. I smelled the familiar scent of leather and knew immediately Julian was around. I attempted to sit up but the world was dizzy around me.

"I'm right here, little bear."

He came and kneeled next to me.

"Do not get up fast." He put his head into my lap and instinctually, I started caressing his hair.

I felt the warm red blood before I saw it. I was covered in blood splatter. The oversized shirt I wore to bed was inked with deep crimson to maroon specks.

"Are you—?" I could barely register Julian's voice.

"Okay? Yes and no. I can't believe it's over. I can't believe I ended it. I did." I looked at my shaking hands and took a few deep breaths to steady myself.

"You did so well. I'm so proud of you." Julian grabbed my hands and laid kisses on top of them.

"It's done?"

"Christian and James are fixing the issue. It is done."

His lips worked their way up my arms as he pulled me closer. Finally, I could feel the warmth of his breath against my lips.

"It's all over. Forever." All I wanted to do was be consumed by the freedom I felt. I wanted to devour it into my bloodstream.

I slipped my tongue into his mouth, deepening the kiss. We were dirty and covered in our sins.

I let him stand and yank me up.

"I missed you so much. I thought I would die without you when you didn't make it home." He pulled me into his arms and lifted the hem of my shirt.

"I thought I would die without seeing you again," I confessed.

"Never, little bear. If you die, I will go with you. If you want to go to the other side of the world, I'll follow. If you jump off a cliff, I'll ask to hold your hand on the way down. You are mine."

I put my arms around his neck, and he lifted me. We devoured each other while he walked to the bedroom. He dropped me on the white duvet cover and took my shirt with him. My nipples hardened in the cool air.

"My god, I missed these while you were gone." He leaned down and rolled my nipples with his teeth. I pushed against him and scooted back toward the headboard.

I watched as he took off his shirt and pants. My body responded with a thrill down my spine.

"Tell me. Who does this belong to, little bear?" He pulled my underwear down and slapped the top of my sex.

"Wait," I murmured. "I have a tampon in. It's just the end of my period, but I kept using them so I didn't have to have sex with him."

Julian chuckled.

"You think this scares me, little bear? Look at us. We're covered in blood. A little more won't hurt me."

He brought his face to my core and gave me a sensual lick. His teeth gripped my tampon string, and he pulled it out. It dangled from his teeth before he spat it on the ground.

"A little blood wouldn't deter me."

"Oh fuck," I sobbed.

My pulse was unsteady as he flicked his tongue over my most sensitive parts.

"Need. More." I gritted out. I didn't want to deny him, but the craving was so intense. His erection ground against me. Our chests heaved in unison as our mouths collided with each other. Desperate pressure building and I was sure I was getting the sheets wet underneath me.

"Look at what a mess you are, little bear. So desperate."

His voice was soft and full of primal need. I reached down to push his boxers off, but he grabbed my hands and held them against the bed above my head. I loved how dirty and raw we were in a room this luxurious.

He ran a rough palm across my cheek before speaking. "Your wish is my command."

Without warning, he thrust his length inside me. It stole the air from my lungs because I forgot how large he was. He kissed me and nipped on my lower lip. A cry escaped me, and I held onto him as he pulled in and out. He let go of my hands while my fingers ripped through his skin as he let out a strangled howl. His hands pinning tight against mine above my head, the raging fire inside of me builds.

I milked him in. He was my downfall and I was happy to let him be.

"Look at yourself." He grabbed my jaw and forced me to look at the tinted floor-to-ceiling window next to us, at our bodies melting into one. In the darkness, we looked erotic.

"Do you like how dirty we look? Do you like seeing what a mess you make?"

As I looked around, I noticed the bed was awash with a rainbow of red hues. The white sheets were now covered in the vibrant color, and Julian's tattooed skin was marked with crimson handprints. My body was slick with blood, sweat, and arousal, bringing me closer to the edge of ecstasy.

"See all that blood, little bear? That's all you. Your power. That's all you," he spoke languidly.

"Freedom," I gasped out breathlessly. He gazed at me, his hands kneading my breasts, our bodies generating enough heat to warm the room. Suddenly, he moved his hands down to my waist and forcefully flipped me onto all fours.

"On your hands and knees. Grab the headboard with your free hand."

His length felt so much bigger from behind, but he slid in with ease because of the liquid heat dripping from me. His pace quickened, and I pushed my hips back, asking for more.

"Say my name, little bear."

He pulled away slightly and began more of a leisurely pace.

"More," I begged.

"Little bear. That is not what I wanted. Bad girls get punished."

He paused his thrusts. I looked behind me and saw his hand raised. I knew he was asking for consent to spank me, and with a quick nod, he brought a stinging slap down on my ass. I felt his other hand placed perfectly over my tattoo. I didn't fault him for not wanting to look at it while he was inside me. He swiped a wetter patch of blood that hadn't dried from my lower back and smeared it over the tattoo.

It was so erotic watching him claim me like that that I drove my hips back into him.

"Julian, please."

"Good job listening."

In an instant, a tingling sensation released inside me, and I exploded. Feeling his cum fill me up was crude yet such a turn-on. I moaned loudly and screamed his name over and over again.

"Julian. *Julian.*"

We collapsed on the bed and stared at the ceiling. I felt his fingers reach for mine and interlock.

"Let's clean you up," he finally said.

I let him lift me off the bed. I glanced back at the bed, where a combination of our flesh was on display. I knew it would be the last time I ever had the remnants of the dirty life I used to live. It was a symbol of the end of the era.

My freedom was in the arms wrapped around me, caring for me. It was time for me to wash away my past.

He kissed my forehead and walked me into the shower. I closed my eyes and tears fell, mixing with the dripping red-stained water.

"Shh. You're safe," he murmured, adjusting me so I was straddling his waist.

"It's all over."

"It's just you and me." He pressed the tenderest of kisses against my nose.

When we got out, he dried me off and brought me to the other room.

"How convenient that there are two bedrooms." I laughed.

"I pay extra for this cleaning service."

He set me on a cloud-like bed and climbed in next to me. I turned so we were face-to-face.

"My friends are probably worried. I don't even know where my phone went."

"We'll call them tomorrow when we go back to San Diego. Then you can come home."

"Home?" I asked. I loved my casita, but I wouldn't call that home. I knew where home was, but I hesitated to say it aloud.

"Yes, *our* home. We'll move your stuff out this week, and you'll stay with me. I'm never letting you go again."

"I feel bad. I don't want to leave Tony without a tenant."

"Christian is looking for a place, so he can move in. It'll all work out, little bear." He placed a tender kiss on my cheek.

His rough hands pulled me into him, and I could hear his heart thumping in his chest.

"I wanted to tell you something before I left for the wedding that day," I mustered up enough confidence to say.

"Mm-hmm. And what would that be?" With the slight quirk of his lips, I knew he knew. He just wanted to make me say it. I gave him a playful push.

"You're going to make me say it first after everything I just went through?" I teased.

I looked at him, knowing he was also teasing me. Neither of us wanted to be the first to say it.

"I love you," I whispered while staring into his eyes.

"I love you more than there are trees in the forest, little bear."

He delicately kissed me again.

The following day we woke up and met Christian and James at the airport to fly back to San Diego.

I cornered Christian on the plane.

"I hear you might be moving in at Tony and Samuel's place," I asked.

"Oh yeah. I was going to move closer to LA where Julian's associate, but I think I like San Diego better. Cleaner air."

"Sure. Cleaner air and also a tall, blonde single mom." I winked. He acted like a protective dad around her.

"Hey, thanks for everything. Saving my life and whatnot." I looked down and felt a rush of embarrassment on my cheeks.

"Julian's my brother, and I'd do anything for him. You're his family now, so you're mine too. Plus, it's the most action I've gotten in a while." He winked.

"Ditto," James shouted from the back after looking up from his phone.

"Thank you both, truly."

I slid over to Julian and spent the rest of the hour-long plane ride in and out of restless sleep.

When the plane landed, I saw three large signs out of the window.

"Wha—?" I squinted to see what the signs said.

YAY FOR NOT BEING DEAD.

WE MISSED YOU.

BADDEST BITCH AROUND.

"Oh my god. Did you do this?" I turned toward Julian. He smiled at my friends waiting for us with large glitter signs.

"I called them and filled them in on what happened. I might have also mentioned what time we were landing."

I jumped off the steps of the plane and ran toward my friends. I hadn't seen them since Big Bear, and we had so much catching up to do. We texted over the holidays, but I hadn't seen them in a while since I got stuck in my love bubble.

"I am so happy you're okay." Chels squeezed me first. The rest of the girls followed suit.

"We were so worried about you," Daphne chimed in.

"I thought I lost you forever," Maeve quietly whispered, joining us in our group hug.

I pulled back from them and looked at the signs they had ditched on the concrete.

"You guys really got creative with those." I laughed, and we wrapped our arms around each other again.

Someone cleared their throat, and I saw my beautiful protector standing beside an open car door.

"Ladies, I hate to cut this reunion short, but I want to take my girlfriend back home." My eyes bugged out of my head. I assumed when you let someone kill their ex-boyfriend in front of you, labels didn't matter, but knowing he felt that way was amazing.

Chels was the first to lean into my ear. "Boyfriend? Ooh, la la."

I said goodbye and promised to get together soon. I slid into the car where Julian was waiting. Christian drove off the tarmac and onto the highway. I looked at Julian, who was staring at his phone, his mouth turned up in amusement.

"Do you have something to say, little bear?"

"Girlfriend, huh?" He laughed like I told him the funniest joke ever. "I think we're a little past labels."

"Yeah, sure. I get that, but you could have talked to me about it first."

He looked up and shut his phone off.

"Do you want me to ask you to be my girlfriend?" It sounded childish, especially when he said it aloud, but I did. "I mean kinda, yeah."

His gaze burned a hole through my soul. He unbuckled his seatbelt and knelt as far as possible while holding my hand up to his mouth.

"Tatum Sloane, will you do me the absolute honor of being my girlfriend?" Now I laughed.

"Of course." I shook my head. "Now, put your seatbelt on."

We sat there on opposite sides of the car but Julian was so large our knees touched, and just as I always have done, I reached out and placed my hand on his knee. He looked out the window but interlaced his fingers with mine. A few moments of silence passed before I whispered.

"For someone who's never had a girlfriend and hates commitment, you're not so bad at it."

30

JULIAN

Present

After I ransacked my house, I had a few people put it back together. I made Christian move all her things to the house and even folded her clothes into drawers again. I had a crew paint a godforsaken wall for her.

I had anticipated this moment since the day I spotted her at that wedding. Her allure was addicting. I spent the last thirty-two years vowing off women, but this person sitting next to me in the car was the center of my world. I died when I thought she did.

We pulled up to the house, and I brought her inside, watching her face go from happy to an emotion I couldn't quite recognize.

"Do you like it?" I asked, sliding next to her. I slipped my hand around her waist and pulled her into me.

"You painted the wall of the foyer yellow." Her voice was quiet, but I knew she understood its meaning.

When we were in the bathroom the day she told me what had happened to her, she mentioned missing the yellow wall she had in her apartment before Cameron took her away from it. I decided my front hallway needed a reminder of her when I thought she was gone, so I picked the brightest yellow I could. It was obnoxious and didn't match the inside aesthetic, but I didn't give a flying fuck about that.

It reminded me of Tatum's warmth. It reminded me of her.

She rose to her toes to give me a kiss.

"I don't just like it. I love it. Thank you for thinking of me."

"Wait, there's more." I walked her into the family room, where I had another bookshelf brought in. This one matched the floor-to-ceiling glass doors, and I filled it with the entire romance section from the bookstore.

"I wanted to make sure if you needed an escape, you could have it anytime," I whispered into her hair.

She turned around.

"I don't have the words. This is too much." Her eyes teared up again. I wiped the wetness from her cheek.

"Don't cry."

"I don't need an escape. My escape is right in front of me. You." She looked at the bookshelf. "But that doesn't mean I want you to throw these away." We laughed.

I sat her on the couch so her legs were laced between mine.

"I can't believe I get to call this place home."

"Anything you want to change, tell me. It's your home now, little bear." I noticed the small silver chain on her neck for the first time since I found her.

"I thought he—" The words got stuck in my throat.

"Anytime I wanted to remember you, I held onto it and closed my eyes. I thought about you every single moment. I spent hours floating in the water imagining your eyes, lips, jawline." Her hands went to my face, and her eyes closed as if she was doing the same right now with me.

"I couldn't stop thinking about you. The way your body pressed against mine. Your smile when you're happy. The glow that seeps through your warm skin."

"I need to tell you something." She pulled back, but I held her waist tightly.

"Yes, little bear." I circled my hand on her lower back.

"Just because I did. . . that... to him, doesn't mean I want to be involved in your world. I know being associated with you means I need a level of protection, but I can't be bound to the underworld again."

I thought about what she was saying. Being photographed with me and publicly acknowledging that we lived together came with many security issues. She would always be at risk at any point in time, but I would never purposefully bring her to meetings.

"I understand, but I won't negotiate your protection and security."

"But—"

"Absolutely not up for a debate. You can have your freedoms, but you are mine. And I protect what's mine. I failed to do that once, but I'll never let that happen again. I vow to protect you not because you need to be protected but because I cannot imagine my world without you." I softened my tone. "You'll have to get used to it because when you share my last name, you'll always carry a piece of me." She melted into my arms.

"You can have Christian or James," I said to lighten the mood.

Her eyes glistened. "Fine. But tell them to keep their distance."

"Of course, precious."

I nuzzled her neck. We stayed there, letting the silence surround us.

"You never told me those eight letters."

Her eyes were once again filled with striking luminosity. Her body snuggled into the crooks of my arms like they were molded for her. The one sentiment that she wanted was the one thing I thought I would never be able to give because of my past, because of her past, because I didn't know what our future looked like. Yet today, I knew I could promise her the world.

"I love you," she whispered.

"I would sell my soul to the devil to walk this earth with you. I will follow you until the end of time and then I'll still be there with you after that. I don't just love you. I love your being," I spoke softly because saying I love you back wasn't enough.

"Good thing, I always loved villains in the fairytales I read growing up." She pressed her lips against mine before pulling away. "I guess fucking and falling in love are connected after all?" She giggled as I grabbed her plush lips and gave the bottom one a little nibble.

"Falling in love with you was the easiest thing I've ever done. You brought me color," I murmured.

"And you brought me a new color of gray." She whispered inside the crook of my arms.

"I will always be yours, and you will be mine."

"I love you, Julian Marchetti." She pressed her mouth to mine, letting me feel her warm tongue slip in momentarily. This woman.

"I love you, little bear."

And that is when I knew.

Per Aspera Ad Astra.

EPILOGUE

TATUM

Six Months Later

"There you are." A rough, calloused hand touched my shoulder, my skin heated from the summer sun. I saw my handsome boyfriend blocking the sun with his commanding form.

I was outside typing on my laptop. I had become obsessed with telling my story, and Julian was the only one who understood the depths of my passion. He supported, encouraged, and believed in me when I couldn't believe in myself. And now, he was my muse, my inspiration, my everything.

"Sorry, I didn't hear you come in." He leaned down to press a kiss to my lips.

"I talked to you about being more aware and not escaping into your world," he chided and sat next to me.

"Ugh, I know. I'm trying." I often became engrossed in my writing. I still worked on my photography but quit working for Lacey with Julian's encouragement. She was only holding me back from flourishing in my own business.

"I love how passionate you are, little bear," he spoke softly. "Are you still going out with your friend today?"

I don't know why he was so concerned with where I was going, but he must have mentioned my nail appointment with Maeve a thousand times. She had asked if I wanted to spend some girl time with her, Daphne, and Chels, and I happily obliged. Once I became busier with photography and writing, I stopped working at the restaurant and didn't really get to see them much. Still, when we got together, no time had passed.

"Yes, yes. I'm going now." I laughed and said, "Maybe I'll convince Christian to get a mani, too so he doesn't sulk in the corner and scare everyone again."

Julian just laughed as I got up to change. I wore a white flowy dress and pulled my hair into a sleek bun. Julian had mentioned going to dinner afterward, so I figured I might as well get dressed now. I said goodbye and slipped out the door.

With each passing day, it became easier for me to leave him. The first few months were difficult, and he worried about me constantly. Christian and James constantly reassured him that I was safe.

When I got to the salon, my friends were already seated.

"Long time!" Chels exclaimed.

"Sit in the middle." Daphne pointed to a chair in the center of them. I picked a bright pink color, and we chatted about our lives. The girls filled me in on the restaurant gossip.

"How's domesticated life?" Maeve asked, knowing I hated when she teased me.

"He's perfect, you guys. I really just don't have words." I sighed.

"I can literally smell the love exploding from your skin," Daphne said sarcastically. We all laughed.

"I don't know how you do it, babe. I just don't think I could ever settle down." Chels leaned back in her chair.

"Says the queen of Vegas." Daphne snorted.

On the drive home, I marveled at the beauty of my life. I would have laughed if you had told me five years ago that I would be standing here. Being in a healthy relationship was also something I was still working on.

It took a lot of therapy to help me not fall back into the submissive role I was forced to have. For example, I constantly did the dishes, and I picked up my mess immediately. Julian had to sit me down and remind me I wasn't there to clean. I was his partner, and a little mess was okay.

I pulled up to the house at twilight, and the exterior lights had clicked on, illuminating a dim path to the front door. I pushed my key into the door and stepped into a dark house. Strange. Julian was home earlier and usually left a light on.

I saw a candle flicker outside and went to follow it. The glass pocket doors had been stored away, and the entire outside was lit with thousands of candles.

"Look familiar?" a husky voice asked.

I turned and saw the love of my life standing next to the pool and a white table and chairs. Cream rose petals were scattered all around.

"From the night we came home from the casita." I gasped. My chest was constricting in my chest. Julian was a romantic, but this was over the top, even for him.

"Will you have dinner with me?" I looked at the table set for two. I must have been so enamored that I didn't realize there was food.

"This is for me?" Shock still hadn't worn off, and I couldn't move my feet.

"For us." Julian just shrugged like this was an everyday ordeal for him and walked over to guide me to the table.

"Wait. This looks familiar." I looked down at the plate to see steak and risotto. It didn't look like Lola's typical menu.

"It's from our first date. I sold a few shares of my investment today and grabbed dinner for us." Again, he acted like this was an extremely casual thing to do.

I looked down, then back up at him.

"What is happening here?" I shook my head in disbelief. I still hadn't sat down, but my legs were shaking.

Suddenly, it clicked. Maeve insisting I needed my nails done today, this over-the-top romantic gesture, my boyfriend who was so nervous, his right hand was fidgeting inside his jacket pocket.

His jacket pocket. . . Oh my god.

"Tatum."

"Julian. What are you doing?"

His tell was always his eyes. I knew what he was feeling if I looked at his eyes. Today they were darting everywhere, especially to the pocket in his jacket. He was going to...

"Tatum Marie Sloane, from the moment you fell into my life, the world has never been brighter. Six months ago, I thought I was going to lose you forever. The day you came home, I bought something. I tried to wait for the right moment, but when it never came, I realized I was waiting for the impossible. Every moment with you felt right.

"Julian. . ." I choked.

"Let me use my words here." He continued, "This house is something we may call home, but home the nights spent together playing footsie and reading books. Home is holding hands in the car and pretending neither of us realizes it. Home is falling in love with you."

He dropped down to one knee and pulled out a little black box. Inside it, a large, emerald-cut solitaire diamond glistened.

"Will you do me the absolute honor of being mine forever?"

I dropped to my knees to meet him at eye level.

"Of course. Yes," I whispered. He slipped the ring on my finger and pulled me up.

"Mrs. Marchetti has a nice ring to it. There hasn't been one of those for a while." He smiled slowly.

"I have big boots to fill then." I kissed him tenderly.

He deepened the kiss, and his eagerness grew. He grabbed me around my waist and lowered me to one of the loungers on the pool deck.

"The food" I breathlessly pulled away from him.

"It's called an oven for a reason." He laughed and pulled me together into him. I could feel his erection through his pants.

"Let me see what a good girl you are." He slipped his hands up my skirt.

"Ah, no underwear. Just as I hoped," he whispered, driving his fingers into me. "And wet. It's like you knew what to do to tease me."

He circled my clit, using a finger to tease it. I let out an unrestrained snarl. It was only a touch.

"More," I begged.

"Take off your dress, little bear." I reached up and pulled it over my head. I had just a lace bralette on.

Julian stood and slowly removed his jacket and shirt, taking his time with each button. He pulled off his belt.

"Turn around," he commanded.

There wasn't a fence around the back of the house as it overlooked the ocean. A small part of me wished someone would be watching this erotic scene.

I obliged and turned around, my hands bracing against the top of the lounge chair.

"You get me so hard on all fours." He took his belt and looped it around his hand.

He teased me by dragging it along my butt before he stopped.

"You got it covered up."

"Surprise" was all I could manage to get out. This morning, I went to a tattoo studio and had the eagle tattoo with a tiny fineline forest. It was still covered in second skin and a bit red, but something I wanted to do. I wanted to change it to a bear but didn't want to feel like I was covering up one man with another, so a forest felt safe. A forest represented growth and life, all things I wanted to attain in myself. It was also where bears lived.

"It felt fitting. You once told me you loved me more than the amount of trees in the forest."

He pulled the belt away and gently smacked my ass cheek with it.

"Harder," I begged.

"As my lady desires." He pulled the belt back and smacked my bottom harder. I twisted beneath the sting, and my core leaked.

Within seconds, he was pressed inside me, thrusting in and out. He grabbed the belt between thrusts and smacked me a little harder until I screamed in pain and pleasure.

"I'm so close," I cried in anguish.

As he continued to thrust through my orgasm, I erupted. My hands sank down, our juices dripping down my thigh.

"Seems like we made a mess."

I turned around and saw a glint of humor in his eyes. I laughed in return, and we sat back together.

I dressed in Julian's oversized tee and realized how silly I must look surrounded by this beautiful dinner in a plain shirt.

"I even dressed up for dinner tonight, but you had to go ruin it." I gestured to his oversized shirt.

"Little bear, I just had dinner. It's time for dessert now." He leaned over and pulled up the hem of my shirt.

"You are insatiable." I laughed.

The silence of the night drifted over us before I felt Julian rustle beneath me.

"The tattoo," he started.

"Do you like it?" I asked hesitantly.

"Why?" he asked.

"It just made sense, you know? You always called me "little bear," and bears are all about living in the wild. They stand for strength, growth, and the need to protect oneself. So, I thought it was a perfect fit."

"It's beautiful, little bear. I'm glad you did that for you." He kissed me softly on my forehead.

I closed my eyes and let the refreshing scent of the sea blend with the sweet aroma of lavender that surrounded us. It was hard to believe that I was about to become this man's wife. He was my protector, my love, my everything. Despite my lingering wariness of the world, having Julian by my side made it all worthwhile. If this was my one shot at truly living, I was ready to embrace it because this was what it truly meant to be alive.

I craved freedom, independence, and strength like never before. What I didn't realize was that I had a cheerleader, someone who would always support me. Julian wasn't here to control me; he was my partner. Together, we were embarking on this journey as equals, and now it was going to be official. With him, I had found a place I could call home, a sense of belonging I had never experienced before.

And in that moment, I knew I was finally free.

Follow Me On My Adventures

Thank you so much for reading and supporting this little adventure of mine. Your support is beyond words on the page. I would love it if you kept up with the next adventure by following my socials below.

Follow me on Goodreads HERE

Follow me on Facebook
Join my Vee's Vixens on Facebook to join a chat group about this book

Follow me on Instagram

Follow me on Tiktok

Listen to the Soundtrack
Click HERE to listen to a playlist

ACKNOWLEDGEMENTS

I would be amiss to say this was probably the hardest part for me to write because there are so many people I want to thank and so many words I want to say. I took a ten year break from writing and the last few months have been consumed by Tatum and Julian's story. I want to thank first and foremost these two for showing me a new world. For letting the words that have lived and festered inside my brain grow and flourish.

Thank you to the world of wedding photography and my photography community family. I have loved being apart of all of your beautiful days for the last six years.

I want to thank my best friend, Morgan for answering my calls at all hours of the day asking the most absurd questions (Jansport backpack). I didn't know what friendship felt like until I met you.

I want to thank my amazing friend and alpha reader Madison. You have worked so hard to help me professionally in all aspects of my life. The word thank you doesn't even begin to cover the debt I feel for you. Paris 2024 baby. Thank you for rooting me on. You believed so hard in this series. I cannot believe we are here.

Thank you to Molly at Novel Mechanic for your incredibly thourough read-through and bringing the story to life.

Thank you to Haya with Haya inDesigns for the absolutely beautiful cover and always listening to my re-edits!

Thank you to my new friend, Windy, for creating designs for the shirt. Thank you for listening to me vent and supporting me!

Christina, thank you for our phone calls. If it weren't for our conversations about the wedding industry, this story wouldn't have come to life.

Raven, you have been the best beta reader I have ever had the pleasure of knowing. I am so glad I found you on Fiverr!

Good Girls PR for your endless marketing tactics. Thank you for pushing this book out and showing the world Tatum and Julian's story.

Badd Bi*ch PA for helping me run my Facebook page and helping with my Insta/Tiktok teams.

My family, even though you are banned from actually reading this, thank you for your support always. I know its been interesting to jump back in, but I appreciate the help as I push this out.

To my Tiktok friends, instagrammers, readers it is all because of you that I get to live my dream. This book was created by an extreme amount of therapy bills and came from the depths of my own personal growth, so thank you for relating.

Lastly, to my husband. Thank you for reading all my smut scenes and rating them for me (LOL). Thank you for always supporting me even though my ideas may seem crazy. I love you more than words can describe.

Turn the page for a sneak peek into the first few pages of the next novel in the series.

1

CHELSEA

Present

subject to change

SIN CITY.

The city that never sleeps, where fantasies and nightmares come to life, and where dreams are made and shattered equally. Las Vegas, the city of sin, had a grip on me that I couldn't shake off. I felt alive here amongst the chaos and decadence. This was my playground, my kingdom, and nothing could stand in my way.

I'd vacationed here with my family every summer since I could remember. Growing up in San Diego, the weather was endless sunshine, so going to a place where vices wander freely opened a world for me.

I was born the perfect child. The only girl. A vision of golden locks and tanned skin. I was treated like the queen and always got whatever I needed and wanted. I lived in a bubble that my parents claimed was to protect me from the world. I never went to a traditional school, had friends outside our family, or never ate at a restaurant. I hated it. I never felt like I was meant to be thrown into a role I didn't fit.

It was when my parents passed away for a tragic unknown reason when I was in high school that this image shattered. I remember feeling bittersweet the day they died because I felt free from this person I was forced to be the last few years. I could finally be myself.

I started partying and drinking the day my parents died. I got so fucked up at their funeral I spent the next morning in a stranger's bed when I lost my virginity. I was seventeen when I first popped my first molly. My bedpost was practically broken with how many men I loved to use for pleasure. I lived and breathed in that world, so it made sense why Las Vegas drew such a pull for me. I was obsessed with sinning.

Growing up as the golden child and being seen as the perfect little girl was old fast. As a young kid, everyone always commented on my beach blonde locks that flowed down my back or my bright blue eyes. I had a 'Cali-girl' accent and how perfect I must have been to my parents. I hated that I was molded and like a prisoner stuck behind metal bars. I wanted to prove to everyone how different I was.

My brother was five years older than me, but at the age of twenty-one, he was forced to take care of his fucked up younger sister. In hindsight, I know he had a lot on his plate and I was grateful he dropped out of college to stay with me. It forced him to grow up quickly; honestly, he became a major square. I am too consumed with avenging the image that everyone saw me as I didn't have time to appreciate what he did for me.

Now, if it wasn't for my three friends, I can almost guarantee I would be in a ditch somewhere. Daphne, Maeve and Tatum worked at the same breakfast spot I did. Although we were all very different personality-wise. None of them knew that I worked, so I had something to do during the day. My parents died and left us with a boatload of cash. I didn't have access to it until I turned twenty-one, but there was no need to work when I did.

I heard a light knock at the door and quickly escaped my thoughts. I pulled it open to see my bags had been delivered.

"Thanks!" I squealed at the valet. He looked at me and rolled his eyes.

It was a common response to my personality. I was boisterous and loud and often came off as phony and vapid. It was my hidden tool, though. Come off looking like a bimbo, and then suddenly you're whipping out insults that are gut-wrenching and they never saw it coming.

"Welcome back to the Penthouse, Ms. O'Brien." After dropping off my bag, the man bowed and scurried out of the room. This trip wasn't any different than the other times I had been here. I lied to my friends, telling them I had to help my brother this weekend and took off work to have a little taste of sin city. I was craving something that would put me over the edge. When I thought about it too long, it was pathetic to be coming to a city alone, to party, alone.

"Let's find out what little dress you could conjure up this time."

I pulled on a taught baby blue mini dress that pulled out the ice from my eyes. It was low cut and I ran a hand down my body when I slipped it on. I was blessed with curves that looked like a porn star. My large hips, bottom and breasts were spilling out of the dress from all directions. I was going to be the envy of every girl at the club and the object of desire for every man. It was perfect.

I curled my long blonde hair into loose waves and threw on more makeup that I had in my bag. I was only here for twenty-four hours, but you would think I was taking a week-long trip. Once, I dated a guy in my good girl phase, and he told me he loved women who weren't high maintenance. I dumped him on the spot.

I obsessed over my hair, makeup, skin, shoes and nails. I wasn't easy to be with, and quite frankly, I didn't care, nor did I need a male companion to be on my arm. I know a therapist would tell me it was part of my trauma from my parents dying, my incessant image to look perfect and then my quick obsession with the underworld and what it stands for. I didn't care because I didn't have a therapist.

I glided in my five-inch heels down the long hallway carpeting before I pressed the lobby on the elevator. The clock told me it was well into the early hours of the night, which meant the perfect time for immortality to come to play.

The club was inside the lobby, so I didn't have to walk far and when I got to the entrance, I noticed the line wrapped around the corner. Instead, I walked right up to the bouncer.

I batted my eyelashes and said, "Chelsea O'Brien."

He looked down at his list and nodded. As he opened the velvet rope to let me in, I heard a roar of groans and annoyances from the line.

I batted my lashes at them and threw my hair over my shoulder as I walked into the club's darkness.

"Ah." I inhaled a crisp scent of spilled vodka and sweaty people wafted through my nose.

"Home." I just laughed and walked over to the bar.

I was here for one reason. I hadn't had a good fuck in a couple weeks since the last time I was here and my core was desperate for a release. There was one big problem.

Vanilla sex didn't do it for me. I needed some excitement because the threw me over the bed and gave me a few little thrusts was the most painful experience. These experiences for me were like hunting in the club. I had the whole thing down to a science, really.

Sit at the bar and sip a few vodka sodas while chatting aimlessly with the bartender. Once I gained enough liquid courage, I turned toward the club's center and leaned my elbows against the back of the bar. Hoisting my breasts over my dress and letting them spill down while radiating the golden girl energy I gave off usually allowed a mark to come slithering toward me.

It took me ten minutes to decide if they would give me even a taste of excitement. Usually, I could tell by the crudeness of their approach. The more docile puppy dog would fuck me missionary into old age. The grittier, the closer the mark was able to satisfy me sexually. It was a challenge of sorts.

To this day, I've never had an orgasm. I just wanted to find someone who would be able to appease me in the bedroom. Yet, they all seem to look at me and see ditzy barbie. It was often a failure that just created a darker circle of frustration.

I leaned my elbows back on the bar and with the blue dress radiating in the club's glow, a golden puppy came crawling to mama. In the darkness, he had the same kind of golden locks I did, except he was pulled up into a tight bun on top of his head. He had a thick beard and the physique of a wrestler. He wasn't tall but very broad-shouldered. I looked down at his hands and saw ink swirls around his plain t-shirt.

He would do.

"You here alone?" He asked, sliding in next to me.

"No." I giggled. I leaned into his ear so he could hear me. "My friends are just out there. It's so hot." I drawled.

I would never let the men know I was here alone. For one, because of well safety, duh. Second, because I don't know a part of me, I guess I still wanted to maintain the good girl façade I kept. I liked keeping my dark side a little secret. I enjoyed walking the line between good and evil in the morally gray shade in between.

"You are so hot." His alcohol-infused breath reeked of desire.

"Thanks." I giggled.

I took a deep look at him. He was good to look enough, but I was desperate for a means to an end. None of these pleasantries were really quite necessary. Plus, I was already feeling tired from the pulsing music in the club and social atmosphere.

"Wanna go to the bathroom?" I winked at him and whispered loudly.

He grabbed my hand and his touch didn't do anything for me. Shit, this wasn't a good sign. I attempted to trick my brain into believing his fire and appetite would bring me through the robes of pleasure.

I looked up and realized he was guiding me toward the club exit.

"Wait," I pulled back on his arm, forcing him to stop, "where are we going?" I gestured to the dark shadowy corner of the club.

"Let's go up to my room. I've got one of the suites in this hotel. It's not far."

Ugh. I rolled my eyes back, thankful the dark lights of the club didn't show my exasperation. Staying inside this club was where sin grew. If we went out to the bright lights of the casino was a major cockblock. I appreciated living my dark self into this deep world of sin and drugs, but the real world? They still got to enjoy the golden child and that person certainly would never admit they wanted an audience to watch while they took cock deep into the back of their throat.

I turned on my charm and pulled my chest closer to his. I heaved my breasts onto his body, pushing in closer to him. My hand slid to his hands, where I circled the hem of his jeans.

"I don't want to go out there." I bit the very top of his ear. "I want you to take me in here."

I pulled him into the shadowed corner. I wish I could say I hadn't been here before, but the darkness and I are good friends. It was hidden from any onlookers on the dance floor. Still, if you were exiting the bathroom and paying attention to where you were going, you would see two shadowed figures getting it on.

But my favorite part? It was the security camera pointed right at us. In a perfect line of vision, the person sitting behind it could see every inch of our bodies enmeshing. They could hear every groan over the thread of music.

I immediately let the stranger rip down my dress and he sucked hard on my pebbled nipples.

"These are so fucking big and perky." Most men were enthralled immediately with my breasts. While I appreciated them, they didn't serve me in the way I needed. I saw them all day long. I get there big, there in my face all day too. Why would I want them in yours?

Instead of saying anything, I feigned a moan, "Yes, you like that."

"Fuck yeah. You are such a babe."

Come on. Rip off my clothes, take me in your mouth, and do something I feigned in my head. This dance was exhausting to me.

"Put on a show for them," I whispered while biting hard on his lower, drawing a bead of blood.

"What the fuck?" the guy lifted a hand to examine the pain I had left behind. My doe eyes just exaggerated, feigning innocence.

"Oops." I thrust my tongue deep into his and lapped up the very hint of iron as I swallowed our saliva.

Quickly, he unzipped his pants and his large erection sprouted through. Ugh, he couldn't even take them off all the way. Snooze. I guess I had to switch directions in my mind. Clearly, this man wouldn't be able to give me the show I desired, but maybe a good lay would take the edge off my system. God, I felt like such a dude saying this.

I let him edge inside of me. My eyes heated in fevered passion. He's got one thing going for him. At least he was big and girthy.

I turned on the heat. My eyes blazed straight into the direction the camera was pointed. I threw my head back in a lustful moan as his appetite grew. The pounding against my core quickened.

My lips parted. My eyes grew. I cried louder, hoping that someone from the bathroom would hear us and get curious to see. But I couldn't take my eyes off the camera. Knowing that the hotel had a 24/7 security staff that always watched the cameras. Knowing someone behind, there was watching me desperately unfurling from the good girl persona.

My attention snapped to the man who was calling me.

"Hello?!" His thrust slowed to a languid pace.

"Why did you stop?" I puffed my lips out at him in disappointment.

"What are you watching?" He turned toward the camera while pulling out. The liquid dripped down my thigh.

When he realized what I was doing and who I was performing for, he looked back at me.

"Are you watching the security camera while I fuck you?" There was no point in fighting this with him. This guy wasn't going to do it for me anyway.

"Yeah."

"Why?" he questioned, his erection still hard and leaking precum onto the floor. God, what a picture this must have been. My lips turned into a small smile.

"Because I like people-watching."

The man looked at me and then pulled up his zipper. He looked at me, his eyes filled with a dark fury.

"You are fucking weird." I laughed at him maniacally. I can't say he was the first person to tell me this.

"Fucking disgusting." He added for effect before stomping off.

Before pulling my dress up, I looked straight at the camera and licked my lips. I threw two fingers into my core and leaned against the cold black wall. Deep into the shadows, I shoved them inside of me and continued thrusting. The heat exploded from me as my ravenous hunger increased. Propelling my compulsion, I dove deep inside. As the pressure burned inside me, I exploded all over my fingers.

"Ah." I just exclaimed, writhing onto my fingers.

The itch to taste the sin diminishing and cool satiation passed over me. I opened my eyes and looked up at the cameras while pulling my fingers out. One by one, I licked myself off of them, my lips turned on the corner, knowing the person behind it was aching to touch. Call me cocky, but my confidence was one of my favorite features.

I moved my dress back into position and fluffed up my hair. After taking a few steps forward, I blew a kiss at the camera before following the exit sign out.

I threw my hair over my shoulders as the bright casino lights beckoned me back into the light. I adjusted the look on my face, and within moments the dark shadows left, and the golden girl was back.

With one look back at the dark pulsating club, I gave a sad smile. In another lifetime...

Preorder HERE

ABOUT THE AUTHOR

Vee Taylor is a passionate writer based in Temecula, a beautiful suburb located outside of San Diego, California. With a lovingly supportive husband, two dogs, and two children, she finds inspiration in her daily life and uses it to fuel her writing. Her passion for reading and writing began ten years ago, and she hasn't looked back since.

As an avid book lover, Vee is obsessed with all things bookish. She loves exploring new worlds, discovering new characters, and delving into different genres. Her favorite genres include dark romance, romantasy, and good ole smut. When she's not writing, she can often be found with her nose buried in a book or scrolling aimlessly on social media.

Aside from writing, Vee is also a talented photographer that worked for years in the wedding industry. She loves spending time with her friends and family, and enjoys trying new things. With a zest for life and an unwavering passion for writing, Vee Taylor is so excited that you are here on this journey with her.

www.veetaylorauthor.com

CPSIA information can be obtained
at www.ICGtesting.com
Printed in the USA
JSHW052154120723
44650JS00007B/63